WILDER

WILDER

Andrew Simonet

Farrar Straus Giroux · New York

Farrar Straus Giroux Books for Young Readers
An imprint of Macmillan Publishing Group, LLC
175 Fifth Avenue, New York, NY 10010

1 3 5 7 9 10 8 6 4 2

fiercereads.com

Library of Congress Cataloging-in-Publication Data

Names: Simonet, Andrew, author.
Title: Wilder / by Andrew Simonet.
Description: First edition. | New York : Farrar Straus Giroux, 2018. |
    Summary: The lives of Jason Wilder and Meili Wen intersect in the
    delinquent-proof room for in-school suspension, known as the Rubber Room,
    and Jason's growing, fierce protectiveness of Meili explodes into violence
    when her chance to return to her wealthy lifestyle in Hong Kong—and his
    opportunity to escape poverty, loneliness, and the past—is threatened.
Identifiers: LCCN 2017045252 | ISBN 9780374309251 (hardcover) |
    ISBN 9780374309282 (ebook)
Subjects: | CYAC: Juvenile delinquency—Fiction. | Student
    suspension—Fiction. | Chinese—United States—Fiction. |
    Violence—Fiction. | Family problems—Fiction. | Dating (Social
    customs)—Fiction. | High schools—Fiction. | Schools—Fiction.
Classification: LCC PZ7.1.S565 Wi 2018 | DDC [Fic]—dc23
LC record available at https://lccn.loc.gov/2017045252

Our books may be purchased in bulk for promotional, educational,
or business use. Please contact your local bookseller or the Macmillan Corporate
and Premium Sales Department at (800) 221-7945 ext. 5442 or by e-mail at
MacmillanSpecialMarkets@macmillan.com.

for e
my true north

WILDER

ONE

I WAS IN THE RUBBER ROOM FOR MY OWN protection. Meili got there by breaking Laura Fenton's middle finger.

The story got retold and exaggerated, but I think it went like this: Laura's boyfriend was seen talking to Meili. Laura confronted Meili outside our high school and grabbed her arm.

Meili famously said, "You ought to remove that hand." Her British-y accent made it "thaht hahnd." It became a saying around school, silly but threatening.

Laura started to say, "Well, you—" and she was on the ground, wailing, her middle finger flopping like a deflated balloon.

Meili—it's May-LEE—was marched into the Rubber Room the next morning by the counselor. Except she wasn't Meili Wen, she was Melissa Young.

"Melissa, you will sit at this table, and you will not

converse or otherwise interact with Mr. Wilder. Is that understood?" Ms. Davies addressed Meili but looked at me.

I nodded.

"Perfectly," Meili said, head tilted, condescending as always.

Ms. Davies gave the aide on duty some papers and hustled out. Meili dumped a stack of books on her table and opened one.

I tried to go back to reading but couldn't. Maybe I never went back to reading.

Instead, I watched Meili.

Deep in her book, she played with the top button of her yellow sweater, twisting it and releasing. Twisting and releasing. The sweater had a faint background pattern, a swirl you didn't notice at first; you had to stare. I stared. Like all her clothes, that sweater made it seem like everyone else in Unionville, everyone I'd ever met, shopped at the same boring store.

Kids who broke the rules got sent to the Rubber Room. Mike Kosnicki was banned from Spanish because he had said something obscene and possibly threatening to Señor Treadway at a school dance. His defense was that he said it in Spanish. Kids who got in fights or sent out of class for using their phones spent time in the Rubber Room. I was the only all-day resident until Meili.

We didn't speak the first day, not a word.

Or the second day.

Officially, it was In-School Suspension, but kids called it the Rubber Room. It wasn't covered in rubber, but it was delinquent-proof. It was a science lab before they built the addition on the school, so it had long tables with empty racks for lab gear. The windows were Plexiglas instead of glass, permanently scratched up and foggy. There was a list of things that were not allowed: mirrors (could be broken and used as a weapon or to slit your wrists), scissors (same), phones, and key chains, though keys were permitted. There was a box of stubby mini-golf pencils; you used one till it was dull, then threw it out and got another. Real pens and pencils were too dangerous. The Rubber Room was set up to prevent tragedies like school shootings, or at least to make it look like you could prevent them. It was actually an ordinary classroom, echoing with boredom. Ex*cru*ciating, as Meili would say.

Rubber Room monitor was not a coveted job. Ms. Davies or an off-duty aide sat at the front to "supervise," eating or staring at their phones. Occasionally no one was there, and we were reminded there was a camera above the door. When no adult was present, you could talk as long as you kept a book open and looked down at it. This was a major flaw in the tragedy-prevention system. A couple times a day, a Rubber Room maniac could slip into the hallway—can't lock the door, fire hazard—and do whatever he wanted. Or whatever *she* wanted, since Meili was and always will be the dangerous one.

5

At the end of Meili's third day in the Rubber Room, Ms. Davies excused herself. "Jason, I'm going to the office to make a call, but I will be watching," she said, pointing at the camera.

I nodded.

"Melissa?" she said. No response. "No talking and no getting up." Ms. Davies stopped halfway out the door. "Melissa?" Nothing. "Melissa, did you hear me?"

"Yes, of course," she said, finally looking up.

Ms. Davies left the door open. The window in the door was papered over to keep curious students from gawking at us. But now, two kids, small and sneaky, probably freshmen, slowed down and peered in, eager for a glimpse they could recount to their friends. Sometimes I snarled at the tourists to give them something juicy to report. But I wasn't sure what Meili would make of that—turns out, of course, she would have loved it—so I stared them down.

Silence.

Meili chewed her lip.

Silence.

"That's not your name," I said. I looked at the page of my biology textbook I'd been pretending to read for twenty minutes.

Big silence.

"Are you talking to me?" she said, not looking up.

"Yup."

"And what did you say?"

6

"I said that's not your name."

Silence.

"What's not my name?"

"Melissa. You don't answer when people say 'Melissa.'"

"Perhaps because I'm reading and not scratching my testicles all day." The word sounded like "testicools."

"People respond when their name gets said. You don't respond to Melissa."

She turned fully toward me, a move that could bring Ms. Davies back. "Shouldn't you be burning something down?" She smiled.

She went for the lowest possible blow and connected.

"Fuck you." I put my fantasy novel right on the table and tried to read.

She stared.

"So you dish it out, but you can't take it. Very attractive quality," she said, and went back to her book.

First thing the next day, she dropped an envelope on my table.

I ignored it.

At ten, the aide left to go to the bathroom.

I still ignored it.

I read a novel hidden inside my history textbook. When I started in the Rubber Room in January, I had homework and check-ins. That quietly went away, like all the promises of *getting you back in class so you graduate in June.* Fine with me. Now it was May, my senior year, and I was killing time.

Meili, without looking up, said, "Really?" Pause. *"Really?"* Pause. "You're not going to read it?"

I wanted to open it the moment she put it down. But I was terrified it would be some cruel thing, mocking me. I pictured the newspaper article about the fire.

But the way she asked, I had a feeling it wasn't cruel. I opened it and took out a girly little card, a kitten blowing out candles on a cake. Inside, she had crossed out ~~Happy Seventh Birthday to One Cool Cat~~ and written:

Dear Firebug,

Still angry?

Your cellmate,
Esmerelda (aka Melissa)

I put the card back in the envelope and saw the money: ten dollars folded into a tight rectangle.

"Well?" she said.

"Well, what?"

"Are you still angry?"

"Why did you call me fire*fly*?"

"I didn't call you fire*fly*, I called you fire*bug*."

"Same thing."

"No, a firebug is someone who starts a lot of fires. What d'you call that here?"

I took a deep breath. "Pyromaniac." That was a word I heard a lot.

"Ooh, much scarier. I prefer firebug. A bit sweeter, isn't it?" She smiled. "So, still angry?"

Confusing. She mentioned the fire but didn't judge me for it. "I guess not. Firebug forgives Esmerelda."

"Cheers. But I didn't ask to be forgiven, OK? Let's be clear about that. And now that you aren't mad, mind doing me a favor?"

I would have done pretty much anything for her, as evidenced by what happened later.

"Depends."

"You have a motorbike?"

"Yeah." She had noticed.

"So you might could pick up a cable for me?" "Might could" was the kind of Meili phrase I immediately loved and never tired of. "It's on the back."

That explained the money. On the back of the card was *⅛ inch to RCA cable, at least three foot please. Cheers!* A cord which, I came to learn, connects a computer to a stereo. Her apology card was (a) not an apology and (b) actually to get me to do something for her. Very Meili.

"Why can't you get it?" I said.

"No car, I'm 'fraid."

"You could order it."

"No credit card. And I'm a bit restricted. My aunt and uncle don't want me going online so much. They think I might waste time communicating with my real friends overseas. They want me to focus on my brilliant life here, engage with the local floorenfawna." I had to look that up later. It's two words: "flora" and "fauna," plants and animals.

"How's that going?"

"Absolutely marvelous. I'm best friends with Laura Fenton. And I've met a firemaniac in the Rubber Room."

"Pyromaniac."

"So you *are* a pyromaniac."

I tried to put on a British accent and failed completely. "No, I just hate it when you rednecks use the wrong word."

"Snob." She tried to sound American—"Snaaab"—and failed completely.

I continued in my fake British voice. "I can't help it if I've sailed the world and dined with heads of state. It's not snobbery if I actually am better than everyone else."

She spoke in her regular voice. "Heads of state. See, that's nice, actually. That's the type of phrase you don't hear in Alabama very much."

"We're not in Alabama."

"May as well be."

"Snob."

She put on an even snootier British voice, lisping and

over the top. "It's not snobbery if I actually am better than everyone else."

I was still laughing my ass off when Ms. Davies walked in. And that made Melissa, or Esmerelda, or Meili, quite pleased.

I have lots of time now to think about what happened. I'm straightening out how one thing led to the next, how I got drawn in, how things became inevitable.

Other people have their ideas, what should have happened, what I did and didn't do. Meili has her version. This is my story, what it's like inside my skin. If it doesn't line up with what other people believe, I'm sorry, but I'm not surprised. Or as Meili would say, "Who cares what they think? They're all half-asleep, trying to fit the rest of us into some twisted dream they're having." She'd back me up. But then she'd point at me, raise her eyebrows. "On the other hand, don't believe a word this one says. Complete lunatic, such a pain in the arse. Even if he can make me laugh so hard I lit'rally piss my knickers." And she'd stand up, pointing at her crotch. "D'you remember, Jason? When I had to go in the bathroom and, like, dry myself out?"

All that is to say: Meili swerves. And so do I now. And so does this story. If you want facts, read a newspaper. If you want truth, read this.

The next day, I came into the Rubber Room with an

audio connector for Meili and a shiny cut over my lip. Ronny and Dmitri and a couple other guys had caught me getting a hot dog at Stewart's. Again. And messed with me. Again.

Meili saw the cut before she saw the adaptor. We had three minutes till the bell.

"Shit, what happened?"

"Got in an argument." I wanted to talk about the favor I'd done, not my face.

"Argument? Bout what?" Meili's shimmery blue T-shirt showed off the dips behind her collarbones. Do those have a name? Hers should.

"About whether I'm allowed to eat at Stewart's."

"You're not allowed to eat at Stewart's? What does that mean?" She folded her arms, deepening those collarbone indentations. You have no idea.

"It means, when I go there, I get this."

"Not from the workers." A statement, but actually a question.

"No, from some guys who don't want me there."

"So they told you not to go to Stewart's, but you go." I nodded. "Bit stupid, isn't it?" She noticed my stare and looked down to see if she was showing cleavage. She wasn't. She didn't really have cleavage.

"Yup."

"Why d'you do it then?"

It seemed so obvious, but it was tricky to find the words.

"Because if I let them tell me what I can't do, it never ends." I didn't mention the fighting, how I craved it, waited for it.

"Bit of a shame that it's all for some crap hot dogs, though. Couldn't you fight over something more important, like a girl or a horse or something?"

Ms. Davies came through the door, and the conversation ended.

She hadn't thanked me. Driving to Winslow to get the cable had taken a silly amount of time, and it was all leading to a moment with her. Except it wasn't. I had an experience I would have a lot: expect Meili to do something, she veers off and does something else.

Did she really need me to get that adaptor? She could have figured out a way, right? Looking back, so much seems flimsy, "unsupported by the evidence," as my lawyer would say. But in the moment, I didn't ask questions. The right questions, anyway.

Before lunch, we got a few minutes to ourselves. "Thanks, Firebug. If there's ever anything you need, you go ahead and ask." Pause. "I'll say no, but you can certainly ask."

"Come for a ride," I said too quickly.

"What sort of ride?"

"On my bike. My motorcycle." I'd been thinking about this for days. Me and Meili on the motorcycle.

A pause. She was writing in her notebook. "That sounds terribly uncomfortable and dirty and dangerous. And certainly my aunt and uncle wouldn't allow it."

Fuck. Of course she wouldn't do a redneck-y thing with a pyromaniac.

We didn't speak again before the last bell. I walked out without looking at her.

I'll say no, but you can certainly ask. She told me up front, and I didn't listen. Maybe that's the whole story.

TWO

TWO HOURS LATER, I WAS IN MY BOXER shorts watching TV. I'm not even going to say what. Someone knocked.

I looked out the window and saw the side of Meili's head.

What?

Shit.

I needed to turn off the TV, hide the onion dip, and put on some pants. And maybe get nicer furniture.

"Hold on!" I yelled, grabbing sweatpants from the dirty pile.

I couldn't even begin to clean up, so I cracked the door open. Seeing Meili's face reminded me I'd made an ass of myself by asking her out.

"Hey, Melissa." I was not inviting her in. My house was somehow both depressingly empty and a total mess.

She half turned away. "I'm here for my ride." She pulled

her blue coat tight around her, an old-fashioned army coat, something Napoléon would have worn.

"Your ride?" I asked.

"On the *motorbike*," she said, exasperated that she had to remind me.

"You said you didn't want to." I pulled the door closed behind me. We were definitely not going in.

"No, I said it sounded dirty and dangerous. That's different." She checked the bottom of her shoe for something.

"Now you want to go?"

"I'm here, aren't I?" she said, not exactly answering my question.

A milk tanker truck turned the corner on Black Rock, air brakes barking.

"OK. Give me a couple minutes."

"Take your time," she said with a sarcastic smile.

I grabbed my helmet and my mom's helmet for Meili, which I worried might smell like my mom. I went out back to the shed, where I locked up my bike. Too many people who didn't like me here.

I had to run-start it, and I didn't want her to see, so I tried running it in the backyard. It didn't start, and she came around.

"It does work, doesn't it?" she asked. She was smoking a cigarette now. Or maybe a joint.

"It just needs a little help when you start it cold." I pushed the bike past her on the dirt driveway, and it turned over.

Not bad. Some days, I'd get halfway to the Maroneys' before it started. I revved it and blew out the lines: loud pops, blue smoke. I handed her my mom's helmet.

"Do I have to?" she asked. I nodded. She carefully placed her cigarette (not a joint, a roll-your-own) on the ground, pulled her hair back, and slid the helmet on. She picked up the cigarette, took a puff, and climbed on.

"Please don't grievously injure me," she said.

"I'll try not to."

"It's fine if I die. I just really, really don't want to get paralyzed, d'yaknowwahmean?"

I gunned it, showing off a bit. She grabbed my waist with her nonsmoking arm. She didn't have an ounce of warmth toward me, but she held on tight. I felt the stone of her necklace—I found out later it was a shark tooth—press into my shoulder blade.

She didn't yell or tell me to slow down. In fact, right as we hit the pavement, dipping down to turn left, she took a drag off her cigarette.

We rolled past farms and used-to-be farms. Corn, feed crops, dairy cows. We cut through clouds of manure smell, thick enough to taste, through our small downtown, with the houses huddled together, out past the Sunoco and the creek. Early May, mud season was over. I turned onto the dirt track that went up Brandt Hill. It was more fun, and we were less likely to get pulled over. The air cooled in the woods, snaking under my helmet and through the holes in my jeans.

We bumped over some divots, and she went with it, leaning in, never complaining. This was the thing I had pictured: Meili on the back of my bike, the wind, the open fields, her holding me tight enough that I felt her fingers on my ribs. But it was lonely and off. She didn't want to be here. It was that gap between what you tell yourself and what actually happens. I hate that gap. I want to destroy that gap.

We passed through the woods into the clearing at the top of Brandt Hill. She climbed off first, removed her helmet.

"What's this?" She looked down at the bowl with the dirt-bike trails and jumps. She was rolling another cigarette, pulling tobacco out of a dark-blue pouch.

"It's trails you can ride."

Most of them you wouldn't want to do with two people, though. I didn't know why I'd brought us here. But this was what I'd pictured: me and Meili on Brandt Hill, her laughing at something I said. There's that moment when a girl laughs at your joke so hard she looks away, and then, right as the laugh is ending, her eyes dart back to you, and she has this sweet, lit-up smile cause you cracked her up. That's the moment I'd pictured.

Not this.

"Imagine that," she said, bored as hell.

I heard the strain of a motor. A tractor, thankfully, not a bike on its way up the hill.

"Look, I'll take you home. Where do you live?" I was sick of her.

"We just got here."

"You hate being here. Why did you even come?"

"I dunno," she said, licking the paper and sealing it. "I mean, it's complicated, y'know?"

"No, it's not. I asked you to come for a ride and you said no, and then you came anyway, even though you don't want to be here. That's not complicated, it's stupid." I was pissed. Enough.

She laughed, and smoke came out of the first non-sarcastic smile I'd seen from her all day. "You're right. It's fucking stupid, isn't it?" She looked down into the bowl. "D'you mind if I have a go?"

"On the bike?"

"Yeah."

"Have you ridden before?"

"Uhhhh . . . once."

She was already climbing on, cigarette in her mouth. She cranked the throttle, and I had to yell to be heard. "So, that foot is the gears, and it's in neutral, which—"

"Do you mind?" She leaned over, wanting me to hold her cigarette. I reached out and carefully pulled it from between her lips. That was sexy. Dead sexy, as Meili would say.

"You should wear a helmet," I said, bending to pick it up.

"Yeah, you're right," she said, and peeled out.

She headed down into the bowl, a move that isn't easy. She wobbled but then sped through the cut and up the far side. She flushed some birds out of the bushes, and they briefly flew above her, a nature goddess on a Yamaha. She rode the rim, then turned toward a small ramp. She slowed before she hit it, almost too much, because if you hit it slow, you tip forward. But she cleared it. She wasn't ripping it up, but she wasn't bad at all.

She did a last run up to the edge and got a tiny bit of air coming over the top. She put her feet down to steady the bike as she landed, then gunned it back to me and slid to a stop.

"That's not bad," she said, smiling and looking to see if I was impressed. I was.

I could hear the tractor again, now that the bike was off. That was Unionville: shut off one motor and you heard the one behind it.

"You call me fag?" she said.

"What?"

"You got my fag? The cigarette?" I passed her the now-extinguished cigarette. "Proper etiquette says you puff on a girl's cigarette to keep it lit until she comes back." She took out her lighter.

"I don't smoke."

She was off the bike now, and I put the kickstand down.

"You don't have to *inhale*, silly." She relit the half cigarette, her face haloed by the lighter. I liked looking at her face.

"You've done that before," I said.

"Yeah, in Malaysia we used to ride everywhere. Lit'rally. On the beach, in the jungle. It was mad." She brushed her hair back, took a long drag, and looked out over the bowl. "You want to know why I came?" I didn't answer. "I was having a fight with my aunt, and she was saying I didn't have any friends here, and it was all my fault, so I said: 'Actually, someone did ask me to . . . to do something today,' and she tells me I absolutely *have* to go, I have *no* choice, so then I thought I'd tell her that it was a motorbike ride with a pyromaniac—I mean, no offense, I don't know if you're a pyromaniac, but that's the sort of thing that would terrify my aunt—and then I realized she would never let me go if she heard that, so I said, 'Fine,' and I fuckin walked out and came to your house." She said it in one breathless sentence. Meili talked in short, bored bursts or long, unbroken paragraphs.

The fact that she knew where I lived could have been creepy, but it felt flattering. I'm not hard to find; anybody in town could tell you where Jason Wilder lives. But it means she asked.

"It's amazing you don't have friends," I said. "You're so sweet."

She laughed, coughed up smoke. "That's what's great

about you, Firebug: you're sarcastic as fuck, and I fuckin love it. Everybody here is so goddamn genuine, it's sick. But riding in there"—she pointed in the bowl—"that was the dog's bollocks. So, cheers."

Her smoke—not the car exhaust of a regular cigarette but intense and organic like a grass fire—was overwhelming, nauseating, and I turned my head. She noticed and waved the smoke off, exhaled out of the corner of her mouth.

"The what?" I said.

"Dog's balls, something amazing. 'Bollocks' means a load of crap. Like, 'Oh, bollocks!' But 'the dog's bollocks' is really, really good." And then with only the slightest pause: "So, what about this fire?"

"What fire?" My heart started racing.

"The fire you're in trouble for."

"What about it?" Smoke, cigarettes, burning grass, burning houses. I was dizzy.

"What happened?" She left it open. "Before you answer that, did you bring any snacks?"

"Snacks? No."

"Great, cause I did." She reached into her coat pocket and offered me a bunch of red grapes. "I'm a bit scratchy at first, but look, I brought fags, I brought snacks. I'm pretty good long-term."

I took a few grapes and started eating—that helped—hoping she would forget her question.

But when I looked back at her, she raised her eyebrows and said, "So. The fire."

Big breath. Finish the grape. "It was stupid. I was getting back at these guys who did all this stuff to me and my house. It was part of a fight I've been in." Meili munched her grapes and nodded, as if I was describing a vacation. "Last summer, some stuff happened with my mom, then I got involved, and it kind of escalated. Six months ago, day after Halloween, these guys shot bottle rockets into our house. They cut the screen window and shot eight bottle rockets in."

"What's a bottle rocket?"

"It's a firework, a little stick with a firecracker, and it shoots through the air, and then the firecracker explodes."

"Right, OK."

"I freaked out. I went to this one kid's house, and I opened the window and put this huge firework canister in there, this cardboard tube that shoots all these different things, and it was fuckin stupid, cause I didn't think about how it could start a real fire. Which it did. And the fire trucks came, and all this shit happened and . . ." I stopped. Meili was still eating and listening happily. "This is the part I can't tell without crying. So, I'm sorry, but I'm gonna cry."

Her eyes went fake-wide. "It *will* be the first time I've seen someone cry, but I think I can handle it."

"There was a boy who got hurt, he got burned. A little

23

kid." A sob welled up, as always. "Seven years old, just a little guy, and he got burned kinda bad." I leaned my head back and squeezed my eyes shut. "He's OK, he's gonna be OK, but he was in the hospital. And . . . that's how I ruined my life."

We were quiet. No more tractor. A breeze pushed Meili's hair toward her mouth.

"Not *ruined*, exactly. A bit dramatic, don't you think?" she said.

"What do you mean?"

"It's not like you killed someone or, you know, went paralyzed or something. Just sounds like you fucked up."

"Tell that to people around here."

"Are you going to jail?"

"I was in for twenty-four days. I'm on probation, a suspended sentence. If I mess up again, I go to juvenile detention for a long time."

"Brilliant. So you're basically free."

"Doesn't feel that way."

"You'll get over it." She finished her grapes and got out a fresh rolling paper. "D'you know when I was twelve, me and my girlfriend stole a taxi—a fucking *taxi*—cause this shit driver kept us waiting in his cab while he drank or whatever, so, finally, we jumped in the front seat and took off. It was absolutely mad." She smiled. "Until we hit an old lady, like, a *really* old lady. Too old to even, like, walk down the street. It was a complete disaaaahster. And I cried for days.

Lit'rally. My dad had to, like, hold me for two days. I wouldn't let go of him." She squinted her eyes closed, shook her head. "But it was alright in the end. She went to hospital, she came back out, it wasn't so bad. And I thought my life was over. But, unfortunately, it wasn't." She grinned and curtsied. "Instead, I'm in beautiful Unionville." She lit the cigarette, blew a swirl of blue smoke through the hair in front of her mouth. How did she not set her hair on fire? "But it is nice to cry a bit. Anyway, sh'we go back?"

That was it. No discussion. Just: tell me your most heart-breaking story, I'll tell you mine, and then, great, let's go. Meili swerved fast.

"Uh, yeah. If you want."

"Mind if I drive?"

"Prolly not a good idea."

She was already climbing on. "It's like *that*, is it? The girl can ride up here in the woods, but not in the real world, right?"

"No, I have to be careful—"

"God forbid anyone sees you being driven around by a girl."

"No. Bullshit." I was conceding and climbing on the back now, but I wasn't done with the argument. "Don't turn this into a gender thing. If you aren't licensed, we—"

"It was bullshit, wasn't it? I only said it so I could get what I wanted. I am *so* crap. How can you stand being with me? Don't fucking answer that or I *will* crash this piece of shit with both of us on it, swear to fucking god, are you ready?"

No. Yes. Didn't matter.

I reached both arms around Meili's waist. She started up fast, and we zoomed down Brandt Hill.

The gap was gone: this was what I pictured, only reversed. Meili driving the bike, me behind. Holding on to her—tightly because she showed off by riding a little too fast—was the sexiest thing I'd done in years, maybe ever.

If you're a good person, this won't make sense to you. For the past four months, my only physical contact with people had been fighting. The crunch of my elbow on Dmitri's cheek. The burn of a well-done headlock. Putting my chin on Meili's shoulder reminded me of that, scratched a similar itch. Scratched it better, of course. I'd forgotten what a friendly body felt like.

I shifted my arms, pulled closer to her. Meili's body was kind of blocky, thick in the middle like a boy's. She didn't have boobs, or much of a butt. Her gorgeousness was beyond that. She was sexy because she smelled real and talked real and chewed her food real. Other girls looked like girls; Meili *was* a girl.

I held on to her as we bumped down through the woods. It was warmer on the back, shielded from the wind. I enjoyed it so much I didn't mind when she passed my street. A longer ride.

"You missed the turn," I yelled. She was opening it up on the paved road.

"What?"

"You missed the turn. My house is back there."

"We're not going to your house," she yelled, and I grabbed on tighter as she cranked the throttle. She let up a bit and signaled a left turn.

"OK, not funny," I said.

Where did she turn?

"No, Melissa, we can't stop here."

Stewart's Root Beer.

THREE

SHE STOPPED THE BIKE AWKWARDLY IN THE
gravel parking lot, and we half stepped, half fell off.

"This is stupid," I said, keeping my helmet on as if I
might not be recognized. The orange Stewart's sign behind
Meili, chronically short of letters, announced: NOW OP
WEKND T 10. It was Friday, a big night for Stewart's, but it
was early yet, not crowded.

"I'm hungry. What d'you want?" She was walking to
the front door, past two pickups, one of which I recognized.
Unfortunately. Polaris sticker and a custom hitch.

I couldn't retreat now that I was here. Shit. I hung my
helmet on the handlebars and followed her through the
glass doors. A two-tone bell chimed whenever the door
opened. *Ding-dong.* To me, it meant: next round, come out
fighting.

"Mark! Tammy! How you doin'?" Meili was chatting up
a table of four by the windows. "Mind if we sit?" She could

talk to anyone, although she basically hated everyone. And people were curious about her.

Mark, who wasn't part of my battle, hesitated. "Uh, well—"

"Fab. And let me get you something, what d'you want, Tammy? Hot dog? One of those foot-long fuckers?" This made Tammy laugh. "No, right? It's like, 'No thank you.' You blokes have got it all wrong, you think girls want some donkey-size monster. I mean, it's gotta be big enough, right, Tammy? You don't want some little sausage-link fucker." She wiggled her pinkie, and now Mark laughed, too. "But, no, I don't want a fuckin bloated horse dick, OK? Thanks."

She glanced over at me. I was by the door, watching but not exactly looking at James Bouchard, aka Butchie. The gray linoleum had a path worn into it from the door to the counter, cows to the feed trough. I was at one end of the path, and Butchie was at the other, ordering, not yet aware of me. He was part of my battle, not central, but definitely in it.

"Foot-longs for everybody, then? Jason, what d'you like? We're all getting . . . horse wieners." Even she started giggling now. "I can't believe you say 'wiener' here. It's appalling."

Tammy said, "Jason, come sit." Some people liked me from before the fire. It was easy to forget that.

I pulled a chair over. I vaguely recognized the other two girls. Sophomores?

Mark gave me a chin chuck. "Sup?" School hoodie with

the hood on for some reason. Dressed like a jock though he wasn't. Not useful in a fight. I'm just saying.

Tammy said, "Jason, do you know Ann-Marie and Marcy?" Big girls with straightened hair, not popular but not *not*. Like a lot of thick girls at my school, they wore tight clothes all the time. They smiled, but with an edge: *I'm meeting the pyromaniac.*

"How you doin'?" I said.

They both said "Good" right away and then giggled. I made people nervous.

Butchie was texting, which would bring other boys here. And I would fight and get my ass kicked. In front of Meili. God*damn.*

"How are you, Jason? I heard you're on probation or something, right?" Tammy, glittery eye makeup and two different earrings, as alternative as it got in Unionville, was being nice and maybe a little nosy.

"Yeah, I have to be a good boy. They check up on me, but—"

"Alright, they're a bit skinny for horse cocks, but they are plenty long, aren't they?" Meili put down three footlongs, overflowing their red-and-white cardboard trays, and went back for more.

"When are they gonna let you back in class?" Tammy asked. After a bunch of fights at school, all because of the fire, I had been pulled out of class four months ago,

January 12, and sent to the Rubber Room. For my own protection.

"I don't know. They don't tell me stuff."

"That's messed up," Mark said, shaking his head.

Meili dropped two more enormous hot dogs on the table. "Who needs one?"

Mark shook his head.

"Someone's having two, then." She pushed one toward Tammy. "Have you ever taken on two at once, Tammy? Don't answer that. I found out the hard way you do not want people telling tales about you at this school. Isn't that right?"

"You mean that whole Darren thing," Tammy said. "That was so crazy!"

"It was ridiculous. I'll tell you one thing I learned, it's like . . . like, Tammy, you're fucking gorgeous, right? Seriously, look at you, you're so cute. And then, look at me. I'm a chubby ten-year-old boy, right? But around here, it's like, 'Asian girl. Must chat her up.' " She moved her arms robotically.

"Yeah, guys go crazy for Asian girls," Tammy said. "We call it the Asian Persuasion."

"That's good," Meili said. "Or even Persu*Asian*, you know, if you put the A in there to make it 'Asian.' "

"There's already an A in 'persuasion,' " Tammy said. "That's why we call it the Asian Persuasion. Asian girls have magical powers."

"Yeah." Meili cringed a little. "That is . . . better, isn't it?"

I saw her profound disappointment. Being surrounded by people who couldn't keep up, who didn't appreciate PersuAsian, was physically painful for her.

"But, seriously," Meili said. "Laura whatever-her-name-is is so gorgeous. She's a *knock*out, right? I was like, sorry, Laura, I'm not even in your *league*. I've got *nothing*. Now, are either of you boys ever going to interrupt me and tell me I'm not ugly? Cause it seems to me I've been saying I'm ugly for a while now, and I'm waiting for a little, like: 'Hey, Melissa, you're not that bad.'"

"Ohmygod, you're totally cute," Tammy said, and Marcy and Ann-Marie nodded. "You have such a pretty face . . ."

"And your hair . . ." Marcy or Ann-Marie said.

"Your hair is amazing, it's so shiny and dark," the other one said.

"You're very kind. But you boys." Meili pointed at Mark. "F. And for you." She pointed at me. "F minus."

Tammy socked Mark in the shoulder. "Come on, isn't she pretty?"

"Yeah, no, she is. But I can't tell another girl she's pretty in front of you," Mark said, a credible defense.

Butchie was standing. Leaving? Walking over here?

"Here's what you say, Mark," Meili said. "'Oh, Melissa, you are such a pretty girl. Of course, you can't hold a candle to my gorgeous Tammy, but you are attractive.' Got it?"

32

She turned to me. "You don't even have that excuse, do you? Have you got a girlfriend? How could I not know that? Have you got one?"

Someone pulled into the parking lot. Not a car I recognized.

"Can't remember."

"Oh, fuck off. You couldn't possibly, the way you act. Such a pain in the arse. You should see him in the Rubber Room. Though he did teach me how to ride a motorbike today, which was amazing. Ever done it?"

"Jason, man, you can't be here." Butchie was standing next to me now, and I braced for a punch or a grab.

"I'm here, aren't I?" I said. Exactly what Meili said on my front step. Same tone and everything. Weird.

"Come on, man, you and the girl should go." He was giving me a chance to get out of the fight, which was nice, considering.

"I'll go when I'm finished."

"Just take your food and go, man," Butchie said. "Don't make it a thing."

"Shit, I do need to get home, Jason," Meili said, checking the time. "Gawd, my aunt's gonna have a cow." She took a bite of her hot dog and stood up.

"I can't leave now," I said.

Mark absorbed himself in his phone to avoid taking sides, but Tammy jumped in. "Come on, Butchie, don't be a dick. We're all hanging out."

"It's not me, it's Ronny and those guys."

"So don't tell them Jason's here."

Meili was pulling me. "I do need a ride. Come back and arm wrestle your little friends after you drop me home, 'K?"

I stood up. This wasn't good.

"It's nothing personal, Jason," Butchie said, shrugging.

"Fuck you, it's not personal," I said, turning around, ready to get in his face. But Meili pulled my wrist hard, and I stumbled toward the door.

"See you guys later!" Tammy called after us.

Ding-dong. Round over.

We were in the parking lot.

"Why are you doing this?" I said. An older dude was getting out of his car. Not part of it.

"Doing what?" Meili asked.

"If I come here, I have to stand my ground."

"Take me home, and then you can come back and do whatever you want, can't you?" She was on the back of the bike. At least I wouldn't ride bitch out of the parking lot.

"Fine." That's exactly what I would do. Ride her home and come back to get my ass kicked. Fuck.

I put my helmet on my lap and gunned it out of the parking lot. Meili held on extra tight, but the thrill of touching her was gone. I was in fighting mode.

"Where do you live?" I yelled.

"Drop me at MacArthur Street."

"You're really fucking things up for me, you know that?"

"Come on, that was fun. Who cares what they think?"

"Now, it's gonna be: 'Jason showed up at Stewart's and had to be rescued by the weird girl with the accent.' Now I'm a pyro *and* a pussy."

We rode on in silence.

I pulled off by MacArthur. "You live here?"

"Up the road a bit. But it won't do to be dropped off on a motorbike." She handed me her helmet. "You really care what people say? It's so stupid. It's like . . . it's like sport." (She never said sports, always sport.) "If you follow it, if you spend all your time thinking about it, then it's like: 'Oh no, my favorite player got injured, what a tragedy.' But if you don't follow it, it's like: 'Football *who*?' Doesn't exist."

"I care what people say because I'm in danger."

"Oh, please, you're in danger cause you want to be. You love it. And did you even hear the conversation back there? All these white people talking about how I'm Asian and desirable and have secret powers. And meanwhile lit'rally every man in this town stares at me, and half of them say something nasty. Now that's fucking dangerous."

That was deep. It wasn't the spelling of PersuAsian that pained Meili. Why hadn't I been more disturbed by that conversation?

An SUV roared by. Ronny?

"Yeah, that sucks, but you'll be out of here in a few

months." I didn't know that, but I assumed it was true. "I live here. And you're making that a lot harder."

"I'm so sorry. Is your life hard? That's certainly got to be my fault."

"You're impossible." I put my helmet back on.

"And unattractive, don't forget. And I'm a weird girl with an accent."

I backed the bike up. I was done talking.

"Thanks for the ride," she said, and gave me a gesture, a two-finger peace sign with the back of her hand, which I later learned was her version of the middle finger.

I rode back toward Stewart's wishing she was still holding on to me.

The evening sun pushed shadows across the road, strobing faster as I accelerated. Alone.

Goddammit.

Before I got to Stewart's, I turned onto my road and went home.

Meili and I didn't speak Monday in the Rubber Room.

That night was the first time I saw Manny.

I was home, rereading *The Fallen Queen*, the first book in my favorite series, and listening to hip-hop.

He may have been knocking for a while; I heard him when the song ended. It was after nine, I had to be careful. I looked out and saw a guy I didn't recognize. He wasn't white or black, maybe Chinese. Hawaiian? Super short hair, arm tatts, clean-cut but muscled. Not someone I open the door for.

I yelled, "Who is it?"

"Hello, Jason. My name is Manny."

"What do you want?"

I checked the back window and the side yard. Could be more of them ready to rush in.

"I'm here about Melissa."

"Yeah?"

"I want to talk." He paused. "I'm Melissa's friend. Please." His calm voice made my two dead bolts plus a knob lock seem absurd. And he used the magic word: Melissa.

I cracked the door. "What?"

"May I come in? I have a gift." He held up a dirty cardboard box. Nice gift.

I opened the door, and Manny walked in. Glided in. He stood in my barren living room, the kitchen fluorescents glaring in sideways. I didn't want him to sit. I had already broken my first rule: never let anyone in the house you can't forcibly remove. Manny would be hard to evict, maybe impossible.

"This is for you." He handed me the box. Inside was a carburetor, the same as my bike's. He smiled when he saw me recognize it. "I understand you're having starter problems. This will help."

Manny was warm. Manny was generous. Behind all that, Manny could kick your ass.

"Uh, yeah. Thank you. How did you—"

"I need to talk to you about Melissa." He sat on the faded pink, fake-leather sofa. "Please, sit. This is a conversation."

I pulled a folding chair over and sat with the carburetor in my lap, not relaxing.

"I have to ask a favor. And, please, it's nothing personal." He sounded like Butchie. "You need to stop seeing Melissa."

Was I *seeing* her? As in dating? God, I wished I was.

"Says who?"

He dodged that one. "Melissa is in a delicate situation with her citizenship. She needs to keep to herself for the time being. If her situation becomes more . . . stable, then of course you would be welcome to visit with her whenever you want."

Huh.

"And who are you?"

"I'm a friend. I watch after her. And trust me, if you want what's best for her, and I know you do, you will leave her alone."

"And if I don't?"

He dodged this one, too. "Jason, I'm sure you don't like being told what to do. I wouldn't either, if I were you." He stopped, and his voice changed. "But you'll do as I ask. Because you aren't foolish, and you have a lot to lose. Especially now."

"Is that a threat?"

He smiled and shook his head slightly. "When I threaten you, you won't need to ask if it's a threat."

I've heard a lot of guys talk shit and act hard, and 99 percent of them are faking. Manny wasn't. Manny was understating how hard he was, I could feel it. It kind of made me want to hug him, and it kind of made me want to punch him in the fucking mouth.

"It won't come to that," he said, smiling but still in charge. He stood up and extended his hand. "Good luck with the bike. If you have more engine problems, come to Gorman's. I'm sure I can help."

I didn't shake his hand. We stared a bit too long, then he walked out, closing the door carefully. "Good night, Jason."

I put the cold, heavy carburetor on the floor. What the hell just happened?

The next day, it took forever to get a moment with Meili.

Sometimes when Meili was absorbed in a book, she would drag her top teeth across her bottom lip: a silent, slow-motion "Fffff." There was this moment when her lip would release from her teeth and pop out. I timed my nonchalant looks at the clock to catch the end of the "Fffff."

"Fffff."

9:57.

"Fffff."

Still 9:57.

At 11:30, this classroom assistant (she recognized me

from Algebra but pretended she didn't, like most people in those days) finally left us alone. Not completely alone. A boy came in crying during third period and sat way off to the side, sniffling and occasionally shaking his head, arguing silently with whatever had just happened.

"Got a message from Manny last night," I said.

Meili didn't look up. "Who's that?"

The other boy stopped his mental fight and stared: *Talking in the Rubber Room?*

"Funny, I was going to ask you the same thing," I said.

She kept fake-reading. "Don't think I know a Manny."

"Works at Gorman's," I said. "And you're a shitty liar. I expected better."

She ignored that. "What did he say?"

"He told me I'm not allowed to talk to you anymore." I didn't say "see you," because that would sound like we were dating, which I desperately wanted to be true.

"That's a pity. Why not?"

"You tell me."

"I have no clue."

"Is he in charge of you?"

"Sure, why not? Everybody's in charge of me. My aunt and uncle, Ms. Davies, the fucking principal. I get to decide, let's see, basically fuckall about my life." There was a long silence. "What are you staring at, cry boy?"

The poor kid looked away. He didn't sniffle again.

"So what should I do?" I asked.

"How should I know? Do whatever you want. It's not like you're talking to me anyway, is it?" The Algebra assistant waddled back in. Conversation over.

Twenty minutes later, Meili said she had a stomachache and asked to go to the nurse. I didn't see her again that day.

FOUR

AT 3:45, I STOOD IN FRONT OF GORMAN'S
Auto in a chilly drizzle. I held the box with the carburetor,
now soggy from the rain.

A pudgy man with a shaved head, the guy who'd bought
the shop from Ray Gorman two years ago, stepped out of
the office. "Help you?" he said, not sounding eager to.

"I'm looking for Manny."

"What do you need?" He didn't like me mentioning the
name.

"I'm returning this part."

The guy was unsure about me, and he did that man
thing of taking a long pause. A trick I've learned is: don't
fill the pause. Don't jump in and say some crap or apologize
or back down. Wait, let them answer.

"He's around back," he said finally. See? It works. "Blue
door."

I walked around to a blue garage door with a smaller,

people-size door built into it. Manny had knocked, so I knocked.

"Yeah?" a voice shouted.

"I'm here to see Manny!" I yelled, pretty sure it was him.

The door opened with a loud scrape, recutting an arc on the concrete. Manny looked smaller in his gray coveralls, his hands too greasy for a handshake.

"Jason. Hello." He gestured me inside. "Problem with the carburetor?"

I handed him the box, which had fallen apart. "I don't want it."

He looked at me carefully. "OK." He placed the carb on a shelf over the workbench and carefully folded the wet cardboard into a trash can. Dude was neat.

I did need that carb, which was one bad thing about this visit. Now it was time for the other one.

"I made my decision," I said.

"Decision," he repeated.

"I'm gonna keep seeing Melissa." I liked that phrase. "Keep seeing" made me hopeful I might *start* seeing.

"That's why you came here? To tell me this?"

"Yep."

He was going to hit me. I'd been hit a lot recently, but I had the sense this would be much worse.

Fine. Bring it.

"You're gonna mess with my Melissa, huh? You're gonna put my Melissa in danger?" *My Melissa*.

He did this sharp motion with his head, and I brought my arms up to brace. But he just smiled. A little fake-out. And then, somehow, I was on the ground. Like I had done a backflip and ended up on my face. He had me pinned in negative one seconds.

The fuck just happened?

"You're not so tough after all. You're down right away, huh?" He pulled my right arm back, and my whole body screamed in pain.

"Aaaaaaaaaaauuuuhhhh!" I yelled involuntarily.

Pain does strange things to your mind. It's a reset. That's part of what I like about it. With my cheek on the cold concrete, I saw an empty chip bag under the workbench and thought: Manny eats Doritos.

"You're not gonna see Melissa. You're done." He increased the pressure, and I started seeing black spots.

When I finally got some breath, I growled, "Fuck. You." I tried to roll over with all my strength, though I thought it might dislocate my arm. This was some ultimate fighting shit. We didn't fight like this in Unionville.

He laughed. "Pretty good. But you're going the wrong way. You know that, right? You need to go *with* my push. Elevate that shoulder." He tapped my left shoulder and eased up a bit.

Sure enough, I was able roll the other way, which felt completely wrong but somehow extracted my arm from his grasp. I tried to come with an elbow, but he caught it and twisted it, and I was stuck again.

He hopped up and stepped away. "Sloppy but determined. Very American." He chuckled and picked up a gallon jug of water, taking a sip and offering it to me. "Time-out, OK? No more fighting. We are on time-out."

We are on time-out is, in retrospect, a funny-ass phrase. In the moment, it was pure relief. My shoulder had been re-aligned in an unfortunate way, and I had to hold the jug in my left arm.

He stared as I panted and tried to remember how to move my right side. An air gun pulsed in another garage. Then music, someone listening to a radio. Had that been on the whole time?

"She said the same." He grinned. "She will keep seeing you. She was here at lunch. I guess school was dismissed early today?"

I shrugged. "For some people."

"Not many guys can take that hold. Almost all submit quickly," he said, nodding his approval. "You need that. To be with Melissa, you need that." Was he talking about what a pain she was? Or something else? "And take the carburetor. Can't have you riding her around on a broken bike."

"OK." That was it? "So we're cool?" This whole inter-action, including the fight, had been maybe ninety seconds.

He frowned and growled, "Cool? I don't think so." Then he laughed. "Look, man, don't take this the wrong way, I've been hearing stuff about you." Oh, great. "Not all of it bad, OK? Some of it very . . . encouraging." That was a surprise. I wanted to talk to those people. "Melissa and I have to be careful, OK? Some things you've done have been sloppy. Dumb stuff. So watch the dumb stuff, OK? I've got enough problems with Melissa. I can't be cleaning up your messes."

He said "OK" a lot. So I said, "Alright."

Silence.

"OK," he said. Again.

Maybe Manny was the key to all of it. I don't regret much, but if I could go back, I would ask Manny a lot more questions.

We stood there, awkward but intent. Maybe we were sizing each other up. Maybe I had a question I couldn't ask and he wouldn't answer. Maybe he wanted me to leave but was too polite to say so.

All of the above.

"I should probably . . ." I started.

"Yeah, thanks for coming down," he said. Which was crazy considering he had nearly broken my arm a minute ago.

I walked out into the now-heavy rain with an aching shoulder, a carburetor I would never install, a new acquaintance I would see a total of four times in my life, and a fierce desire to talk to Meili immediately.

"Talked to Manny again," I said.

"Did you?" Meili said, calm and casual as if our speaking again was no big deal. We were enjoying a long unsupervised period in the Rubber Room.

"He said he spoke to you," I said.

"Maybe. Can't remember." Meili stared at her book.

"Bullshit. You told him the same thing I did."

"And what's that?"

"That I won't stop seeing you." I used the phrase. Screw it. If she pointed it out, I could say I meant it literally.

"Don't exactly have a choice, do we? Erasing Room and all that."

Meili said "rubber" was a word for eraser. ("Yes, I *know* it means condom here in the States.") You rub out your pencil mark with a *rubber*. So she called the Rubber Room the Erasing Room. It erased us from school, erased our days slowly, grindingly.

"Now we have Manny's permission," I said.

We had both confronted Manny to say we wanted to see each other. Wasn't that a bond, a commitment?

"What a relief." Bored as hell.

"And, in case you're wondering, he half kicked my ass."

"He's like that." She looked up, swerved. "Where's your mother?"

"Right now? She's at work," I said.

"Mmm. Bullshit. Where is she?"

"I don't know. Probably at work. Or shopping."

"I've been 'round your house a dozen times, and I've never seen a car in the driveway or anyone inside but you. Where is she?" Meili said.

No one was supposed to know about my mother. My probation required living with her. But more important: A dozen times? That was interesting.

"So you're a stalker *and* a finger breaker."

"I think you live alone." She paused. I didn't deny it. "Don't worry, I won't tell. And . . ." she added quietly, "I'm jealous."

"Don't be. It's not great."

The bell rang for fourth period, and the hallway was instantly clogged.

"If you get tired of reheated macaroni and cheese, you should come by the house for a proper meal. Served by some utterly uptight people."

Had she seen me eating mac and cheese, or was that a guess?

"You're serious," I said.

"Rarely. But yes, you should come by Sunday. I'm sure my aunt and uncle would love to meet a real live firebug.

And you're very cute for blushing. I mean, it would be cute if you were twelve. At your age, it's a bit sad, isn't it?"

I didn't care. We had gone from not speaking to a dinner invitation.

The endless boredom of the Rubber Room, the lunch I'd forgotten to bring, the aide's loud, wet breathing (did she need medical attention?), none of that could touch me.

Meili had invited me over.

I waited for her after school. Meili had to stay in the Rubber Room until Laura Fenton was on her bus home. Nobody made the guys who threatened me wait in the school building. I'm just saying.

The kids with trucks and SUVs lingered in the parking lot, cranking their music. Preppies drove off in their Hondas, but rednecks flaunted their rides.

"Look who it is," Meili said. "Six and a half hours not enough time together?"

"I thought we could go read near each other without talking."

"Promise you won't keep staring, though? 'S a bit unnerving after the first four hours." Joke? Flirtation? I pretty much did look at her every chance I got. "And I'm 'fraid I'm booked today. Little trip with my aunt, who's right over there." She pointed at a silver Toyota. "Wave, Firebug. Now you've ruined my carefully planned introduction to my custodials. It was going to happen at dinner, remember? Nice, controlled environment, everybody polite and done up."

Done up. "Yeah, should I bring something or, like, wear something?" That didn't come out right.

"Definitely wear *something*. At least a thong and some boots, yeah?" She stepped back and eyed me. "You'd do alright in a thong, wouldn't you? Make a fortune dancing at a gay club. Is there one in town?" I didn't mind being checked out by Meili. It was only fair, given how much I stared at her.

"Seriously, should I dress up?"

"Please, Bug, come as you are. You're not going to fool anyone."

"What does that mean?"

"It means you, Mr. Firemaniac, are a somewhat good-hearted human being. Shockingly and rather tragically for your sake. And people can tell. Now, no mushy goodbyes, 'K? I'd hate for my aunt to see me kiss a felon."

If Meili wanted to get inside my head, if she wanted me to do nothing but wonder about her, she was succeeding.

The third time I saw Manny, and the last time I saw him calm, we were in his hoopty old Ford Tempo. Guy knew cars, and he drove a faded family sedan. Go figure. To make it even more pathetic, he had four-point restraints in both front seats, serious racing stuff, like: "Hey, I can't afford a decent ride, but I have fierce seat belts." I didn't put mine on.

He came by my house Friday afternoon, said he needed help. I figured this was progress—there were no blindingly painful holds involved—and, of course, anything related to Meili came first.

He drove us out to the fairgrounds, empty until August when the rides and the show pigs and the demolition derby gave Unionville its two weeks of glory. It started raining as we rolled into the parking lot behind the grandstand, a great place to find drugs or fights on summer weekends, but deserted today. What could Manny need help with back here?

"Buckle up, Jason."

"What are we doing?"

"Buckle up."

I reached back and pulled the harness over me. "No offense, man, but the seat belts are a little over the top. Around here, people are gonna laugh if you—"

The car roared to life, and I was pinned against my seat. We rocketed across the parking lot as I strained to fasten my harness. We were heading right toward a row of stables. My first real makeout session, in sixth grade with Allison Robbey, was in those stables. We were about to demolish them.

I braced against the dashboard.

"Manny!"

He popped the emergency brake and cut the wheel hard

left. The car spun a precise 180, and we were heading back the other way.

This was a "bootlegger's turn," the kind of spin you see in movies. Turns out, it's a real thing.

"Yeeeeeeeeah!" Manny yelled. He had his mature side, but, in a car, dude was a redneck thirteen-year-old.

I caught my breath. Manny floored it again. He looked over at me, which was a terrible idea.

This time he braked hard (brake pedal, not emergency brake) as he turned left, and we started a controlled skid, a rubber-burning donut, three times faster than I'd ever seen a donut done, Manny grinning at me the whole time. I was pinned against the passenger door, the blood in my head rushing to one side.

The car straightened and stopped short. My organs returned to their assigned seats.

"What?! What the hell is this?" I meant that in every sense.

"Not bad, right?" He put the car in neutral, revving it and listening closely.

"I take back what I said about the seat belts. In fact, I want a helmet. And a fire suit."

Manny laughed. "That's good. I like your sense of humor." He turned the car off, got still. He talked to the dashboard now, a little speech he had rehearsed, probably while talking to that same dashboard. "Seriously, I like you, Jason. And I trust you. So does Melissa. But. She is in a difficult situation. If you expose her in any way, if you tell anyone about her, I will burn you." Weird word choice. "You're on probation. One phone call to the police—maybe you hit me or stole my money or grabbed Melissa's knickers— one phone call and you're back in jail."

"You've done your research." Knickers. That meant underpants, right? Meili's underpants. Sexy.

"But it's not going to come to that. I just need you to understand, if you're going to be with Melissa, you must be careful."

"Look, I don't know what's going on," I said, hoping he might enlighten me. He didn't. "But, yeah, I would never do anything to put her in danger."

Still facing the steering wheel, he said, "She is already in danger, Jason. We all are. Know that."

The toughest thing about a bootlegger is going for it. It feels so wrong to turn hard at full speed, my whole body fought against doing it. But once you do it, and pop the hand brake at the right moment, it's like skid-stopping a BMX bike. You use the car's weight to stop and turn at the same time. Manny called his car a *sleeper*, a boring sedan modded out for high performance, a rocket hiding in plain sight. It had excellent tires (the most important mod, he said) so it was easy to get the right amount of cut to make the 180.

"Alright! That's it! You feel that?" Manny yelled when I finally nailed it, flooring it out of the spin.

"Yeah, I get where the weight is."

"Exactly. Feel the weight of the car, and you can make it do anything."

I stopped by the boarded-up concession stands. The adrenaline, the speed, the screw-it-go-faster, it all made me blurt out a question. The question.

"What is this all about?"

"What is what all about?" He leaned out the passenger window, checking a tire.

"Melissa, the danger, all that."

He came back in, faced his friend the dashboard again. "I can't tell you. Obviously. It puts Melissa and me at risk, but even more, it puts you at risk. I don't want you to know anything valuable enough that someone might"—he paused, and my mind inserted a variety of horrifying verbs—"come after you, so to speak."

So to speak? That was a creepy phrase to put there.

Manny was a sleeper. A quiet mechanic who was really what? A bodyguard? A spy trained in evasive driving and hand-to-hand combat?

"People are after her," I said. A statement, but actually a question. Something I'd picked up from Meili.

Manny spoke carefully. "People have threatened Melissa's family. More than threatened. So we had to disappear. And to disappear, you have to be careful."

"And Melissa isn't careful," I said.

"Not always."

"She broke that girl's finger."

He shook his head, closed his eyes like the memory was physically painful. "And this isn't the first school where we've had an incident."

"She's tough," I said, meaning both senses of the word. Let him choose.

"She is. Very strong. I wish she'd save it for the real fight."

Good phrase. *Save it for the real fight.* I'd wear that shirt.

"Hopefully, it all gets . . . resolved, and we can start over." He stared out the window. "We don't want to live like this forever."

Like this. In Unionville, pulling donuts in the drizzle behind the gray metal grandstand.

Really, he meant: "We don't want to live like *you* forever."

I felt the same way.

FIVE

I PARKED MY MOTORCYCLE DOWN THE STREET.
I know, I know, *come as you are*. But I remembered dropping Meili off several blocks away so her aunt wouldn't see my bike.

They lived in a ranch house with a well-mowed lawn. Extremely well-mowed. The lawn mower made perfect lines parallel to the street, with no stray tire tracks. Did they pick the mower up and carry it back when they finished?

I rang the bell, stood up straight in my light-blue UHS sweatshirt and my cleanest black jeans (which had little holes in the back, hopefully covered by the sweatshirt). I had showered, shaved, and, weirdly, flossed. Combination of sprucing up for the aunt and uncle and dreaming of making out with Meili. I even cleaned my house on the astonishingly optimistic hope that Meili and I might end up back there. Meili got me to do what parental lectures and Life Skills classes never did: I was taking care of myself.

"You must be Jason," Meili's aunt said, opening the door, more accusation than greeting. Like: you must be kidding. Like: you're *that* Jason.

"Hello," I said, forcing a smile.

"You're early," she said.

I was. It was Sunday, and I couldn't sit home for another minute anticipating this dinner. I had to jump in.

Mrs. Jenkins, like her husband, looked white and sounded American. That intrigued me but didn't shock me. In my world, "aunt" and "uncle" can mean people you're related to or people you're staying with.

Meili appeared behind her and crossed her eyes. My smile became genuine. The aunt saw this and, annoyed, turned around to Meili, "He's here." Oh, really? "I suppose you can sit in the living room till dinner."

"And you are?" I asked.

Caught in her own rudeness, she tilted her head at me. "I am Melissa's aunt Sophie. But you may call me Mrs. Jenkins."

Wow. This was gonna be painful.

"Thanks, Auntie. I think we'll sit out back since it's such a lovely evening." Meili took me by the arm—she touched me—and escorted me out to a picnic table.

The grass under the table was, yes, mowed in perfectly straight lines.

"Isn't she mahvelous?" Meili whispered.

"The bear hug was nice, but those kisses were a bit much," I said.

Meili laughed. It wasn't easy to make her laugh. She had a high standard for cleverness and cynicism. But when she did find something funny, she laughed her ass off. So gratifying.

"You can see," she said, "how the Erasing Room is no big adjustment for me. I'm well used to living in the glare of the prison guard. Feels natural."

"How long has it been?" I asked, leaving the question open.

"How long has what been?" she asked.

"Living with the prison guards."

She didn't love this question, so she changed it. "Been living here since January. And loving every second."

I remembered seeing *the new girl from overseas* a few times before I was banished to the Rubber Room. But I had been preoccupied in January, scanning the halls for Ronny and his crew.

"How long will you be here?"

"Who knows? Somewhere between forever and a few more days. Especially if I keep annoying them by bringing rednecks around."

The neighbors' back door opened, and a tiny dog ran out, yapping through the chain-link fence.

"God, I still can't believe how much space there is here," she said. "In Hong Kong, this would be a fucking park, seriously, a nature preserve."

"You're from Hong Kong," I said.

She smiled, nodded, a little tense. "Mostly." Was she not supposed to say that?

"And I'm here to annoy your aunt and uncle," I said.

She grimaced and raised her shoulders to her ears. "Can I say: definitely yes, but also no. You are here to annoy them, obviously, and you're doing a great job. Please continue. But that's not the only reason."

"What's the other reason?"

"Because you are not a stupid, pathetic redneck like every other boy in this town." I smiled, a little too early. "You are a smart, pathetic redneck. You can annoy my custodials *and* keep me entertained. Rare combination, that."

So tricky, her cruelty. It drew me to her, and that made it hurt more.

Dinner was delicious and agonizing. Noodles, sorry, *pasta* with tomato sauce that was homemade and spicy. Garlic bread and salad. Did people eat this way every night?

Mrs. Jenkins said grace so fast I only caught "blessing" and "we humbly."

Mr. Jenkins—thinning red hair, digital watch, and a huge appetite—made an effort. "So, Jason, what are you into? Sports?" he asked.

"Uh." I stalled. What was I into? "Motorcycles, mostly." That was a stretch. I mean, I rode a motorcycle, but was I *into* them?

"I trust Melissa isn't riding on any motorcycles," Mrs. Jenkins said, looking squarely at Meili.

"Certainly not," Meili said, shaking her head gravely.

"Melissa did say she used to ride a lot," I said. "Back in . . . where was that?"

Meili smiled a big "fuck you" at me and said, "You must be thinking of another girl."

"Right, the other girl with the British accent."

"The little one who died in that tragic fire?"

"After her grandmother got run over by a taxi." I turned to Mrs. Jenkins and quoted Meili: "She went to hospital, she came back out, it wasn't so bad."

Meili's eyes burned from across the table.

I loved quoting Meili. I loved how my language got tangled up with hers. Even now, a sentence comes to me, and I think: Did Meili say that? Did I steal it from her? Did we both say it? Or did I make it up? Language was one way Meili captured my mind.

Mr. Jenkins sopped up sauce with his garlic bread. "Whareyoudarrsmember?" he asked with his mouth full. I liked that.

"Sorry?" I said.

"He said: 'What are you doing in September?'" Mrs. Jenkins did full-mouth translation.

September. What happened in September? There was the Labor Day cookout I never went to, and "Hogs for the Cause," a bike rally that benefited some kids' disease.

Oh, college. Of course.

"That's a good question," I said. "Still working that out.

Been talking to my guidance counselor a lot about . . . what's next." Factually accurate, totally a lie. "And what about Melissa? Is she heading off to college?"

Fun to talk about her in the third person. If nothing else, I could use this excruciating dinner to get more information.

"Melissa's plans are also in flux. We aren't sure what's next for her," Mrs. Jenkins said. She strained a smile, passed the salad.

"It must be hard, being a senior in a brand-new place," I said.

"It's an adjustment," Mrs. Jenkins said.

"And it's not the most welcoming school." I was enjoying this.

Mrs. Jenkins sniffed. "Say what you will about the high school, they were very accommodating when Melissa arrived midyear."

"Not everyone was," Mr. Jenkins said, shaking the blue cheese dressing.

"Well, violence is hardly the way to make new friends," Mrs. Jenkins said.

Oh, that. This was an opening for me. I spoke right to Mr. Jenkins now. He was the one to convince. "Look, I don't know what Melissa told you, but I promise you that incident was a hundred percent the other kid's fault. Melissa defended herself. And to be honest, at our school, if she didn't stand up for herself, they'd keep coming after her. That's the way these kids work, especially with someone new. They push and push until you fight back."

Mr. Jenkins chewed and nodded. "I certainly remember that growing up. We used to throw hands sometimes." Wow. Great term for fighting. Stealing it. "That was guys, though. Guess I'm naïve. I'm surprised to hear girls are fighting."

"Not all of them," I said. "Definitely some." I shook my head. I was having a how-times-have-changed moment with Meili's uncle. Nice.

"For the record," Meili said, twirling noodles onto her fork. "I did tell them exactly what happened, but for some reason they didn't believe *me*."

"It's not that we don't believe you, we're concerned about the consequences," Mrs. Jenkins said.

"And it's . . . uh . . . reassuring to hear it from a local," Mr. Jenkins said.

Locals was what preppies called us, to our faces at least. Behind our backs, we were rednecks, drunks, trash.

"Maylorgaspees. Amen." He stood to clear his dishes. Turns out, that's how dinner ends at the Jenkins home.

Later, as Meili walked me out, she squeezed my arm. "That was brutally funny at the table, that bit about the taxi and the motorbike, be*lieve* me, no one appreciates inappropriate humor more than I do, Bug, but you should be aware that Auntie and Uncle know fuckall about my past, and that's how I prefer it. Reduces my exposure." Weird word. "So if I make the horrid mistake of telling you anything about myself, which I fear I may, let's keep it between us, shall we? Keep the morbid jokes between us, 'K? But *do* keep them, please, god, let there be someone who can horrify me with his jokes, 's a dream come true. Ta." She gave me the fastest, stealthiest peck on the cheek, so unexpected and sudden there was no way I could turn it into a real kiss. Or even experience it. By the time I understood what was happening, she was back through the screen door, walking down the hall, her blue dress hugging a body I couldn't stop thinking about.

That night, I sat in my neat living room with my clean shirt and my flossed teeth. I replayed the night and Meili's touches, especially that shocking kiss on the cheek. I'd gone a lot further with other girls and barely been affected. Meili squeezed my arm, and I sat dumbfounded on my couch.

My messy, thoughtless world was converging to a point. Everything moved to Meili.

That seemed wonderful, until it didn't.

The Rubber Room became, to use a Meili word, exquisite. She used the word to amplify her dislike. "She's an exquisite arsehole." Or "What an exquisite waste of time."

For six hours and thirty-four minutes every day, I sat near, but not too near, the person I couldn't stop thinking about. I pretended to read but actually obsessed over her every action or nonaction. Meili was doing her lip-chewing thing. Meili turned toward me a little. Or did she? Meili was writing. Meili caught me staring and bared her teeth like a dog.

I measured days by the number and length of our un-supervised periods. That Monday, a great day, had five teacherless stretches, some lasting more than ten minutes. Tuesday was agonizing. A substitute, or anyway a teacher I'd never seen and never saw again, treated the job as if it mattered. Mr. Harris, tall and shiny bald, ate lunch at the desk, graded essays, and timed his bladder for the moments I went to pee, accompanying me to the bathroom and leaving Meili alone, which did me no good. There was a note in my American lit anthology when I returned: *Damn Harris!* in angry letters. That became our shorthand for ridiculously unfair situations.

Meili read, quickly and devotedly. She finished two books that Monday, one on Tuesday. I rarely got through a full page without staring at her out of the corner of my eye.

Wednesday, Meili dropped a card on my desk when she arrived. I remembered her first note, the not-apology that I'd wanted to open but didn't. That feeling, so intense the first time, was a thousand times stronger now. *A note from Meili.* Since having dinner at her house, I had done exactly two things: thought about Meili, and been briefly distracted from thinking about her. It was out of control. I was out of control.

I didn't open it.

During an aide pee break, she said, "Oh, please, Fire-bug, read it. We've got work to do."

"Work?" I said, not opening the card.

"I've got a legitimate—*we've* got—a legitimate gig this weekend."

"A gig?"

"DJing. Some crap metal band, and I'm the opening act," she said. "Don't ask me why, but a certain fabulous boy has decided I'm the savior of Unionville, sent to enlighten you."

"What fabulous boy?"

"My boy Stephen. He's booked me as a DJ, though, technically, I haven't got *so* so much experience, but it's not like the crowd will know, because they'll be too busy throwing cans of tallboy at me as soon as they hear the shite I'm going to play, which I can't possibly play till you obtain some very specific equipment for me. Thaink ewe vurr much." She finished in her fake Southern accent. Not that we lived in the South. "Cans of tallboy" was Meili's misunderstanding of tallboys, sixteen-ounce beers that were a slightly cheaper way to get drunk.

More favors. I opened the card. A white butterfly on a white flower, *With deepest sympathy.* Inside, she had crossed out ~~You are surrounded by thoughts of love and care, today and in the days to come~~ and written: *Dynamix 2-Channel Compact DJ Controller! Right away please! Melissa xoxozzzzzzzzzzz.* There were four crisp twenties folded into a triangle.

"That's a lot of cash."

"Yes, and the address is on the back. And the thing is, I need to have it to practice, so . . ." The door opened—conversation over.

The back of the card had an address in Wells, a good hour away.

You're welcome, Meili.

xoxo

I didn't go to Wells. I didn't get the DJ controller.

Not that day or the next day.

I was proving something. Something hard and heavy and made of wanting Meili so badly.

I was so desperate to ride to Wells—it was all I could think about—that I had to resist. I had to disappoint her, turn away. She had to see me turn away.

Needing people was never a good idea. Letting them know you need them was worse.

I got a phone call, which was shocking. The phone had been shut off for two weeks. More shocking: it was my mom.

"Hey, J," she said when I picked up. Her voice was slowed down like she'd been drinking some, but not blurry like she'd been drinking a lot.

"Hi, Mom. What's going on?"

There's a mode you go into when your mom's a drunk or an addict or otherwise a mess. Whenever she called, my first thought was: What's wrong? What is she gonna ask me for?

"Hey, baby, I miss you so much."

My second thought, when the call was not an emergency, was: How much lovey mother-son talk does she need to reassure her that she's not a total disaster as a parent? I was willing to provide the minimum to get off the phone.

"Yeah, what . . . um . . . how's Florida?" She missed me so much at a specific point in her drunk. Two drinks later, she regretted everything, and two drinks after that, no one understood her.

"It's good. It's real warm, you know. I was just thinking about my boy, worrying about my boy. I don't care what happened, you know you're my boy, right?"

This was where I had to grit my teeth. "Of course, Mom. I always will be."

"Yeah, you will, baby." She took a drag off her cigarette. "Things are coming together, I want you to know that. They're coming together."

"Like what?" I said, stupidly hoping for good news. I always paced when I talked to her, stretching the cord from the couch to the fridge and back.

"I got the phone back on, didn't I?" she said, as if a working phone was a triumph. A cell phone was out of the question in my world. We only ever had the discounted poor-people landline with no long distance, so we always had calling cards from Redi-Mart taped to the kitchen wall. They had pictures of the globe or maps of Central America or logos of Mexican soccer teams. And they stayed up long after they were used, so making a long-distance call meant trying three or four till you found one that had minutes. "And Al and I are getting it together down here. We just needed a little space. He's got some terrific ideas for starting things and, you know, making a little money."

"Make a little money" was a classic Al-ism, used either to whine about unfairness ("I just want to live my life, make a little money, and have some fun, OK? Why can't [bosses, landlords, banks, cops] understand that?") or to promote his latest doomed scheme ("I'm just gonna [open a lunch cart, start a music festival for Spanish-speaking people, buy cigarettes on the Indian reservation and sell them outside bars], make a little money, and start over.")

"Is he clean?" I said, knowing the answer but needing my mom to say it, needing her to hear herself say it. I warmed my feet in a square of sunlight by the back door.

"He's getting there, I'll tell you, he's really taking steps. I wish you two could forget what happened. He's a good man, J, and I'm so lucky to have him. And you, I'm so blessed with you, my sweet boy." Another drag. "How are things in Oniontown?"

"You know, moving along. I still can't go to class, so it's pretty boring at school." Truth was, the Rubber Room and Meili were the least boring things in my world. Maybe ever.

"Everything OK with probation?"

"Yeah, I go in once a month. He's on me about finding a job, but he hasn't visited or anything."

"Al says they never visit unless there's an issue. So I think we're in the clear on that one." We. She can live in Florida, and I can stay out of jail. "And I'm betting the whole . . ." The rest of her sentence was drowned out by loud music on her end. I heard a couple swear words and some banging, then her voice came back. "Sorry, I had to step outside. You there, babe?"

"Yeah."

"Anyway, I just want us all to get along. That's all I wanted to say. I love you, babe."

This was the beginning of the wind-down, as my mom laid the groundwork for hanging up. Next was the part I hated, where I had to ask for money that wasn't coming.

"Love you, too, Mom. Hey, did you get a chance to send that money?"

"Yeah, we definitely did. You didn't get it?" Bullshit.

"Not yet."

"Tell you what, let me ask Al, cause I'm sure we sent a check. And I asked your father to send something, too, but I don't guess he did."

My biological. Eight years since I'd seen the man, maybe five since I got a birthday call. I used to defend him to my mom. *No, Mom, he was late, but he was really excited to be here.* Then we switched, and she stood up for him. *He does*

what he can, Jason, and at the end of the day, he is your father.
Now we tried not to mention him.

"No, nothing. And it's getting kinda tight, Mom."

"Don't worry, babe. It's gonna work out. It's all gonna work out." Pause, then back to the wind-down. "And I do love you, J."

In December, when she first went to Florida, the wind-down included promises of when she was coming back or how we'd all live together again. That had quietly disappeared, like all those promises of summer camps and dogs and vacations and even, in the crazed grip of some AI scheme two years ago, a promise to buy me a car.

"I love you, too, Mom."

"Let's talk soon, OK?" As if I hadn't been returning her calls.

"Yeah, definitely. Take care of yourself, Mom."

"You too, babe. Bye-bye."

My drunk mom, a thousand miles away, hangs up after not speaking to me for three weeks, and what's my feeling? Sorrow? Anger? Loneliness? No, relief. She's not here. Her bullshit and her boyfriend's bullshit are not in the house with me, and I'm free to do what I want for the rest of the night.

Except that Meili arrived five minutes later.

"Knock, knock!" she yelled, trying to open the door, which was, of course, double bolted. "DJ Esmerelda is here!"

I opened the door to Meili and Stephen Morse. Stephen

70

(Stevie in grade school, Steve in middle school, and now Stephen) was a tall, big-eyed kid I sort of knew. We'd played on the same tee-ball team. I remember doing a history project with him in eighth grade and thinking: this kid is so nice to everyone. That hadn't lasted into high school.

"Hey, Bug. Here for the gear," Meili said, waiting for me to let her in.

"Hey, Jason," Stephen said, fake-smiling, as he always did, though I think he liked me.

"Hi. Um, yeah, I don't have it. Sorry." I blocked the door. Couldn't let them walk in and see the pathetic state of my life.

I liked living in chaos. No one could say anything about my house. It was mine. The crappiness was my crappiness. But that depended on one thing: if I cared about your opinion, you couldn't see it.

"'K." Meili paused, reading my face for clues. "Can you get it?"

"No, I'm busy. Sorry." I was letting her down, proving myself. Why didn't I feel righteous?

Stephen was looking past me into the house. He drove here; couldn't he get the stuff?

"Busy." A Meili statement-question.

"Is everything alright, Jason?" Stephen asked, wide-eyed at my behavior and what he could see of my living room.

I ducked inside, grabbed the envelope out of my bag, and hustled back. "Yeah. What do you mean?"

71

"I mean . . ." Stephen waved his hand at the barren and trashed living room.

I handed the envelope with the cash to Meili, but I talked to Stephen. "I'm fine. I'm . . . there's stuff . . . there's someone here. That's all." What? Where the hell did that come from?

"Ooooooh. 'K. Bit awkward." Meili's eyes widened, and she grabbed the envelope. "We'll have our little DJ session somewhere else, then. Ta."

Stephen waved halfheartedly, said, "OK," and walked after her.

Crap. What had I done?

"Hey," I called out. "I would love to hear your music, though. You know, soon." Jesus.

Meili's face as she turned around said: *Don't you dare fucking pity me. Ever.*

I didn't like it in the moment, but that was a good face. I support that face.

I fucking agree with that face.

SIX

THE NEXT DAY I CUT SCHOOL. BECAUSE SCREW it. Because sitting in the Rubber Room was no more educational than sitting at home. Because I should scrounge gas money and try to get to Florida. Because I didn't want to face Meili.

But it turned out sitting at home, not going to Florida, and not facing Meili was worse. Daytime TV goes from Excitement of Playing Hooky to Depressed Confusion of Person with No Life in three shows. At 2:30, I was outside the rear door of the school, the one Meili and I used so we remained "segregated from the general student population."

Students rushed out the front doors into buses and cars. At 2:50, our door popped open. I stood up and nearly bumped into Meili.

"You're a bit late, aren't you?" she said, unfazed. Always unfazed. " 'Fraid the Rubber Room's closed."

"Yeah, I wanted to tell you . . ." What? "I'm sorry about yesterday."

She shifted her book-filled bag to her other shoulder. "Christ, leave it go. You're being awkward. It's nothing to do with me."

The parking lot was clogged with people trying to exit and people cruising. Honking and counter-honking. Sammy the security guard was on the move, ordering cars to "get the hell out."

"No, I was . . . I was in a weird mood. There wasn't anyone there."

She dropped her bag. "Please. Don't do that, OK? Don't lie. You can be a freak and an arsehole and that's fine, but don't fucking lie to me. I can't abide lying fucking liars."

Somewhere in that sentence was a clue, a ping from the black box of Meili. In the moment, I was too flustered to hear it.

"I'm not lying. I mean, I did lie. Yesterday. No one was there, I just didn't want you to come in and see my house and how messed up it is."

"Really? You hadn't tidied up? Curtains don't match the sofa, that sort of thing?"

The gridlock eased as Sammy waved a long line of cars onto the road. Kids yelled out plans to meet at Stewart's or Redi-Mart or some other boring-ass place.

"Seriously, Melissa, it's bad. My whole situation is bad."

"A bad situation? Wow, I can't possibly imagine. Mine is so ideal."

"You're the fanciest person I know, OK? And my life right now is pretty messed up."

"I'm fancy? The fuck are you talking about?" That wasn't what I wanted to say. Ugh. Finally, she said, "I should go."

"No," I said. "Listen. I live alone. My mom's a drunk and some other things, too. She got into trouble, and she left. Her and her sketchy boyfriend went to Florida five months ago to get clean." After the fire, before the Rubber Room. "So I'm living alone. I don't have money. I do eat cold macaroni and cheese. And if the court knew about all this, I'd be in jail."

She didn't physically step back, but her eyes did. "It's quite lovely, you know."

"What?"

"Florida. It's gorgeous. I was down on the little islands when I was a kid, the Keys, absolutely magical. You might should take a trip."

Here's a difference between me and Meili: I need a certain reaction from people. Not everyone, not all the time. But if I say something real to you, acknowledge it. Meili never waited for reactions, never expected anything in conversation. She gave surprise and wanted surprise and figured the whole thing was so arbitrary and broken that expecting anything was ludicrous.

"Great. I'll think about that." Everything was a sick little joke to her. I got on my bike.

"What?"

"I tell you some deep, crazy shit, stuff that could get me arrested, and all you can say is: 'Florida is lovely'?" I hoped I could start the bike without pushing it.

"If you're looking for pity, you're knocking on the wrong door. I don't do pity. And in my defense, I was right about the macaroni and cheese."

"Pity's not the same as understanding." I didn't know where that came from. I didn't know that I thought there was a difference. But there was.

The bike wouldn't turn over. I should have put that carburetor in. I started pushing. Maybe I should ride south and find my mom. No, then I'd be taking Meili's advice to go to Florida. I ran it halfway across the parking lot and still nothing. What a nightmare. Goddamn, I wanted her to see me speed away. I wanted to end this conversation by roaring off. But, no, I was pathetically still there, too broke and incompetent to have a working bike.

I pushed farther so it was clear we were done talking, turned off the gas line, and tilted the bike, since it was probably flooded. I was wiping out the carb with my sleeve when I heard her behind me.

"May Lee," she said. I ignored her. "It's May Lee."

I stopped working and turned around. "What?" Couldn't I leave?

"M-E-I-L-I," she said. "My name. 'S not Melissa. So you were right about the macaroni, too."

Whoa. "You changed your name."

"Not changed, exactly. A little alias. Temporary, I should think, but who's to say?" She had her tobacco out, pinching and rolling. Not allowed on school grounds. "We totally blew it, right? 'Melissa' looks like 'Meili' on paper, but it sounds totally different, especially when you rednecks say it, it's basically 'Lissa,' you know, which sounds nothing like Meili. 'Hey, M'*Lissa*!' It's a completely different name and a crap one at that. Being called Lissa is like being named Mandy or Pony or Frosting or something." That made me laugh. Dammit. "Except it's *not* funny, not really, because it's a huge fucking problem, and if my real name got out, I'd be . . . y'know . . . worse than in jail."

"Because . . ."

She lit her cigarette and picked a piece of tobacco off her lip, which reminded me of girls who dip tobacco, a thing I always found attractive. "That's just it, isn't it? It's a secret. Talking about why it's a secret's no different than telling the secret. But, on the positive, now we can *both* wreck each other's lives. 'S nice, right?"

"Yes, it is, Meili."

"Wow. OK. Shit." She was wide-eyed. "That's, um . . . wasn't ready for that." It was the first time I'd seen Meili thrown. And like every other time I'd see that expression, it had to do with this. With her name, her secret. Then it was gone. "Don't ever fucking say that in public."

"Got it. I'll stick with Frosting."

And right there, in the heat of the back parking lot on a Friday, stinking of gasoline, I stepped into Meili's maze. Not sure I ever found my way out.

"Appreciate that." She didn't walk away.

I got on my bike.

"You're a bit precious, aren't you? Underneath it all," she said.

Maybe, Meili. Maybe I am.

Over the weekend, I heard about a job. Family FunZone was hiring preseason workers to clean out the arcade and batting cages, prep the go-karts, and whatever else Big Don could think of. I'd done it two years ago and made decent money. It was also an audition for working there during the season—I hadn't passed the audition, apparently—which was a sought-after job, not because of the pay (minimum wage) or the working conditions (harsh), but because you could give your friends free tokens and rides and generally treat your job as a chance to meet girls.

I needed money. I also needed to show my probation officer that I had applied for jobs, which I had been faking for two months.

It's easy to see now that bringing Meili was a terrible idea. It's like when I was in sixth grade, and Mitchell, this older kid who lived behind us, said: "Your mom's boyfriend is a drug dealer." Of course he was. And of course I knew it. I just didn't *know* that I knew it.

"Family what?" Tuesday morning, Meili was searching through her bag before the bell rang.

"FunZone. It's go-karts and arcades and stuff. They're hiring people to get the place ready for summer."

"And I'm coming along why, exactly?"

"Cause it'll be fun," I said with a fake grin. "Not really. But it might help me get the job."

"Help you how?"

I didn't want to say: because Don flirts with girls. And I didn't want to say the real, *real* reason: because I am using any excuse to be close to you, to feel you pressed against me on my bike. "Cause then it's two high-school kids looking for work, not a felon on probation who needs a favor."

She squinted at me, then smiled. "Actually, it's brilliant. I need the money. And it might could get my aunt off my back. If I tell her I'm applying for a job, she'll stop panicking about the DJ thing. Apparently, in America, 'DJ' is a synonym for 'Takes Date-Rape Drug and Loses Mind.' " The aide walked in and heard the last bit. Meili put on a huge smile and said, "And a good morning to you as well!"

"Don't s'pose I can drive this time," Meili said or asked.

We went right from school Thursday afternoon. If people weren't already talking about Pyro and the Finger

Breaker, they would start now. Pulling out of the school parking lot with a girl on my bike was an announcement.

"No," I said, climbing on. "You're not legal."

"And you've got to look macho here at school, don't you?" She said "macho" with a short A, like "satchel." "Want me to cling to you like a little girl?"

Yes.

"Try not to fall off," I said.

"I'm *not* getting paralyzed, OK, so—"

"I know, I know. If you fall off and get paralyzed, I'll turn around and run you over repeatedly."

She lit her cigarette. Still not allowed on school grounds.

"Horrid thing to joke about. I so appreciate that, Bug. As a thank-you, I'll be super girly on the back of the bike. You'd like that, wouldn't you?"

She was. And I did.

That's Meili in a moment. I shock her with a joke the way she shocks everyone else. That makes her so happy she sarcastically acts girly "to please me," but actually to mock me. But then I do like it. And she knows I like it. And she enjoys that. Plus a few more layers I'm not smart enough to understand.

"Girly enough?" she called out as we hit the pavement, hugging me tight.

Family FunZone was at an otherwise desolate crossroads on Route 12. It had expanded over the years: laser tag, mini golf, and, the real breakthrough, a liquor license and a beer garden. That made it a huge hit in Unionville: basically a bar with childcare. My mom would take me there and give me, like, a dollar twenty-five, telling me to bum tokens off my friends while she partied.

Riding into the dirt parking lot, overgrown with grass from the wet spring, I realized I desperately wanted this job, and for the whole summer, not just preseason. I would have money, something to tell my PO, and an actual social life. I got my hopes up.

I never knew with the fire. Did people hear about it? How big of a deal was it? Seen one way, burning a seven-year-old is no recommendation for working at an amusement park. Seen another way, being on probation is pretty common around here.

I got off the bike feeling positive. Meili would insulate me from my reputation. I could ride her charm to an opportunity, work my ass off, and earn the job.

Some older guys were already hired. I approached a guy power-washing the awnings. He saw me, but it took him a while to turn it off.

"Is Big Don around?" I asked.

"What do you need?"

"I'm here about a job."

He looked at Meili and kept looking at her as he said, "He's out. Should be back soon if you wanna wait."

"Thanks, man," I said, but he had already started the power washer.

We sat at a picnic table scarred by cigarette burns and

carved names. She took out her tobacco, but I shook my head.

"Big Don doesn't like smokers. They take too many breaks."

"Do they? Good to know." She put it back in her bag and looked around. "God, this place is amazing. To'ally American. This is what we picture you Americans doing: you drive a huge pickup truck here and drink beer and shoot guns and race a go-kart, and then you get all rowdy and decide to invade a country or something."

"Sometimes we invade first."

"And celebrate here."

"Yup."

"Nice." A long exhale. "So strange."

"What's that?" I childishly hoped she was about to confess feelings for me. Seriously? At Family FunZone in the middle of the day?

"I've been so many different places. Lived so many places. And every one of them is . . . permanent. People were living there, and they're still living there. Like this place, it's been here for ages, and it'll be here forever. But I'm floating." She reached instinctively for her tobacco, then remembered. "It's like, what a hellhole, right? I would hate to spend my whole life here. I can't be*lieve* people live their whole lives in this depressing place. Sorry, Unionville, no offense. But really."

"None taken. Unless you're saying I'm depressing because I spent my life here."

"Your life isn't over yet."

"Depends who you ask."

"Seriously, it's not a place I want to live at all, and still, I'm sitting here"—she looked around and then at me—"jealous. I'm actually jealous you live here, and every year the FunHole opens up, and you go back, and it's yours, you get to keep it. That's the thing, you get to keep it, even . . . what?"

I was grinning. "Nothing."

"No, what?"

"You said 'FunHole.'"

"What is it?" She looked around. "FunZone? Sorry. Stupid name." She switched to her bad Southern accent. "Ah'm een mah Fun Zown naow."

"Stupid name, but don't go around talking about your FunHole."

"None of you blokes are getting near my FunHole. I don't care how big this Big Don is, all my FunHoles are off-limits." I laughed. Big Don's SUV—not a pickup truck, for the record—pulled in. "D'you want this job?" Meili asked.

"I do."

"Badly?"

"Very."

"Right. I'm going to pull out all the stops, 'K? Don't

judge me." She stood and shifted into a different body, all posture and alertness. "And I said 'FunHole' on purpose. I think I did anyway. So you were laughing at my joke, not at me. Probably."

Big Don walked past, uh-huhing into his phone. He looked Meili up and down but didn't stop. I would have waited meekly outside, but Meili went striding in after him, so I followed. The arcade was empty and windowless, more like a garage. The games were stored in shipping containers behind the mini golf. Rolling those huge machines over bumpy grass was one of the many sucky tasks of opening the FunZone.

Big Don leaned over a table covered with papers and tools and empty Big Gulps, his baggy no-name jeans sagging while I tried not to look. I was afraid Meili would be horrified by the place, but she was still at full attention, slight smile, bright eyes.

"Alright, yup," was Don's goodbye. He put the phone down and kept writing. After a long while, and without turning around, he said, "What can I do for you?"

"Hello," Meili said brightly. "I'm Melissa Young, and this is Jason Wilder. We understand you're hiring, and we are very interested in working at Family FunZone."

"OK." Don was still writing. He finally turned around and, pleased to be reminded that a cute girl was here, gave a half smile to Meili. "You know what the work is?"

"Yes, Jason worked here two years ago, isn't that right?" She turned to me.

"Yeah," I said. Don didn't seem to remember.

Silence. Then Meili jumped back in. "He described the work in great detail, and we are both eager to start as soon as you might need us."

"It's dirty, sweaty work, sweetheart. Sure you're interested?"

Sweetheart. I braced for Meili's sarcastic comment.

"Don't let my appearance fool you," she said, smiling. "I'm stronger than most men."

"It's not like working the arcade," he said, still talking only to her. "We aren't hiring for the season yet. This is manual labor."

"I was taught you get hired for one thing: to do exactly what you say you'll do," she said. "That is what I promise. When you see how dedicated and responsible we are, I have no doubt you'll want us working here all season."

"Where'd you get this one?" he asked me.

I didn't even know how to answer that honestly, let alone how to answer it in the middle of begging an asshole for a job.

"Oh, she, uh . . ."

"I'm an exchange student," Meili said, saving me.

"Where you from?" Don asked.

"Hong Kong."

"I was gonna say China," Don said.

"Right."

"But you're from Hong Kong."

"It's part of China, actually."

"Is it? Why don't you sound Chinese?"

"I'm sorry?"

"You look Chinese, but you sound like you're from England."

"Oh, right. At my school in Hong Kong, we learn English from British people. So we, you know, talk like them."

Don looked at me. "You'd never expect that, would you? A British voice coming out of a Chinese face."

Oh, shit. Here it comes. This is where Meili lays into him.

But she kept smiling, which she never did unless you made her laugh.

Don pointed vaguely at the table. "Write down your names and phone numbers. We'll call if we need you."

"Thank you, sir," Meili said. "Any opportunity you give me will be hugely appreciated."

Me.

He nodded with a quick "OK" and started looking through a pile on the desk. Meili took a notebook out of her bag and started writing.

Now came the part I hated. "Sir, I was wondering if you could sign this. It shows that I applied for a job, which I'm required to do because of a program I'm in." Keep it vague. Could be vocational.

"Program?" he asked.

"It's adjudication, something I'm required to do," I said, hoping the term would be meaningless. I was an Adjudicated Juvenile Delinquent.

"Yeah, I heard you got in trouble. Pretty serious, huh?"

What do you say to that? "Yes" means you are in serious trouble. "No" means you don't take it seriously.

"I made a mistake, and now I'm getting right." I handed him the crumpled paper.

"Good luck with that," he said, which sounded like: no job for you here. He scribbled a meaningless mark on the signature line. I could have done that.

These goddamn papers. So many people gave me papers, and the papers had all the power, told you who you were. Teachers, cops, social workers, lawyers, counselors. The people act powerful, but it's the papers. Until the lawyer hands you the court order, he's just a self-important prick with a bald spot. The paper makes him real. Paper says you owe money? Pay up. Paper says you threw the first punch? You did. Paper says you're a screwup who has to apply for jobs or go to jail? Put on the SCREWUP hat, cause it's true.

That's why I'm writing things down. You think papers are truth? I'll give you some damn papers. Here's my over-due notice, assholes; here's my summons.

"Name and phone number," Meili said coldly, pushing

the notebook on me, then turning brightly to Don. "Thank you so much for your time. I'm sure you must be busy. And we look forward to hearing from you." She extended her hand.

Don looked confused, unanchored. He usually flirted from a position of power, leering at teenage girls who needed work. Meili was young and female, but not submissive.

"Yeah, fine," he mumbled, shaking Meili's hand and turning to walk out. He was back on the phone within five steps.

Meili had written *MOTIVATED, HARDWORKING EMPLOYEES* across the page, which seemed over the top. I put it on Don's desk. Meili grabbed it and taped it to the wall.

"Don't get lost in the shuffle." She looked around, testing to see how visible our names were, then moved them up to eye level.

We walked out into the blinding sun. Big Don, still on his phone, sped around on his mini-forklift, carrying a roll of fencing across the parking lot. Zooming around on the mini-fork was a favorite pastime of his, something he wrongly thought looked manly.

Back at the bike, Meili returned to her pre–job search self. "God, I want to put a cig in my Chinese face, but I s'pose I should wait, shouldn't I? Can you believe he said that?"

"That was so creepy."

"Right? Thank you."

"The whole conversation was crazy," I said. "What happened in there?"

"Honestly? Americans say stuff like that all the time."

"But what happened with you?"

"Me?" She looked at me. "Oh, that's called getting a job. I said: don't judge me. I know what I'm doing."

"Clearly."

"Piss off. You likely ruined it with your little prison paper."

"I had to get that signed," I said.

"Right now? You needed it signed this minute?"

"Yeah, I have to show my PO."

She shook her head and got out her tobacco, forgetting again. "You don't mention it when you're applying. Either he gives you the job, in which case you don't need it, or he doesn't, and you go back later and get him to sign. Ending a job interview by saying you're a criminal and you're only applying for the job because you're required to? Ludicrous."

Was that a job interview? "That's not the only reason I'm applying."

"But it sounds that way, doesn't it? Every boss meets twenty people a day who want work, and you gave him a reason to cross you off the list. You have to give him reasons to put you at the top of the list." She shook her head. "You didn't even smile."

"Why would I smile?"

"Because it makes people want to hire you."

"Where do you get all this stuff?"

"What do you mean?"

"Smiling, and twenty people a day, and 'the only job is doing what you say you'll do.'"

She grinned. "That's nice, isn't it? That's all my dad. He's brilliant. I've seen him take complete country people, uneducated people, and train them up; like, three months after leaving their villages, they're building managers, project managers. Swear, he should write a book." She put the rolled cigarette behind her ear. "What?"

"You were a whole different person in there."

"I said 'no judgment,' OK? And how many jobs have you gotten, Mr. SurlyPants?"

"A few."

"From friends and family?"

Had to think. "Mostly." Maybe all. FunZone two years ago was because one of Al's friends put in a word.

"Exactly." She climbed on the bike without demanding to drive. "Maybe you need to be a whole different person, too."

Great idea, Meili.

SEVEN

I WANTED HER TO REMAKE ME. I WANTED TO learn what she knew, think the way she thought, go to the places she had been. I would have happily jumped into her world.

And that disgusted her. She didn't want me to be like her; she wanted me to be like me. She sensed that I would give myself away to her and was repulsed. She invited it, maybe even craved it, but despised it.

I didn't know all this at the time. Back then, I lurched forward and back, disoriented, angry when she swerved. I learned her swerve, anticipated it. Every time I wanted to move closer, connect with her, even become her, I felt disgusted, pivoted away.

I tried to be the Meili version of me: strong, unpredictable, cynical all the way down. It was exhausting. I was helpless in front of her, and it took insane effort to hide that from both of us.

The next day, Meili was out of the Rubber Room most of the morning. When she came back, it was clear she had been crying. She dropped her pass on the front desk, slid into her seat, and began writing. No glance at me, no eye roll.

I tried to get her attention. Then stopped. Then tried. Then turned away. Then wrote her a note. Got disgusted with myself and asked for a bathroom pass I didn't need. Returned from the bathroom and fell right back into it. Couldn't get Meili's attention, couldn't let go of wanting it.

Goddamn Rubber Room. I got out my Biology notebook. On the inside cover was a red Sharpie cartoon of our Bio teacher drawn by my lab partner, Lainey. Mr. Eagan was diagrammed, and we had taken turns labeling his parts: *Adorable Warts, Distinctive Third Nostril, Knuckle Fur.* This was from that other UHS, the one before the fire and before Meili, the two changes that had merged into a single break. I could feel the old Unionville High in my body, see it in this picture. There were things I loved about that school and that *me*. It wasn't simple, but—look—me and Lainey cracked each other up. Now, I was Against. Against my enemies, against the school, and, with Meili, against the whole stupid, redneck town.

I could walk out of the Rubber Room, down to 214, sit next to Lainey, and listen to Mr. Eagan explain RNA versus DNA.

I could go back before the fire. Before Meili.

Was she saving me from isolation or making it worse? Was she letting me say out loud things I already thought, or was she putting those things in my head, contempt for my town, my people, myself?

(Even now, I can hear her answer: "Anyone who doesn't have contempt for themselves is an arsehole.")

She would leave. Soon, I imagined. She could tell everyone to piss off because she was about to piss off herself, to some other town or other country. A tiny part of me hoped, assumed she would take me with her, but she wouldn't, couldn't. Did people do that? Take their seventeen-year-old friend to live with them in New Jersey or Texas or Hong Kong?

At dismissal, I grabbed my backpack and hustled out the door.

"Jason!" Meili yelled across the parking lot.

I let her walk all the way over. Proud, mean me. I couldn't lose every time.

"Where you going?" she said. The parking lot was clearing out fast, which, in the spring, meant an away game for varsity baseball and softball.

"Home. Got stuff to do." Yeah, right.

She was rolling a cigarette. "What a shite day. Had a conference with Laura Fenton's *mother*, for god's sake. Basically getting bollocksed for forty-five minutes." Did that mean getting screwed? Beaten? It was bad, certainly. She switched to her whiny American voice. "'My daughter has trouble *sleep*ing. She has an*xi*ety. We had to get her a *coun-selor*.'" She tilted her head. "Seriously. Like, Americans, every time someone pinches you, you go see a counselor?"

"Pinch counseling does help." That was funny—Meili funny—but she ignored it.

"They lit'rally just wanted to see me cry. That was the actual reason for the conference. It was crueler than what I did, even. I wasn't trying to hurt anyone, I was defending myself." She was outraged, but, in fact, they had shaken her. "If your daughter has fucking mental problems, first of all, welcome to the planet, we all do, and second, I'm sorry, but I don't think I caused it. Maybe you shouldn't have raised her so fucking soft that she falls apart when someone stands up to her shite." She was falling, trying everything to catch her balance.

I wanted to say something true without simply taking her side. "People want to be safe."

She looked around for her aunt. "If you want your kids to be safe, here's a thought: don't have any." Then, in the same breath: "You're coming to the gig tonight, right? Of course you fucking are because it's the only exciting thing happening in this shite-hole. And you'll protect me from the rednecks, since my set will not have the required portion of Guns or Roses."

"I'll be there." And maybe she could protect me from those same rednecks.

The sun came out, and Meili took off her coat.

"You get a call?" Sounded like "cool."

"Call?"

"From Don. FunZone."

I shook my head.

"I did, last night. I'm going in tomorrow. Hope I'm not hungover."

"You got hired?"

"Seems like it."

"Jeezus. What . . . I can't believe that."

"That I'd get hired?"

"No. But you were there to help me get a job, not to take the job."

"I took your job?"

"Seems like it." I was repeating her again. Stop it.

"No, I got hired because I didn't say anything stupid."

"That's not why you got hired."

"Really? What was it then?"

"Don likes girls, especially cute ones."

"Oh, I see. You brought your little piece of ass and it backfired. Serves you fucking right."

I didn't want to argue about that because she had a point. "I need this job, OK?"

"I do, too."

"No, actually, you don't."

"So glad you know my needs better than I do. What else can you tell me about myself?"

"Really? You *need* this job?"

"Who are you to tell me what I need?"

"You need money for food? And gas to get to school? And to pay the electric bill from six months ago? Bullshit. You're like all the preppies. You need a job for your résumé. I need a job to stay out of jail."

"You're going back to jail because of me? Right, of course. Listen, you fucked up, it's nothing to do with me." She was looking around, floating up a wave of outrage. "But . . . but, how *dare* you . . . like . . . preppies? The fuck does that mean? I can't believe you."

And then, from my little brain, genius: what she said about Laura. "Maybe you shouldn't fall apart when someone stands up to your shite," I said.

Her eyes flashed, and she walked away. A car jerked to a stop two feet from her, and she didn't flinch, kept walking.

Good riddance.

The Unionville VFW had ceremonies on all the war holidays, an upstairs bar that my mom managed to get herself banned from (no small achievement given what happened there every weekend), and a main hall that was rented out for weddings, team banquets, Sweet Sixteens, and all-ages rock shows.

Happily, it wasn't connected to the school, so I would be allowed to mingle with the general population. Unhappily, the crowd would certainly include some of my enemies. My plan was to arrive close to the start, stay for most of Meili's set—no, *Melissa's* set, Melissa, Melissa, Melissa—and leave before any self-respecting rednecks showed up to listen to Sonic Doom, who fancied themselves speed metal and whose main musical idea was volume. I parked around the corner for a quick exit if things went bad.

I never considered staying home. Even if Meili was a preppy who stole my job, she was DJing her weird music for a bunch of VFW rednecks. I had to be there, had to be on her side.

The music was already booming, a mournful Middle Eastern–sounding vocal floating over a thick backbeat. I waited in a surprisingly long line to pay my six bucks. Four ones and eight quarters, sadly. I had two twenties at home, but I had a thing about not breaking my last big bills.

The Gulf Wars had restocked the aging VFW with young, muscled dudes. I didn't recognize the two at the door, but Roger Bartolino was inside and he shouted, "Jason!" with a chin chuck. He was the father of Merribeth Bartolino, a girl I dated freshman year, and he'd always liked me.

He bear-hugged me and, over the impressively loud music, yelled in my ear, "You doing OK, man?"

I nodded. Didn't seem like the moment to yell out an explanation of my parentless, probationed, Rubber Room, Meili-obsessed life.

He leaned in again. "Just stay right, man. We all screw up. Just stay right."

I nodded and smiled, letting him know he was the wiser, older man. I pulled away from his crushing hug, but he yanked me back one last time. "You need anything, you let me know, OK? Just let me know."

The only thing worse than people hating me, avoiding me, or being embarrassed to see me was people being nice. Being helpful. God, I hated that. I wanted to say: "Great, I need three thousand dollars, a car, a truce with Ronny, and a new family. I'd also like to have sex with Meili. Plus a cell phone."

"Thank you. I will," I yelled/mouthed to him as Meili transitioned to a throbbing dancehall beat. Roger smacked me affectionately on the head, and I walked in.

Meili had fans. A good twenty people were dancing in the wide-open center space, with another thirty around the edges. Some kids pressed up against the small stage, where she was DJing on a crappy folding table. They nodded their heads, staring at her, taking pictures like she was Someone.

She looked real. Hair tied in a bun, bright red skirt, and a billowy white shirt with a cartoon pickup truck on the front (I got the joke). A DJ from some other place, not Union-ville, not America. Some place where interesting people knew important music and made culture instead of consuming it like frozen pizza.

Turned out, Unionville needed her, somewhat anyway.

An impressive number of people were lining up to watch a Chinese girl with a British accent play music they'd never heard.

I hadn't seen this coming. Honestly? I'd imagined Stephen and six friends standing around, the VFW guys shaking their heads as Meili defiantly played her beautiful, unloved tracks. I'd be doing her a favor, cheering her up afterward and making jokes. "Next time, I'm sure there will be *nine* people."

Now, I would be lucky to be noticed at all. I found a spot on the side, near-ish the stage. I don't dance. Sorry. No defense for that. I've just never seen a way in.

Kids were still arriving, and it was early, more than an hour before Sonic Doom would soil the stage. My spot was gradually obstructed by people nodding, bouncing, dancing to Meili's undeniable beats.

A sad, predictable thing inside me shifted from Pretend I Don't Need Meili to Oh Crap, What If I Don't Matter to Her? Were those the only two urges I was capable of?

The dancing slowed during a rough transition, then a more familiar electronic beat kicked in. Over top of it, Meili layered some crazy drumming (Indian? African?), so as people bounced to a beat they recognized, this other thing twisted them up, lifted them.

She mostly looked down, nodding her head, occasionally drinking from a metal thermos. They confiscated that kind of thing at the door, but I guess the DJ had privileges.

To drink at the VFW, you had to stash tiny airplane bottles of liquor in your boots or underpants and then transfer it to the plastic water and soda bottles you could buy for two dollars. We called it "taking a flight," and liquor that traveled in the underwear or bras of girls was considered particularly desirable.

Whenever Meili looked up, I raised my hand and pointed at her. Dorky. She would hate it. Didn't matter, cause she never saw me.

The dancing engulfed me now. A Jay-Z sample layered in, and everybody could shout along. I did my thing of nodding my head and moving side to side, approving of the dancing without joining it.

I recognized people, but there were kids I didn't know, too, kids with interesting hair and clothes and attitude. Nobody came to Unionville except at fair time. Kids from Unionville went to Kendall and Walton to do stuff. But tonight, Kendall and Walton came here.

Some kind of line was crossed, and I was the only person not dancing. Tina Welch, a cute jock turned electronic music–head, bounced into me. She turned around to apologize and then jumped on me, wrapping her arms around my head, screaming: "Jaaaaaaaaason!" We had hooked up a couple times sophomore year, but I'd always assumed that was because she got really into drinking and smoking weed, not because she liked me. She spun me around and climbed on my back. I boosted her up, and now she was The Girl Up on the Shoulders, which is something, right? I pushed into the crowd, and Tina's altitude and her pulsing light necklace gave us status, so people let us through. Her powerful thighs squeezed my head, and her feet wrapped around my back. Still a jock, even with a penguin tattoo on her calf.

I didn't know what the lifter was supposed to do, but I bounced a bit, joining her rolling and spinning while keeping myself anchored. She was into it, and it got downright sexy, her lurching and arching up on my shoulders. We were grinding vertically.

Tina put her hands on my head. Oh, crap. She wanted to stand on my shoulders. I bent my knees and spread my feet, grounding myself in the swirling, colliding mass of bodies. She put one foot on my shoulder, and I grabbed it as tightly as I could. She knew what she was doing—did she used to be a gymnast?—and I was strong, or strong enough, anyway. For a good fifteen seconds, Tina waved her arms at a height no one else in the room had attained. Everybody around us was "woo"-ing and reaching up toward her, and when she fell like a tall, red-haired tree, she was caught by dozens of hands and briefly passed toward the stage.

Amazing.

Even I had to bounce up and down and wave my arms around. Screw it. Not dancing, exactly, but not *not* dancing.

Another crowd surfer, this one not so successful, and

101

then three kids climbed onstage to dance. One of them hit something or maybe distracted Meili because the music cut out at a particularly unfortunate peak. The crowd heaved a bodily sigh of disappointment. Meili's shoulders went to her ears as she frantically tried to restore sound.

Embarrassed for Meili, and worried I might get coerced into more dancing, I took a pee break, pushing through the sweaty bodies that reeked of alcohol and weed, down the stairs to the men's room (the women's room was, chivalrously, on the first floor).

I waited for my turn at the communal piss pot, a long rusty tub that was tilted so the piss ran out one end. There used to be running water that flushed it clean, but not anymore, so the entire basement smelled permanently of urine.

The music restarted for a second, then shut off again, with groans and boos from upstairs. We pissed in awkward silence, a mix of metalheads, Goth-looking dudes, and Kendall preppies checking their phones while urinating. When did that start? Phone in one hand, penis in the other.

I headed back to the stairs.

"Look who it is!"

Fucking Ronny. And Mike. And a couple other enemies.

Not a good place to be caught, the basement of the VFW. I probably should have anticipated that and peed outside. I didn't think these guys would show up for this. They'd come for Sonic Doom, sure, but if they got here early, Meili's crazy music would keep them in the parking lot drinking and rolling their eyes, right?

"Sup, Ronny?" I said, watching them all carefully and letting uninvolved kids push past.

"The fuck are you doing here?" Ronny said, as if he'd told me I wasn't supposed to come to the VFW, which, for the record, he hadn't.

"Just here for the DJ, man. That's it." Maybe if I made it clear that I'd be leaving soon, we could let this go. But I had to do it without backing down, cause Ronny was looking for me to back down. Avoid the fight without ducking the fight.

This is the problem with wanting something. You want to see a girl, so you go places, places where you might have to fight. But then you don't want to fight because you're there to see the girl, and if you fight, you'll be kicked out and maybe arrested and definitely messed up. And if you duck the fight, the assholes think they own you, and that's a world of hurt forever. The whole fucking mess starts with wanting something. Otherwise, I could stay home. Or I could come here and happily beat the shit out of Ronny until his boys jump in and beat the shit out of me.

"You like this faggot music?" Ronny said, mostly for his friends.

"I wish it was a little more faggot-y, but yeah, it's alright."

"Lucky you, Jason. Some kids can't go out. Kids like little Kevin can't go out."

That was ridiculous. First of all, little Kevin was seven years old, maybe eight by now, and, obviously, wouldn't party at the VFW. More important, from what I heard, he was fine. He had some scar tissue on his neck and hands, but he was totally back to his regular life.

Normally, I'd keep moving toward the fight by stepping to Ronny, all "What are you saying?" But there was something I wanted, so I tried to smooth it over. "Come on, man, you know how I feel about that whole thing. I think about him every day." I looked over at Mike, Kevin's older brother, who immediately looked away. If it was between me and Mike, we could have been cool months ago. But Ronny, some kind of cousin to Mike and Kevin, not biologically but through marriage or maybe just sympathy, would never let that happen.

Ronny stepped to me. But I could take that. "Yeah, well you should. You go home and fuckin think about what an asshole you are." I could probably even take that. "Instead of comin' here to see your little girlfriend, your little . . ." See, this was gonna be a problem. This is what happens when you back off: they fuckin press and they press until you go off. Cause here it comes. Here comes the thing I can't let pass. ". . . Chinese bitch up there who's got—"

And I was on him.

I drove him back against the fake wood paneling, and everybody started yelling. Before we hit the wall, I had landed two punches on his ribs. I kept my head down because he immediately moved to lock it up and punch my face.

There's this release when you finally cut the crap and start beating someone who deserves it. Everything else is pretending or waiting. All the stuff we do every day to keep ourselves alive and entertained is just so we can get to this moment, this truth. Which is: Ronny Bellman deserves to have every one of his ribs broken, and I get to do it.

You know when you're hot for someone and you go on a date and talk, talk, talk, and finally you start hooking up? Everything on the whole date was in the way of kissing, and now you're finally kissing. That's what beating on Ronny felt like. Even getting hit felt right. It was part of the flow, like getting wet when you step in the ocean. And it never hurt in the moment, only later.

I felt a rib crack finally. Ronny yelled out in pain, which would bring his boys over, and they'd really hurt me. But then, heavy footsteps down the stairs. Three VFW guys pushed everybody out of the way. Ronny and I jumped apart and tried to look normal.

"What the hell is going on down here?" a guy with a potbelly yelled, mostly at me.

"Nothing," I said, sticking to the code. "We were just playing around."

He looked at Ronny, who nodded, though he was having trouble breathing.

Roger Bartolino came down the stairs, and I looked away. There was, it turned out, a lot of blood coming out of my nose and mouth. Ronny must have landed some nice shots while I was cracking his rib.

"Both of you out of here." He sounded harsh, but this was the merciful thing to do. Roger could have called the cops, which, as he undoubtedly knew, would have been very bad for me.

"Come on, we were just playing," Ronny said, like the VFW guys were pussies for thinking this was a real fight.

"Play somewhere else," Roger said, and then looked at me. I coughed, and a mucus-y blood ball splattered on the floor. He shook his head.

I couldn't look at him. What could I say? I'm trying to stay right? I tried harder tonight than I have all year? Didn't matter. My whole life, adults had looked at me with concern, then pity, then disappointment. First, I'm a decent kid in a crappy situation. Then I'm proof that the apple doesn't fall far from the tree.

Fuck that saying, by the way. And fuck you if you've ever said it. You have no idea.

Walking out, kids either stared at me because I was bleeding or looked away because they didn't want me to punch them. People act like fights are a big deal. Fights aren't a big deal. Fights are what happen as soon as you stop trying not to fight. Like a naked body. It's always there, butts and crotches and tits. But take the cover away, and everybody freaks.

Upstairs, I looked into the main hall—still no music—and saw Tina and her flashing necklace trying to start a slow clap. A hundred kids, maybe a hundred and fifty, had their backs to me.

EIGHT

SITTING HOME WAS MISERY. I TURNED AGAINST my house, hating everything about it. The long wait for the kitchen fluorescents to get bright, the gas snaking back and forth, making up its mind whether it wanted to help you tonight. The numbers scrawled on the wall by the phone in Al's impatient, little-boy handwriting, especially the ones where the pen stopped working and he cut inkless, angry circles before switching pens. The toaster that only worked if you held the lever down the whole time.

I considered trying to get beer, but it wasn't worth risking my freedom for a six-pack. At 9:30, I knew Meili was finished, and I was only missing Sonic Doom. That helped, but I was still away from her on her big night. Couldn't things be nice for once? Couldn't I have one good night that didn't involve fighting over the biggest mistake of my life?

I wrote Meili a note. It took a lot of editing because her

standards were so high, and because I was trying to secretly tell her something else, something embarrassing.

~~Dear M.,~~
~~DJ Esmerelda,~~
DJ Frosting,

~~Amazing set!~~ That set was brilliant, to use a word my ~~dear friend~~ cellmate Melissa is fond of. So sorry I left ~~in the middle~~ before the end. ~~There are battles that follow me. I had to defend someone's honor who shall remain nameless.~~ I had an unscheduled meeting with my friends from the hot dog stand.

~~The crowd loved you and I did too.~~
~~The crowd loved you almost as much as I do.~~
~~I fully agree with the crowd's assessment of you.~~
The crowd saw something I already knew. You were, and are, ~~amazing. the dog's bollocks~~ the cat's vagina, or as we say in ~~Unionville America~~ Alabama, pussy pussy.

Please put me on your mailing list for future musical events.

~~Love,~~
~~Your Rubber Roommate,~~
Sincerely,
F.B.

I recopied it, and, by the end, it was fun. I imagined Meili reading it, and I could hear her laughs and groans and edit accordingly. That meant something, right? I got her.

I put it in an envelope and rode to her house. Maybe she would read it and come visit me. Or maybe she'd be there now when I dropped it off.

When I pulled up on her block, there were three cars out front. I got nervous, waited till two of the cars pulled away, and then walked up, envelope in my pocket.

It was Stephen's car, and he stood on the curb, yelling into his phone.

"No! Chris's house. Chris Valentine . . . What? Yeah, whenever . . . Jesus . . . OK." He hung up. "Jason?"

"Hey, Stephen."

"What's up? What are you doing?" Stephen was texting furiously.

"I came by to drop this off," I said, without specifying what "this" was.

The passenger door opened, and a kid with an asymmetrical hairdo got out. "Ben's not coming," he said to Stephen.

"I know. He's such an asshole," Stephen said, face in his phone. "But, whatever. I'm gonna have fun."

The other kid looked at me. "Hey."

"Miles, this is Jason," Stephen said, finally looking up. "Don't worry, he's cool. He just looks scary." Was that about my cut-up face or me in general? "Are you coming, Jason?"

"I'm dropping this off for Melissa."

"She just left." Dammit. I shouldn't have waited. "But you can give it to her in person if you come. Party in Kendall. I'm hoping DJ Esmerelda will bless us with another set." Stephen was walking around to the driver's side. "If I can keep her sober."

"Little late for that," Miles said, looking at me. "Girl can *drink*."

"Girl earned it, OK?" Stephen said. "She killed. That whole show killed, even with the tech problems. And you're welcome, Unionville. No need to thank me for putting it all together and basically teaching her how to DJ." He held the back door open for me. "Coming?"

I got in, leaving my bike since it was technically illegal for me to ride this late.

It took over an hour to get there because we stopped to pick someone up (no one home), at someone else's house to get vodka (they were home, but only gave us a half bottle, which Miles began drinking), and at a third house where we picked up a twenty-year-old and a case of beer.

Chris Valentine lived in a farmhouse that was done up the way people who don't farm do farmhouses. Big windows, wide-open space inside, nice lighting, weird art on the walls, pool out back. This world, more of it in Kendall than Unionville, made me nervous. It was all transplants and preppies, and though they seemed to be doing interesting stuff, it was out of my reach.

Case in point: walking into this party. I was intensely

aware of how fucked-up my face looked: swollen eye, bruise on my cheek. Everybody tried not to stare at the dirty local. And failed. Stephen and Miles immediately found friends and forgot me.

I walked through the living room into the shiny open kitchen, and there she was. Sitting on some long-haired dude's lap and speaking Chinese.

I walked over as she laughed at something Long Hair said.

"Oh my god, look!" Meili jumped up, then swayed a bit. "What happened to you?"

"Some of my old buddies didn't want me at your show," I said, hoping for a hug but not initiating one.

"God, yeah, I heard about the fight." Her eyes were looking toward me but not exactly at me. "I heard you started it." She was a bit drunk. More than a bit.

"Who told you that?" Seeing Meili with another boy pissed me off. And now people were lying about me?

"But you didn't? You didn't start it?"

"God, no! I wanted to see your whole set," I said. "I was pissed off I couldn't stay."

"Damn Harris." That was a glimmer. "You did see some of it, yeah? Before the disaster?"

"It was amazing. I even sort of danced, that should tell you something. What disaster?"

"God, it was a nightmare. Something got overloaded, and it took forever. When we finally got it back, it was like

112

three songs until that horrible band." She said something in Chinese that made Long Hair laugh. "Jason, this is Martin, who speaks fucking Cantonese. My *god*. I've got a whole new faith in the American educational system. Seriously. I can barely find anyone who speaks English around here, and then along comes Martin." She punched his shoulder.

Long Hair said something in Cantonese that included the word "Unionville," and Meili laughed.

Asshole.

"Martin, this is Jason, who's, like, *the* best person at my school. But I must warn you, he will fucking hurt you for, like, absolutely no reason, so watch your step. No sympathy, this one. Tore into me earlier today right when I needed him." I liked that phrase, *when I needed him*.

"Hey, man, nice to meet you." Martin stood and extended his hand in a regular handshake like we were buddies on the golf course. Like meeting a dad.

"Bug, I am in no way agreeing with *what* you said back in the parking lot. I don't fall apart when someone stands up to my shite, but . . ." She was still stuck on that, which felt good. Martin sat back down, and, cruelly, Meili sat on his lap. My face flushed so strongly my black eye pulsed. "That was good. You turned my words right 'round, didn't you? Bravo, you're an arsehole; bravo, you're forgiven."

"Thanks, but I didn't ask to be forgiven. Let's be clear about that."

She got right up in Martin's face. "See, he's good. You

113

don't even know how brilliant that last bit was." Martin nodded, watching her mouth, not listening to her words. "Where's my drink?" Meili looked around on the floor.

Awkward pause. A girl in a tank top that prominently showed off her plaid bra was soaking her friends with the kitchen sink sprayer. They screamed and covered their heads.

Martin turned to me. "You were at the show?"

"Some of it," I said.

"What about this DJ?" he asked, pointing at Meili. "Ridiculous, right? Where has this one been hiding?"

If he only knew how loaded that question was. But he didn't, because he didn't know her. I knew her.

"I got friends up at State, and I'm telling you, she could make five hundred a weekend, easy," Martin said to me, but really to her. "I'm gonna put you in touch with them. Seriously. They're gonna flip their shit. Cause that was: Off. The. Chain." He added something pretentious in Cantonese.

Yes, I could tell it was pretentious.

"I'll want to practice a bit before I go out and humiliate myself again," Meili said.

The music from the living room tripled in volume, physically attacking my ears.

Meili shouted, "Want a drink, Jace?" Since when did she call me Jace? "Thayre's a dayumn kegger yout beeack."

"Yeah, man, keg out by the pool," Martin yelled, all helpful and douchey.

"But we can't go in the pool," Meili shouted, shaking her head.

"Can't go in the pool," Martin agreed, grinning.

"Definitely not allowed," Meili yelled, turning back to Martin, her face right near his, looking mostly at his mouth, not his eyes.

"Not allowed," Martin said to her sternly.

Jeezus.

I went to find the keg.

"Bring me a drinky, luv!" Meili shouted after me, which felt nice till she added something in Cantonese.

I gave her the two-fingered reverse peace sign, a code: I know you.

"I will *not* piss off," she yelled.

I walked through the living room, resisting the urge to cover my ears. Miles sucked on an orange bong, and Stephen was rolling a cigarette, a trick he'd undoubtedly picked up from Meili. Down the hall toward (I hoped) the back door, girls and boys pressed up against the walls to make room for scary me.

What was I doing here?

The keg had a line, with a chatty guy drawing beer into red cups. Not regular beer either, some fancy local brew called "Angry Woodsman," according to the block letters on the side of the barrel.

When I got near the front, beer guy said, "Whoa! Dude,

what happened?" He stared at my face while filling some-one's cup. Everyone turned.

"Stage-diving accident," I said.

"Seriously? At the show?"

"No, I got jumped by some assholes. Yes, at the show."

"No way! You call the cops?"

"Uh, no. I can't."

"What do you mean?"

"I'm on probation."

"Seriously? What'd you do?"

I thought about this one. Why tell the truth? But then again: come as you are.

"Arson."

"Oh, shiiiiiiit. That's real, dawg! I'm getting you two beers."

Arsonist with facial wounds? No waiting. I stepped to the front and took two beers.

"Thanks, man. You're the best thing that's happened to me all night," I said.

"Don't mention it, bro. I got you. Who's next?"

A stronger man would have taken a beer to Meili. A more mature man would have jumped in and made friends with Martin, been charming and tough. Not me.

I took my beers out past the pool, which was, by the way, full. Why no swimming? A couple was hooking up on the lawn in front of the barn, so I headed toward the pasture fence and lay down in the cool grass. Beyond the glow of the house and the thump of the music, the stars glared with no moon to compete.

I had to leave. This night was going to keep breaking my heart. I didn't cry in those days. The closest I ever got was a swelling in my chest that dampened my eyes but not enough to form tears. And that's what happened. All of it—the fight with Ronny, my lonely house, the preppies at this party, Meili on somebody's lap—it all brought that wave up from my belly, and I huffed out a sob. That was as far as it ever went. I don't know why.

Sure, I could smack Martin in his toothy little face. But it was bigger than that. This was Meili's world: smart kids in nice houses, college kids, rich kids. She fit in, I didn't.

I was clever and hip in the Rubber Room, but not here.

"Andy? Is that you?" A tipsy girl staggered past the pool toward me. I sat up and wiped my eyes.

"No, not Andy."

"Who is it? Noah?" She was squinting as she got closer.

"Not him, either. Sorry. My name's Jason."

"Jason, how you doin'? You by yourself?" She was right over me now, bright-orange tank top and intentionally ripped jeans.

"Taking a break."

"Ohmygod, me too. It's so loud in there." She plopped down. "Are these yours?" She pointed at the two beers.

"Yeah, take one. It was for someone else, but I think she left."

"The keg's dead and everybody's like: 'Where's the beer?' Ohmygod, what happened to your face?" Her eyes had finally adjusted, and, of course, I was scary.

This was getting old. "You really wanna know?" She nodded. "There are these guys who hate me, and every time I run into them, they try to beat the crap out of me."

"Seriously? You should call the cops." Everybody in Kendall wanted to call the cops. In all my fights, the concern was *not* having the cops show up.

Change the subject. "Can I ask you a question? For real?"

"Yeah, definitely."

I could flirt with her. And I could talk about my Meili situation because, who the hell was this girl? She was drunk, it was late, she didn't know me.

"Alright, you're a girl, right, you seem smart and pretty and nice." She giggled. I hadn't flirted in a while. God, I hadn't been to a party since the fire. "No, I mean, you're a decent person, right? So, I'm trying to figure out this situation. With a girl."

"I can totally help."

"Great. That's great. What's your name?"

"Stephanie."

"Hey, Stephanie, I'm Jason." She looked for a spot to balance her beer cup. "So, there's this girl—"

"Cause I literally just helped my friend get out of this relationship that was . . . You know when your friend starts acting not like herself? And it's cause of some guy she's seeing? And you totally see the whole thing? But it takes her like a couple weeks to see it? How she's acting and whatnot?" Stephanie was pushing her hair back then pulling it forward and messing it up with her fingers, occasionally looking toward the house like she was expecting someone. "I told her, I said: 'This is *not* you, Erica, and you know it.' So I—like, I get it, Jay. I know how girls are."

"It's Jason."

"Totally. Jason. Sorry. Stephanie." Again, a handshake. Did they teach that in school here? "Nice to meet you."

OK, not drunk. Stoned? Coke? But, I have to say, I liked Stephanie. She was a little ridiculous and a little messed up, but she was trying, you know? Trying to help her friend, trying to talk to me.

"So who's this girl?" Stephanie picked up the other beer and took a gulp. "Is she here?"

"I think she left." I didn't want to get too specific.

"Poor little Jason's all alone?"

I loved it when girls flirted. I can't even tell you. I instantly liked everything about Stephanie. I forgave her uptalk, her tank top, her preppiness. I'm shallow and typical. A girl acting cute and flirty warms me top to bottom.

And it had been a while.

I was ridiculously attracted to Meili, of course, more than I'd ever been to anyone. But Meili didn't flirt, not in a sweet way.

"There's this girl, and we connect. We get each other.

Completely. I told her things right away that I don't tell anybody."

"What about her?" Stephanie interrupted, shifting into Friend Shrink role.

"What do you mean?"

I loved the way she kept flipping her hair. That's a difference between me and Meili. Meili doesn't forgive people. If someone's superficial, they're superficial. Nothing will ever change her mind. I could forgive anything.

"Did she tell you stuff? Did she confide in you the same way?"

Great question. "Eventually, she did. She's slower, though."

"OK, go on."

"I've never known someone who was so real, so able to say how things actually are." I hadn't put that into words, not even to myself.

Stephanie was impatient. "Yeah, yeah. But . . ."

"But what?" I asked.

"What's the problem? She's fabulous and she's real and you get each other. All sounds great."

"Right, but the thing is, she's . . . harsh. She doesn't make things easy. I get the feeling she could turn on you all the sudden." I wasn't sure how to say it. "I'm scared of her." That was honest.

Stephanie laughed.

"What?" I said

"Sorry," she said, unable to stop giggling. "It's just funny, looking at this man with a black eye and a broken nose or whatever, big and tough, and he's scared of a girl." She called me a man, not a boy. "It's like, sorry, but *you* might be the scary one."

I put a lot of work into making myself intimidating so people didn't mess with me. It was a big thing I thought about when I was out in public. Wasn't that normal? I didn't want to do it, I had to.

Someone plunged into the swimming pool. A boy's head popped up in the water, screaming, "So freakin' cold!"

"Ohmygod, that's totally not allowed," Stephanie said. "Anyway, what's your question?" Back to therapist mode.

What was my question? Maybe it was: Do you wanna hook up, Stephanie? But I'm not that brave. Flirting with a girl felt amazing. Being rejected wouldn't.

"My question is," I said, stalling, watching the kid climb out of the pool, shivering in his boxers. "When do you take a risk and go for it?" I tried to say it suggestively, so Stephanie might apply it to this moment and not to Meili.

"Bug!" Meili's voice.

Stephanie didn't know my nickname, so she was still looking at me intently, scheming an answer to my question.

"Bug! Where are you? I've been waiting!"

Maybe that was my answer.

NINE

"OVER HERE!" I CALLED OUT.

"Is that her?" Stephanie said.

"No, that's a friend," I said, trying to keep possibilities open with Stephanie.

"Bullshit." Stephanie was good.

"Bug! Come back, Bug!"

"Over here!" I waved to Meili. She finally saw me and walked over in a super straight line, the kind of path drunk people take.

"Bug, where've you been? I ordered that beer ages ago," Meili said, standing above me. She was a giant, and I could almost see up her skirt. "Hello. Don't believe we've met. I'm Melissa, also known as DJ Esmerelda. *The* DJ, at least until things went quiet, that was someone else, obviously, and you must be Jennifer." Meili complained everyone in America was named Jennifer or David.

"No, I'm Stephanie, nice to meet you." More hand-shaking. "I think one of these beers is yours. Sorry, I drank some." She handed Meili the more full of the two cups.

"Now, I don't want to disturb you, because you seem very cozy." Meili shoved me over with her foot and sat down between me and Stephanie. "And the last thing I want to do is get between Firebug and a Jennifer in a tank top. You do know he's a firebug, don't you?"

"Careful, May," I said, alluding to her real name. "We don't want to go sharing secrets, do we?"

"It's like that, is it?" Meili took a huge gulp of the beer and turned to Stephanie. "Do not trust this one. Whatever he's told you, it's absolute shite. All he cares about is slapping rednecks and getting punched in the face." She poked at my eye, which hurt. I flinched. "And calling people 'preppy.' D'you know what that means, Jen? Preppy? Is it an insult?"

"Depends how you say it."

"Are you a preppy?"

"Some people might say I am, but, no, I don't think so."

"So what are you then? A redneck?"

"I'm a relationship counselor, and I've been giving girl advice." Stephanie could stand her ground. Most kids didn't even try with Meili; they backed away.

"*Girl* advice? *Really?*" Meili looked at me and then Stephanie. "Do share. Lord knows he never talks to me about girls even though I'm his . . . I was going to say 'best friend,' but I think I might be his *only* friend. Am I? Am I your only friend, Bug? Because that would be rather sad, seeing as how we've known each other for about two days."

"I have a second friend named Stephanie."

"More his therapist than his friend." Stephanie was quick.

"Right. So, doctor, who's this girl? She here?" Meili asked.

"She was here, and then she left," Stephanie said carefully. "Right, Jason?"

"Oh, poor boy! Your little hottie stranded you? So unfair. But you're not exactly alone, are you, Bug? Look at this gorgeous psychotherapist. Now, professional boundaries likely prohibit vaginal intercourse, but I'm sure there are practices of a more *rural* nature that could be considered therapeutic. She's quite cute, isn't she, Bug?" This embarrassed Stephanie enough that she covered her mouth.

"She's very cute, Melissa."

"*Very* cute? That's a bit strong. Jen, you will want to watch your step. He's one of those men who end up on the news, and the neighbors say: 'Yup, we seen thayat cummin'.' " She wasn't wrong. I would end up in the news, for a minute anyway. On the other hand, she also called me a man. "Lots of danger signs. Obsession with fire, homoerotic love of fighting, thoughts of harming young boys—"

"OK, Melissa, that's enough," I said.

"You're right. That is enough," she said, and I thought

she was about to leave. "Thanks so much for stopping by, Jen. Really, really appreciate the counseling. Now, I need to speak with my friend Bug here, so prance on back to the party, 'K? Pool seems to be open, and everyone would love to see you in a sopping-wet tank top. It's what dreams are made of. Ta!"

Stephanie, bless her, didn't get offended. She smiled, stood up, and said quietly, "He's right about you, you are rough." She looked at me. "Nice meeting you, Jason. And the answer to your question is: right now."

She walked away.

"Oooh, that's enticing, isn't it?" Meili said, laying back on the grass. Our arms touched, and neither of us moved away. "Sorry if I disrupted your seduction, Bug, I need something from you."

"What?" I asked, ignoring the rest.

"My present. Stevie says you brought me a present." She turned toward me with a fake smile.

"No present, just a note."

"What's it say? Come on, give it a read."

I pulled the envelope out and read it to her. She smiled through the whole thing and laughed hard at "pussy pussy."

"Fuckin love it. Gimme that note. Jeezus, Bug, I got to say: thank goddess you're here. I don't care who you're beating up or hooking up to, you're a fucking gem."

"It's hooking up *with*, not *to*," I said, happy my note was a hit. Screw these preppies. They couldn't write that.

"Speaking of which, who is she? Who were you talking to that dreadfully skinny girl about?"

"You don't want to know." I was officially scared.

"No, of course not. But fucking tell me."

I took a deep breath.

Risk it?

Right now, Stephanie said.

"Her name's Melissa."

Silence.

Shit. She doesn't want to hurt my feelings.

Finally, she spoke, but quieter. "Fuck you. Who is it really?"

"Really. We were talking about you."

"Don't mess with me, Bug. I know you weren't talking about me."

"Really? How do you know?"

"How do I know?" She talked up at the sky. "Oh, let's see, I've got, like, twenty boys in there on my bra strap, while you, on the other hand, have never shown the slightest interest despite numerous—"

I did it. I kissed her.

I leaned over and put my mouth on her mouth. She tasted like whiskey and tobacco and her lips were chapped and it was glorious.

Her eyes got huge, and she whispered, "What are you doing?"

Fuck it. I just said it. I'd never said anything like it before. "You're the most incredible, gorgeous person I've ever met. I can't stop thinking about you. Every minute." I paused and added in a whisper, "Meili."

She squinted her eyes closed like she was in pain. "Are you drunk?" she asked.

"No."

"Well, I am. A bit," she said. "Which gives me permission to do inappropriate things. So say it again."

"What?"

"My name."

"Meili," I said. She winced again, but this time with a smile. "Meili. Meili." She rolled me over and started kissing my neck furiously, almost biting. "Meili. Beautiful Meili." She kissed up toward my face then kissed me hard on my bruised cheek. "Ow!"

"I'm a bit rough. Sorry in advance," she said. "And don't stop saying it."

I whispered her name twice more before she pushed her tongue into my mouth. I grabbed her hair as she climbed on top, her body warm and heavy. I wanted her whole weight, all of her. It was more than lust, more than wanting sex, which was something I wanted a lot. I wanted *her*.

She pulled her mouth away. "Say it."

"Meili." She pulled her shirt up and slid so my face was on her chest. I wondered if I should try to figure out her bra, but she kept sliding up. I was kissing her ribs, her stomach, her belly button.

She reached down and pulled up her skirt, and in one motion, she straddled my face. She pulled her panties to the side and pushed her crotch onto my mouth.

Wow.

I was no expert at this. I tried a couple times with this girl Rachel, and I don't know if it worked. At a certain point, Rachel would push my head away, and we'd do something else.

Not Meili. She grabbed my head and started thrusting her crotch back and forth on my face. It hurt my eye and cheek a lot. I didn't care. When my tongue got to a good spot, she sped up, and I heard her grunting.

"Shit!" she yelled. Was I doing it wrong? I tried moving faster. "Oh, fuck," she said, climbing off.

I heard the whoop of a siren.

"Fucking coppers. I'm fucked," Meili said. She was kneeling beside me now. My face stung from the friction and maybe from the fluids we were exchanging.

Kids were running out the back door past us. I could see the red-and-blue glow of police lights in the trees around the house.

"I gotta go. I'm fucked," she said, then finally noticed me. "That was getting good, wasn't it?"

I stood up. I needed to get the hell out of here. Any dumb bust could land me back in jail.

"Shit, my bag's in there. I gotta get my bag," Meili said.

"Leave it. Let's go. I can't get arrested." I tried to pull Meili toward the barn.

"No, you don't understand," she said, leaning her weight away from me. Two people with the same problem, pulling in opposite directions.

"Don't be stupid. Just leave it."

She snarled, "I can't!" She broke free and staggered toward the house.

"I'll be behind the barn!" I yelled. Meili was drunk-running toward the back door. I saw a flashlight coming around the side of the house, and I sprinted away.

It happened fast, and it changed everything.

At 4:30 a.m., I arrived home. I had hidden in the woods, holding my breath every time a cop shined a light, until everyone had been driven away in various police cars and vans. Then I had walked down the so, so long gravel road to Kendall, eventually persuading someone at the convenience store to give me a ride to my motorcycle. With my swollen face and odd story, it took a few tries.

I felt triumphant. Sure, Meili might be in some trouble, but I wasn't going back to jail. And more important than anything, more important than anything had ever been: I had kissed Meili. And more.

Maybe she was tipsy, but she meant it. I was wired, and I was turned on.

And I was hungry. I made two packs of ramen and drank half a two-liter bottle of orange soda. I was finishing the ramen on the couch, trying to remember Meili's body in detail, when a car roared up.

The hell? It wasn't even light yet.

It was Manny's Ford. He hustled to the front door, banging quickly and loudly.

"Hold on," I said. I put the ramen down, unlatched the several locks.

"Where's Melissa?" He pushed past me into the living room. "What happened to you?"

"She was at a party. I think she got in trouble," I said. "And some guys picked a fight with me. Before the party."

"What do you mean: She got in trouble?" He was furious.

"We were at a party in Kendall, and the cops came. I tried to get Melissa to run away, but she said she had to get her bag, so she went back inside." I paused, but Manny expected more. "I hid in the woods, but she never came out. I think they busted the underage kids and took them away."

"Took them where?"

"Probably to the police station in Kendall. Then they call people's parents to pick them up." Manny tilted his head back. "It's not that big a deal. You get a ticket, and you have to pay a fine. It happens a lot in Kendall, the cops are bored, so they—"

"You have no idea," Manny said. "It's a big deal."

Maybe she had an arrest record? I said, "I don't get it. What's—"

"Yeah, you don't get it, do you? I asked you to look after Melissa, and you failed. What were you thinking? She can't get arrested because her name"—he looked at me cautiously—"her *Chinese* name, will show up in the public record. And if that happens, we have to disappear." His eyes darted around the room, finally landing on me. "What were you thinking?!"

"I didn't know all that. I'm sorry."

"You took her to some wild party?"

"I didn't take her there. She went after the DJ thing. I only ended up there cause this other kid was going." Mostly true, and it made me look better.

"She has one job! One! She has to stay low. That's it. And she can't do it." He took a deep breath. "We have to get her."

"I'm sure the cops called her aunt and uncle. She's probably home now."

"No. Her aunt called me; she doesn't know. Melissa wouldn't give them the phone number." His eyes darted again. "She's at least that smart."

TEN

EVEN COMPLETELY ENRAGED, MANNY DROVE the speed limit. He stayed perfectly legal on public roads, which, the first time I was in the Tempo, had produced a backup of cars that roared past whenever it was safe to pass, and often when it wasn't. It was just after 5 a.m., though, orange glow on the horizon, and we had the road to ourselves.

We drove in silence. I was replaying the party in my head, the moment when the cops arrived. What could I have done?

"You'll talk to the police," Manny said. "I can't go in there. Say you're her stepbrother, and your parents sent you to pick her up. Make sure you get a copy of the complaint, we need that. Understand?"

"Yeah."

"If they give you any problems, tell them you need to get ID out of the car and come back out. We'll think of something else. Don't give them your real name under any circumstances."

"There's a slight chance they might recognize me."

"What do you mean?"

"There's a cop in Kendall who definitely knows who I am."

"OK, if you see that cop, don't mention Melissa. Tell him you're there to pick up someone else, then walk out." He paused. "That's step one. Let's talk about the next two days." Manny looked straight ahead, and his tone changed. Less angry, more logistical. "I'm putting Melissa at your house for the time being. She can't go back to her aunt and uncle's until we clear this up. *If* we clear this up. She stays with you, and she doesn't leave the house. Close the shades, don't tell anyone. Got it?"

He wasn't asking if it was OK, he was asking if I understood the rules.

"Got it."

"There's a lot I have to do, so I won't be around. I need you to stay with her. Watch her, don't leave her side. Don't let anyone in the house except me."

"What do I do if someone comes? Call the police?"

A slight laugh. "No. Police will only cause more problems. Pretend you're not home and hope they go away."

"And if they don't?" I wanted to know what my job was, what it really was.

"Look, I'm not putting her with you because of your

good looks. I'm putting her with you because you know how to handle yourself." He pulled over and turned off the car. "Now, go get her."

I knew how to handle myself? Wow. That was the opposite of what every adult had been telling me since eighth grade.

Maybe, like so many other things, Manny's words became too important. I wanted to live up to his idea of me. When the time came, I would handle myself.

The last of the party was sprawled around the waiting room, kids whose families couldn't be reached or couldn't be bothered. Meili stood immediately, went not to me but to the cop at the window.

"When," she said.

The cop scanned his list, and she pointed.

"And you are?" he asked without looking up.

"Her stepbrother," I said. That brought a stare from the cop. "Our mom can't drive at night cause of her eyes." Simple, convincing stories for people in authority are a specialty of mine. He bought it.

Meili took some papers from the cop, and we walked out. She was unwell, pale and bleary, squinting at me in an annoyed, distant way.

A few hours earlier, my face was in her crotch. You wouldn't have guessed.

In the parking lot, she asked, "Did Manny send you?"

"Yeah, he's here. He drove."

"Shit."

She slid into the backseat and immediately lay down with her eyes closed. Manny waited till we were back on the road and then started barking at her in Cantonese (I remembered that word from the party). She tried to ignore him, but soon she was yelling back, sitting up. At one point she rolled down the window and dry-heaved, but it barely interrupted their argument. She threw her arrest paperwork at him, and I gathered the four sheets and strained to read them in the dawn light. Meili Wen, not When. That's who got arrested.

During a long silence, I said, "Since I'm involved now, could you all speak English? I should probably know what's going on."

Meili said, "What's going on is Secret Agent Manny here has lost touch with reality."

Manny spat some words in Cantonese, and Meili responded.

"So, that's still Cantonese, y'all," I said. "No idea what you're saying."

Manny said, "Melissa has not recognized how serious this is, and she refuses—"

"He knows my name, for god's sake. Call me Meili." Like everything in the past hour, that infuriated Manny. He grimaced, said nothing. Meili said, "We will have to kill you,

Jason, now that I've told you my name. Sorry, that's how Manny operates."

"Shut up," Manny said. In English, though. Progress.

"Gladly," Meili said, lying back down.

Ten silent minutes later, we were in my driveway.

Manny parked on the grass behind my house without asking. I had to go around front and then unlock the back door for them. They stepped into my filthy kitchen as I quickly put as much garbage as possible into the overstuffed trash can.

"Oh, this is lovely," Meili said, not venturing past the doorway. "You could've left me in jail. At least it's sanitary."

Manny cursed at her in Cantonese (it sounded like a curse, anyway), and Meili gave the "piss off" sign to his back. She walked into the living room, carefully stepping over the moldy towels that were there to soak up the leak from the kitchen sink.

"Is the guest suite ready? Or should I sleep on the pizza boxes?" she said. I stopped straightening up and walked over to her. She wouldn't look at me. She tried to defend herself, saying, "Look, I'm drunk and hungover at the same time, and I could use—"

"You can sleep in there," I said, pointing to my bedroom. "I'll sleep on the couch." Mom and Al took their mattress to Florida, so there was only one bed.

"Fabulous," Meili said, and slammed the door behind her.

Manny handed me his car keys and a wad of money. "I'm

136

leaving the car for you. Keep it behind the house. There's food, water, clothes, and money in the trunk and a spare key under the bumper. If you drive it, keep the tank full, premium gas, OK?" I nodded. "We have a lawyer we work with. I'm going to see if he can do anything. Either way, we'll know in forty-eight hours. That's our window." He picked up my kitchen phone. "Does this work?"

"Yup." For the time being.

He wrote down the number. "I'll call you as soon as I know anything. You may need to get her out if I'm not back soon enough." He headed toward the back door.

Get her out?

"That's it?" I said. "Aren't you going to explain what's happening?"

"Ask Meili," he said with a grim smile, the only time he would ever say that name in front of me.

And he was gone.

What did I do next? What was most important, given the intense situation we were in?

I cleaned.

I frantically cleaned the kitchen and living room. I swept, wiped counters, took out the garbage. I got rid of a broken dresser that Al had trash-picked, saying it was "definitely fixable." I scrubbed the bathroom, but the linoleum walls were permanently stained. I took everything in the living room and threw it in my mom's room, already the repository for my unwanted crap. I took a year of old magazines and school papers out to the shed. I considered throwing out the smelly rug in the living room, but the floor underneath had cat-piss stains, so I flipped it over.

At 8:30, I took a break. I lay down on the couch, certain I couldn't sleep.

I woke with a gasp, my face sticking to the fake leather. Meili was climbing onto the couch. She put her head on my chest and curled up next to me.

I held her like that for four hours and seventeen minutes. I know because I watched the clock the whole time.

For four hours and seventeen minutes, I was at peace with the world. Meili's sweet, slow breathing, the smell of cigarettes in her hair. An occasional tremor as she dreamed.

She was comfortable, trusted me enough to sleep in my arms. That felt magnificent, sexier than sex. A thing I didn't know I longed for.

It was massive.

At one point, my arm fell asleep, and I debated whether to move it for ten minutes because I didn't want it to end.

Meili shook awake at 1:39, coughing and quickly rolling off the sofa. She hustled into the bathroom, where she peed and spent a while washing up, hopefully with the fresh bar of hotel soap I'd put out (my mom's job at the Rodeway Inn two years ago was still paying off).

She returned and sat on the folding chair, rolling a cigarette, not looking at me.

"I see the maid's been in," she said.

"I usually have it cleaned before the hostage arrives," I said. "Didn't have time."

"Does the ashtray mean I can smoke?" I'd put my mom's red metal ashtray on the coffee table.

"Yup."

"There's an upside," Meili said, lighting her cigarette. "Can't roll out of bed and smoke at Auntie's house." She exhaled an astonishing amount of blue smoke into the sunlight of the front window. "Things are getting better and better."

She was subdued, troubled in a way I hadn't seen before.

"Hungry?" I asked. I was starving.

"God, no. It's all I can do not to retch," she said. "A glass of water'd be nice, though."

I stood up into a head rush. No food, almost no sleep, some punches to the face, lots of adrenaline. Not good for a growing boy.

I poured Meili some water and noticed how nice it was to have a cabinet full of clean dishes rather than the usual wash-it-when-you-need-it pile of dirties.

I put instant oatmeal in the microwave and brought Meili her glass.

"Cheers," she said, forcing a smile. She drank it in one gulp.

I watched her roll another cigarette. Neither of us spoke. The microwave beeped, and I went to get my oatmeal.

"Did we have sex last night?" Meili said from the living room.

"Uh, I think you had sex with my face," I called back. "At the party."

"Oh shit, I did." She laughed. "That's dead sexy, actually."

I sat on the couch and started eating. "It was."

She looked at me for real now and laughed. That felt good. "It's a real shame, that," she said.

"What?"

"I liked you, Bug." Past tense. "And now it's all fucked."

"Why? What's gonna happen?"

A long drag on her cigarette. "Most likely Supermanny will evacuate us to the next shite town. And you won't be hearing from me. I'll have a new name and a new haircut. I could go blond. You American boys like that, don't you?"

God, I didn't want her to leave. I didn't want any American boys staring at her blond hair. "All because you got a ticket for drinking?"

"Yeah. And it's probably not even necessary. It's all Manny's paranoia at this point. Who knows if they're even looking for us."

"Who are they?"

"That's just it, isn't it? We don't really know. Or I don't, anyway. Manny's the one who communicates with people, I just hear about it."

"Can you explain it? Maybe a little? I'm pretty involved."

She made a grim half smile. "You are, aren't you? Sorry bout that." She stubbed out her cigarette and started rolling another. "Let's see. Starts with my father. My father is . . . amazing. He basically raised me; Mum died when I was tiny."

I knew almost nothing about Meili, but it felt shocking I didn't know that.

She stopped rolling and smiled. "Lit'rally everyone who works for him tells me: your dad's incredible, he saved my life, thank god he exists. Over the top, just adoration. He managed properties, then started developing new buildings. When you do that work, especially where I come from, you have to know the right people and pay the right people. So he did some shady things with construction and bribes, things everybody does, I should think. But he got caught, and he made a deal, testified against some people. Powerful people. That's who we're running from." She struggled to get comfortable on the folding chair. I wanted her to sit next to me. "Didn't tell you how we left, did I? I'm up at boarding school in Hong Kong, and one day Manny, guy who works for my dad, walks right into my lit'rature class. Big, strapping man with tattoos, everybody's pointing and giggling. He'd gone to my dorm and packed my suitcase, did a terrible job, too. Like twenty pairs of panties and no socks. Pervy packing, that's what I called it. We drove to a hotel, and he told me someone burned our apartment." Was she crying? Almost. "Bastards set it on fire. Nobody was home, thank god. Our housekeeper was there, though, completely beside herself, apparently, but she was OK. Manny and I go

141

to this goofy tourist hotel, all these drunk Australians, and we're, like, pulling the blinds and ordering room service. My dad was so sweet, he called every day, had books delivered. He was the one in danger, but he only worried about how I was doing. I was like: 'When can we go home? When's this gonna be done?' It got longer and longer. Then he said he couldn't call for a while, it was too dangerous. One day, we got a package with plane tickets and money, and we flew to America." She wiped her eyes. "Fourteen months and five days ago."

This was the moment to comfort her, right? She might hate it if I tried.

"Was like a vacation at first. Manny's obsessed with American cars, so he was in heaven. But that wore off. And we weren't in New York or Miami, the glamorous places you hear about, we were in New Jersey till Manny got paranoid, then Unionville. Not a top destination for Chinese people."

"Yet."

"Wait till I go home and tell them." She stretched, pulled her shoulders back. "So here we are. Manny's in touch with someone close to my dad. Supposedly. But the story keeps changing. First it was: we're going home soon. Then it was: Dad's joining us here in the States. Then he couldn't get permission. Then he got permission but had to testify first. It's fucking endless, and I'm not allowed to talk to anyone, so it's all based on what Manny says, and who knows, Manny acts like this is some spy movie, there's snipers on every roof, he's totally off it, paranoid as fuck, and I have to go along with it. It's like I'm in a cult, a two-person cult."

"Three now," I said, wanting to join.

"Welcome to the cult. We'll shave your head, get you a robe," she said.

I had one more question. "And Manny said you had . . . an incident at another school."

"Did he? Bit more chatty than I'd have guessed. *Incident.* S'pose he's talking about Suyin. She was at boarding school with me, a year ahead. And, look, most of the talk at school, I really can't be bothered, all the gossip and bullshit. But Suyin started telling people my dad was a crook and my whole family was going to jail. Spoiled little shithead." She finally lit her cigarette. "Love that word, by the way. You Americans really got something with 'shithead.' I'm stealing it."

"You did something to Suyin?"

"I just went to Suyin and told her, look, stop talking about my family or, basically, your life will fucking end." She took a drag. "Didn't go over so well."

"Really? I'm shocked."

"What was it you said? People want to feel safe? At least they didn't get her a fucking counselor." She put her cigarette down. "Anyway, does it freak you out, what I said about leaving Hong Kong?"

"No, I mean, it's crazy."

"But about the fire and, like . . . your fire and all that?"

Jeezus, that hadn't even occurred to me.

Now, when you think about it, it's totally different. I wasn't trying to hurt anyone, I was defending myself. These people, whoever they were, were sick. Still. "Oh. That's . . . that's kinda weird, isn't it?"

"No, but it's not really. It's coincidence. It's not a *thing*." She thought about it, taking the final drag on her cigarette. "Freaked me out a bit at first, to be honest, but no, I'm not like: 'God, is Jason going to burn me up in a fire?'" She stamped it out in the ashtray. "Have you got breakfast? I'm suddenly starving."

Swerve. God. "Uh, yeah," I said, standing up. "Want some oatmeal?"

"Mmmm. Have you got anything else?"

"Not exactly. Not breakfast."

"No cold macaroni and cheese?"

Cruel joke? "I could make you mac and cheese, but it would be hot."

"Would you, though? I know it's weird, but that sounds amazing right now." Meili followed me into the kitchen and refilled her glass. "I remember the first time I saw macaroni and cheese, thinking: Who the hell would eat that? Turns out, I would. Love that shit." She took a long sip of water. "God, you did straighten up, didn't you? You're a treasure, Bug. Seriously." Maybe this was the moment we would hug and make out? She sat at the kitchen table. Nope. "Shame I'll never see you again."

I sat on the other chair, the slightly broken one. "You're really leaving? It's that dangerous?"

"Who knows? The paranoia means I can't talk to anyone, can't get information. It's all a bit circular."

"You're talking to me," I said.

"Because I'm leaving, to be honest. You don't matter anymore."

Thanks.

"Who would you want to talk to?" I said.

"Anybody. My friends, my dad's friends." She was thinking about it now. "Bloke who used to drive my dad around. My dad's old business partner. I have a friend, Rina, she's from India, her mother does some kind of white-collar crime work, I bet she'd know plenty." She took a sip of water and belched. "Ooh, sorry, that was nasty. Anyway, that's the whole point, I'm not allowed to. It's too dangerous."

"But it doesn't matter anymore. Like you said, you're leaving. Call who you want. By the time they figure out you're in Unionville, you'll be gone."

She thought about that, then noticed me staring. "Look at you, Bug. You're not just funny clever, you're clever clever, aren't you? I can't believe I thought you were mental when I met you. So judgey." I laughed and almost spit out my water. "But even if I found out something, Manny wouldn't believe it. He's got his own story, y'know?" But she was thinking it over. The water boiled, and I poured in the macaroni.

145

BRAAAAAAAAANNNNNG.

"Oh, shit!" Meili jumped up. It was the phone. "Jeezus, I thought you didn't have a phone."

"It wasn't working, but then the bill got paid," I said, reaching past her, certain that it would be Manny.

It was a woman.

"Hello, is this Jason?"

"Who's calling?" My heart pounded. I remembered my assignment was to protect Meili at all costs.

"This is Sophie Jenkins, Melissa's aunt." Shit. "Melissa never came home last night, have you seen her?"

"No. I mean, I saw her last night."

"Where?" she asked.

"At her DJ thing. The VFW."

Meili mouthed, "Who is it?"

"Where did she go after that?" her aunt asked.

"I don't know." I pointed at Meili and mouthed, "Your aunt."

She said a silent "fuck" and walked into the living room.

"I'm told you were at the party in Kendall that Melissa was seen at," Aunt Sophie said.

Damn. "Oh, yeah, I stopped by that party. I think she was there. But I went home. I don't know where she is, ma'am."

"Have you heard from Manny?" she asked.

"Who's Manny?" God, I was lying a lot.

"You don't know Manny? Melissa's friend?"

146

"No."

"Well." She didn't believe me. Tough shit. "If you have any contact with Melissa or Manny, please have them call. We're very worried."

"I definitely will."

Meili walked back in, rolling a cigarette, listening intently.

"Thank you, Jason."

"Goodbye, Mrs. Jenkins."

I hung the phone back on the wall. "That was fun," I said.

"Welcome to my world. Lie to fucking everyone. Do it so much you can't remember which lies you've told." She sat down but didn't light her cigarette. "How's Aunt Soph? Worried?"

I nodded. "She's not really your aunt," I said/asked.

She smiled. "Not a lot of family resemblance, is there? No, I'm pretty sure . . ." She diagrammed in the air with her fingers. "Mr. Jenkins has a brother in Hong Kong who married a woman who works for my dad. So, through that, someone asked them to take me in. Maybe as study abroad or maybe as troubled girl who needs to pull herself together, who knows?" She rubbed her temples. "Aunt Soph. Poor thing. She's gonna be absolutely shattered when I disappear. A bit of a cow, but she really really likes me. Not the first one, either. Must have a sign on my back that says: looking for clingy, controlling mother figures."

"Someone crossed that out and wrote: looking to fuck rednecks."

She smiled. "That explains a lot."

I stirred the macaroni.

"These phone cards work?" Meili asked, inspecting the collage of long-expired cards.

"Uh, mostly no," I said. "There might be some time left on the one with the stars."

"You might could get me a phone card. Not s'posed to go out myself."

"Sure. Manny gave me some cash." I pulled it out of my pocket. It was a lot, and it was fifties. Who carries fifties?

"Fuckin hell, give me some of that," Meili said, grabbing the wad. "God, I forgot. The floodgates open when it gets bad." She was counting it.

"I need to get food, too," I said. The patheticness of my food situation, already pretty obvious, would become embarrassingly clear if I didn't shop right away.

"Sure. Let's get a thousand boxes of macaroni and a pickup truck to drive it home." She paused. "Or drive away."

ELEVEN

SHOPPING WHEN YOU HAVE MONEY IS FUN
as hell. I bought orange juice, bananas, fancy cookies, a gallon
of not-powdered milk, frozen ravioli, name-brand English
muffins, eggs, and two cartons of Ben & Jerry's. Two. I
would have bought more, but that was all I could fit in my
backpack.

I got three forty-dollar phone cards—I could use them
if Meili didn't—and a pack of her rolling tobacco. I chose
the checkout line where this girl Carey was working, knowing she wouldn't card me.

When I got back, Meili was on the phone, talking ex-
citedly in Cantonese. She had a different energy, still badass
but younger, less over it.

One sign she felt different: she stood up and kissed me
on the cheek, cradling the phone in her shoulder and muss-
ing my hair with her nonsmoking hand.

I was the sweet husband back from the grocery

store, greeted by his charming wife who gossiped with a friend.

I put away the groceries and drank a glass of orange juice without watering it down the way my mom used to. Then I drank a *second* glass of undiluted juice. Things were changing in my world.

Meili yammered and wrote notes on the back of the takeout menus that hung by the phone. I was surprised the calling card lasted more than a few minutes, so I dropped the new ones on the table along with her tobacco. She made a silent "WOW" then grabbed my hand and held it to her cheek for a while. A long while. Long enough that I started stroking her hair with my other hand. I was in an awkward position, hunched over, but I didn't care. She jumped up to write more Chinese characters on—was it intentional?—the Jade Garden takeout menu.

The house was so neat that I felt filthy. I hadn't slept much or bathed since before the VFW. I got in the shower and rinsed a disconcerting amount of blood out of my hair. Mine? Ronny's? Meili was still talking loudly, so I shaved and brushed my teeth. With a clean T-shirt and not-filthy jeans—hey, now I could hit the laundromat, too—I walked into the kitchen as Meili hung up.

She hugged me. She cried softly at first, then big, heaving sobs, smearing snot on my shirt.

I held her as tightly as I've ever held anything.

I felt that sob build up in my chest and rise to my eyeballs. Just one, then it passed.

Always one.

Her trembling slowed, then stopped. Meili wiped her face on my shirt, muttering a quiet, "Sorry, Bug."

She put a pot of water on to boil. Somehow, she'd found tea (we had tea?) and the sugar packets I kept in the refrigerator so the mice couldn't get them.

"You OK?" I asked. Stupid question.

"Yeah, no, I just, I talked to my friend Jia for the first time in like a million years." She sipped the last of the Lipton in her mug. "It was *so* good. It's five a.m. or something there, but Jia never turns off her phone. Lit'rally since she got the phone, it's been on, right? And I remembered her number, which is scary, and she picked up. I can't *believe* it was that easy."

"The phone card worked?"

"Yeah, I had her call me back, though, cause we had a lot to talk about."

"You gave her my number?"

"Take it easy, Manny. Jia's not about to fly over here and kill us, OK?"

Good. Was there someone who *would* do that?

Meili peeled the Jade Garden menu off the wall, and a fair amount of paint came off with the tape. "Ooh, sorry bout that. I'll fix it up, I promise."

"Ordering Chinese?"

She laughed. "Actually, big confession: I love American Chinese food."

"Not tonight. I'm cooking."

Meili opened the menu. "Manny's always mortified. We'd go to Chinese restaurants here in the States, and when you're Chinese, they give you a totally different menu, it's in Chinese, has different food."

"I didn't know that."

"Well, you wouldn't, would you? I'm always like . . ." She raised a hand timidly, cringed. "'Scuse me, could I get the white-people menu, please? Cause I love that shit, some of it anyway. Manny covers his face, horrified. But he's mainland, it's different."

"What's mainland?"

"Mainland China. Totally different from Hong Kong. Huge divide, stereotypes, all that."

"They don't like Hong Kong?"

"More the other way. Hong Kongers think mainland people are crude, unsophisticated, that sort of thing."

"What do mainland people think?"

"About us? Our stereotype would be: we're snobs, and we're not Chinese enough. Not real Chinese. We order from the white-people menu."

"Are you?"

"Am I what?"

"Real Chinese."

"Wow, dunno. What does that even mean?"

I poured hot water in her mug.

"Cheers," she said. She opened her new tobacco, pulled out the rolling papers. "I think if you'd asked me that a few years back, I'd have said: not really. I went to an international school, friends from all over the world. But in the States, especially here, I'm like: 'Oh shit, I am so Chinese.' A completely white town will do that, I s'pose."

"It's not completely white."

"Oh, please. Yes, it is." She rolled a cigarette and licked the paper. Smoking's nasty, but that lick was always sexy. "Could you get the sugar? Cheers."

"There's people who aren't white."

"Where?"

"There's a black teacher at UHS."

"History teacher?"

"You know him?"

"No, but every time I say this town is white, he's the one black person everyone mentions."

"Well, yeah, there's a lot of white people here."

"Yeeup. Sherr awrr." Her Southern accent. She lit her cigarette. "What about you?"

"What?" I looked in the fridge for a dinner plan. So many options.

"Are you a real American?"

"I don't know. Not so much."

"Oh, please. You're completely fucking American. Like, insanely. Go anywhere else in the world and you'll see."

"I'll see I'm ignorant?"

"Yes, that. But no, it's freeing, actually. Such a big world." She curled her legs onto the chair. "I'd be up at boarding school, tiny school with all the cliques and the talk. Then I'd leave and, like, go to Thailand on holiday, and it was such a relief. All that shit at school, all the drama, it's like: wait, no one cares. No one even knows it exists. It's amazing. You should go, Jason. This town's like boarding school. Too tight."

"How did you do that?"

"What?"

"Go to Thailand."

"It's quite cheap, actually."

I refilled the pot with water and put it back on the stove.

"But how did you know, like, where to go?" I said.

"Where to stay?"

"No, I mean, if you sent me to Thailand, I wouldn't know, like, is this safe? Where should I go and not go?"

"Look at you! So cute, you're scared of Thailand."

"I'm not scared, I'm just saying, how do you know?"

"You're totally frightened of Thailand, it's completely endearing, especially from a man who punches people for sport." She stubbed out her half-smoked cigarette and balanced it on the ashtray. "Come here, cute boy. What are you doing?"

"Making ravioli."

"Please, I couldn't. I just had, like, nine cups of tea. Come on." She took me by the arm and led me to the living room. "Ooh, you're all clean and fresh, aren't you?" She lay on the couch and pulled me on top of her. "Now, I've decided something."

"What?"

"I've decided you like me a lot."

"I do?"

"Yeah, you're really into me."

"Good to know."

"You're basically obsessed."

"Obsessed?"

"Yeah, I'm a goddess. Rainbows out my arsehole, diamonds for nipples." She squeezed her tiny boobs like she was shooting them at me. "Champagne pouring out of my nipple diamonds."

I laughed, and she kept shooting champagne.

"It's time."

"For what?" I asked.

"For a proper snog."

God, I hoped that was slang for sex.

She kissed me and kept her eyes open. She moved her lips back and forth across my mouth, watching me the whole time. I managed to get the first taste of her tongue when the phone rang.

"Oh, shit, gotta get that," she said, pushing up from the couch.

"Leave it," I said. Losing touch with her body was painful.

"It could be Jia. Or somebody else."

"Well, it's my phone, I should answer it."

She pulled the cord as far as she could, and I reached over the back of the couch.

"Hello?" I said.

A female voice spoke what sounded like Cantonese.

"Hold on." I passed the phone to Meili.

Goddammit.

I knew the phone call would end, though. I knew she'd come back, and I'd taste her mouth again.

I didn't know how unlike sex with other people it would be. Sex with Meili involved a lot of position changing (including standing) and, more than anything, talking. Sex with other girls was always an eyes-closed, we're-not-really-here tussle. Meili looked at me a lot and talked about stuff. And tried stuff. "Put your hand right here and press." "What if I put my leg up here? Like that?" "Oooh, that's fuckin great, a bit gentler, 'K?"

We tried stuff on the floor, on the kitchen counter, in a chair. She especially enjoyed doing several things at once: mouth here, hand there, and what if you sucked my toes? (That actually happened.)

Another thing that was different: she came a lot. Other girls came once, or maybe just made a convincing display. I could never tell, and I never asked. Meili came thunderously, heavily, moaning and trembling, many times. And talked about it. I came twice, once in a condom and once a different way. (My mom got pregnant at nineteen, so piles of condoms appeared in my room during middle school.) Meili came repeatedly before and after. Never at the same time, though not for lack of trying.

During a pause on the couch (were we done?), I had my head on her chest. Her naked chest. Casually hanging out with a girl's naked body was a first. Before Meili, a naked girl meant: quick, have as much sex as you can before the opportunity passes.

I played with the shark tooth on her leather necklace, fake biting her with it.

"Plump Bambi," she said.

"Is what?"

"Where I got that. Fat Deer Key, this amazing island off Florida. Went there when I was little, absolutely magical. I couldn't believe it was named Fat Deer Key. I'm picturing, like, this huge, overweight Bambi. It was the most spectacular place. I swear to god I'm going back. We should go. Your mum's in Florida, yeah?"

"North Florida. Pretty far from the Keys, I think."

"You'll love it, Bug. Nothing like here, I'll tell you that."

You'll love it. Fat Deer Key. I'm going back. We should go. Later, I would argue about this in my head. Was she telling me something?

She squeezed my ass. "God, you're so pale. Look at you."

"Um, thanks?"

157

"It's like you're anemic or something. Get this boy some steak, I think he might pass out. Which reminds me, I'm famished, and I'm dying for a fag," she said, popping up from the couch like it was nothing. "That was good fun, though, eh?" So we were done.

"That was amazing."

She put on my T-shirt and smoked at the kitchen table. Very sexy. I opened the fridge and admired our food supply again.

"God, know what I just remembered? FunHole. My first day was today," she said. "Sorry, Big Don. Guess that bit about motivated, hardworking employees wasn't so accurate. I thought of it when we were on the arm of the sofa, you were doing that bit with your fingers." She watched me cook. "You're a bit shy, aren't you?"

"Is that a joke about how I'm naked and making ravioli?"

"No, while we were having sex, sometimes I'd say something, and I'd think: oh god, he's absolutely mortified, I should shut up and get on with it."

"Well . . ." I didn't know where to start. "That was different from other girls. I'm not used to all that . . . communication."

"American girls, like, lie there unconscious or something?"

"Not unconscious, but . . . definitely there's less, um, talking and . . . less trying different things." It was even hard for me to talk about what was hard about it.

"God, maybe it's a cultural thing. Can't imagine just lying there, hoping for the best."

I laughed. "When you say it like that, it does seem like a bad idea."

"I remember one bloke, he kept telling me to stop looking at him, and I was like, 'Where should I look?' He said, 'Close your eyes.' I thought, 'What a terrible idea. Everything we're doing is dead sexy, why wouldn't I look?' "

"American guy?"

"One was American. The other three guys in the orgy were Russian." She sensed the tension in my question. "Yes, Bug. I have had sex with other people, OK? Shocking."

"I know. Me too. I was just wondering if it's an American—"

"You had sex with another girl? Who? Swear to god, I'll kill her."

God, I loved that about Meili. She could laugh at me for being jealous one second—How absurd! We're adults, we have bodies, get over it—and then immediately swerve and be over the top jealous of me. And she meant both of them. Or neither. It made things OK, made them honest. Things that had always felt self-serious and tragic didn't with Meili. She was too quick, too comfortable with the contradictions.

I stirred the ravioli and splashed a bit of boiling water onto my bare belly. "Ow!"

"Don't burn your cock off," Meili said. "It's a quite lovely cock. I know you blokes are always wondering if you're, like, massive enough, and rest assured, you're brilliant down there." I couldn't look at her. "Are you blushing? That's too cute, Bug. Are you totally embarrassed by me?"

"It's just, this is not a conversation I'm used to having."

"What conversation?"

"The one where the girl reviews my cock. I don't talk to girls about sex. Not in that way."

"How d'you make it better then? I'm not saying it needs to get better—it was quite fantastic—but, like, how d'you know if it's going OK?"

"I think most people, or most people I know, don't make it better. They just do it how they do it."

"Their loss. And my cock review is five stars." She held out five fingers. "Three on the shaft and one on each little testicle." She drew my cock in the air with her hand. "Not little. Sorry, can't ever use the word 'little' when you're near a man's crotch. One on each of your massive balls." She spread her arms wide, looking up at my blimp-size nuts. "But really, it's ridiculous, you blokes, all you're ever on about is sex, but the minute a girl talks about it, it's like, 'Oh god! Don't speak of it!' Explain that."

"Can't. Sorry. But you're right, it's uncomfortable."

"Have you got any alcohol? Smoking after sex is unbelievably good, but it'd be even better with a little drinky, wouldn't it?"

"Sorry, no."

"Your mum's a drinker, right? Must be a little stashed away someplace."

"That's not how alcoholics work. They drink it all. Hit the liquor store every day, drink till it's gone." No amount of stockpiled alcohol could survive the twin assault of my mom and Al, so my house was always dry. Other kids would steal a bottle from their parents' liquor cabinet, and I would always think: What's a liquor cabinet?

"Really? What about Sundays? Liquor store's closed on Sundays, I think."

"Sunday, you go to the bar." I knew the whole system.

"Wow, didn't know that. Bit sad, isn't it? We should call your mum."

"We?"

"Yeah, I'll be like . . ." She took the phone off the wall. "Hello, Mrs. Firebug, how you doing? I'm sitting in your kitchen watching your son cook pasta with his cock out. What's that? Oh, yes, it's a lovely cock, five stars."

I covered my ears. "Aaah . . ."

"What? OK, I'll tell him. Your mum says she's sorry for being such a drunk. And you should go out and get a nice bottle of wine for me. Her treat."

"Oh god." I shook my head.

"Is it too much? I'm sorry." She went back to the phone. "Gotta go, Mrs. Bug. Your son is mad now, and we all know what happens when he gets mad, people end up in hospital. I'll talk to you later!"

What?!

I stared at the stove, unable to come up with a response.

"Bit too far?" she said. "I'm too much, aren't I?"

Yes. No. Didn't matter.

"Do you want to see my tits? Would that help?"

That made me laugh.

"Ta-da!" She lifted up her shirt. "Come here, you dirty boy."

Twenty minutes later, we got up from the kitchen floor and ate very overcooked ravioli.

TWELVE

MEILI TALKED ON THE PHONE LONG INTO THE
night. I slept on the couch, intending to get up and ask what
she was learning. But my belly was full, I had just had the
most amazing sex of my life, and when was the last time I'd
slept? Occasionally the phone rang, and every time, I
thought: Manny's gonna be mad.

At some incredibly late hour, I stumbled into the bedroom and passed out.

I woke in the morning with my arm under Meili's head.
She grimaced and rolled away.

The kitchen was bright and messy. Meili had made
macaroni and cheese and eaten a lot of ice cream. The table
had papers on it, phone numbers, Chinese characters, some
circled with question marks. I was relieved that Meili seemed
to be a slob. Less pressure.

I happily cleaned. I washed Meili's dishes, took out the
trash, stacked up her papers, threw out the old phone cards,

wiped out the refrigerator, and chipped some dried barbecue sauce off the counter.

At eleven, I put on music, boiled water for tea, and toasted two English muffins. I didn't have any butter, so I put on cream cheese from two takeout packets I found in the refrigerator door. They smelled fine.

I brought Meili breakfast in bed, or rather, breakfast on mattress, since I didn't have a bed.

"Morning, sunshine. It's tea time."

She sat up, face puffy, eyes squinting in the sunlight. I remembered Manny said I should cover the windows.

She was off balance, unsure. She sat against the wall and looked around, not seeing anything.

"Are you OK?" I asked, laying the plate down beside her.

She nodded but didn't smile. I'd never seen her this off. I'd seen her pissed, distant, exasperated, trashed, but never frightened, always solidly where she was. Now, she was floating.

I handed her the tea. She took a sip and grimaced. "No sugar," she said, not to me, not to anyone.

"I'll get some," I said, hoping she hadn't used it all last night.

I came back with four sugar packets, and Meili was lying down, face in the pillow. She was . . . hiccupping? Every few seconds, her back trembled like a cough.

I put my hand on her shoulder, and she recoiled. "Is

everything alright?" I asked, maybe the stupidest thing I'd ever said.

I wanted her to say: "Yeah, everything's fucking peachy cause I'm hiding out here and I have no idea what's going to happen," etc., etc.

Instead, she said, "Leave me alone." It was quick, cold, purely instructional.

I went to curl in next to her. I wanted to hold her while she cried. But she lifted her head and barked, "Leave me alone!"

There was an animal fear in her voice, a survival instinct that didn't know me or care to know me.

I walked out as she went back to the pillow, the tiny convulsions faster now.

I poured a glass of milk and sat at the kitchen table. Meili occasionally let out a sob I could hear through the wall. I sat there, heart pounding, dizzy with the feeling that this was so wrong. I should be in there, I should hold her. She should want me to.

Of all the messed-up things I'd been through that year, this was the hardest. People fought, people hated, people let each other down, people left. Little bodies got burned in fires. I could live with all of that. But not this. This gutted me. This beautiful person, this person I adored, was crying, and I desperately wanted to comfort her, but I couldn't.

I didn't want to live in a world where that happened.

If I knew how to cry, I would have been bawling. Instead, I put my head on the table and tried to think about other things. We needed more groceries. We could take Manny's car and do a real shop. Another wail. Shit. Meili was still in there sobbing, and it was still ripping my heart out. I walked out, didn't close the door, didn't tell her I was leaving.

Past the car, past the shed, through the row of trees, and into the soggy field behind my house. A farmer hayed it twice a year, and in between the grass would get tall, and I used to hide in it: sometimes a game with my friends, sometimes not a game. When I was ten, my mom grabbed me, and we ran back into the field and lay there for almost an hour because some people were looking for her. I remember thinking: when I get big, I'm not gonna hide. I'm gonna protect her.

The field was stubby, still waking up from winter. I hadn't been out there in a couple years, but I knew exactly where I was going. Out in the second field, a diagonal square off the main field, were the Rocks, three boulders too heavy to move, so farmers had planted around them for generations. As I walked up to the Rocks, my racing heart slowed a bit. Geese nibbled the picked-over grass by the edge of the woods, too far away to notice me.

Big Rock was dome-shaped and steep. Kids needed a boost or a lot of momentum to get up on it. There was one solid grip up top, but you had to know about it, because you couldn't see it from the ground. Tall as I was, getting up wasn't that hard, but I still took a few steps back to get speed.

Big Rock was warm. It was always warm if the sun was out, even in the middle of winter. My friend Gary and I used to take off our coats and sweaters and lay down shirtless on cold days, convincing ourselves that it was *totally warm* as we got goose bumps and chills. I took off my shirt and lay back, adjusting to find the right surface.

I never did things like this anymore. Like Brandt Hill. Riding there with Meili was the first time I'd been there since . . . when?

Meili. Dammit. That thought clenched my breathing. Why couldn't I comfort her?

And why couldn't I let it go?

And behind that, lurking as always, the original question: Why am I so messed up?

When I got back to the house, Meili was on the back stoop, drinking tea and smoking. She barely looked at me.

"Where've you been?" she asked.

"A walk."

She nodded. There was a long silence, and then she moved to one side. "D'you want to go in?"

"No," I said.

She kept smoking as if she was alone, but she was self-conscious, toking more quickly.

"Whot?" she said at last, squinting up at me.

"You OK?"

"Yeah," she said quickly. "No. 'Course not. Whatever. Doesn't matter." She looked down at the grass. "I just really don't like waking up in a place I don't know. I hate it. Really hate it." She stubbed out her cigarette in a beer can that was used for exactly that. "And yesterday was hard. It was all a bit much." Sex with me? Getting arrested? Talking to Jia? I hoped it wasn't sex with me. "I talked to a bunch of people I hadn't spoken to in forever, and it was *so good*. Mostly, like, *so* fucking good. But also, you know, they've changed, they've moved on. I'm this memory to them. It was awful. And then I learned some fucked-up things, really fucked-up. Like, I can't even get into it, it's so bad."

I sat and wrapped my arm around her. She tilted her head toward me briefly but then reached for her tobacco.

"What are we doing?" she said, shaking her head.

"I know what I'm doing," I said.

"What's that?"

"Don't take this the wrong way," I said.

"No, don't," she said quickly. "I can't bear it. I lit'rally can't bear it."

"No, it's not like that. It's good," I said, pulling her over toward me. "I know this is a crazy time, and insane things are happening, and more are about to happen. But, for me," I said, not exactly sure where I was going, "I'm happy to be here with you. I'm happy to be in my house. I hate my house. I hate this town. I hate ninety percent of what my life is. And I am so happy to be here with you." A strange thing happened while I was saying all this: I felt a stirring in my crotch. I was getting emotionally turned on. A love boner. Is there such a thing?

"You little softy," she said, leaning over. "Wait'll I tell people. Then you'll really get your arse kicked."

"Seriously, I've never felt this good at home. Come on, it's a messed-up time, but it's nice here, right? Together?"

"Yeah, Bug. 'Course it is. I'm sorry, I . . ." She let out a long exhale. "I'm sorry, I'm sorry, I'm sorry. I'm fucking sorry for my sorry-ass self," she said, clenching her face up. "I am not going to fucking cry again. But, yeah, it's great. You're an absolute doll. I got tea, I got cigarettes, I got a cute little maid cooking and cleaning, it's brilliant. Seriously. It's just not my moment. Sorry." She covered her face in her hands and leaned over. "Aaaaaaah. God." She stood up suddenly. "Sh'we go inside?"

She moved out of the way of the screen door but didn't go through. She turned toward me, face down, and stepped in to hug me. I held the screen door open for a while, but when she slid her warm hand under my shirt and up my back, I wrapped both arms around her.

We stood there pretty much forever.

"Are you gonna tell me?" I asked.

We had been quiet for a while. Meili had papers spread out on the kitchen table, copying names and phone numbers into a notebook she'd found in my room. I was frying eggs for both of us.

"Tell you what?" she said, scribbling away.

"What you found out," I said.

"God. You really want to know?"

"I'm involved. I need to know."

"You don't have to be involved. Seriously. This is not your mess, and you—"

"Meili. Come on."

"I need to say that, OK? I need you to hear it, because I can't expect—"

"Consider it heard," I said.

"OK. Well. Short version is: Manny's not telling me everything." She pulled out a rolling paper, her last one. "Fair enough, no surprise there. I've known fuckall about what's been going on for a while. But what he's not telling me is massive."

Silence. I flipped the eggs and took them off the heat.

"Maybe I could go home and be with my dad." She lit her cigarette.

I plopped the eggs on the English muffins and sprinkled salt and pepper. I was a pretty good cook.

I carried the plates over. Meili carefully extinguished her cigarette, rested it in the ashtray for later.

"This looks fantastic, Bug. Thank you."

"What you're saying is interesting, but I still have no idea what's going on."

She laughed, her mouth full of egg. "'S true, isn't it? God, it's so weird talking about it. I have to say, it feels completely wrong. I never talk about it. Obviously. And it's been so long, I can't imagine how to explain it all."

"How about I ask questions?"

"Yeah, great. Ask." She dug into her eggs. I loved watching Meili eat. She was undelicate, enthusiastic, and a bit loud.

"Where's your father?"

"Oh god!" She covered her mouth. "It's so wrong. It feels *so wrong* to talk about. It's OK, though, right? Is it? Yeah, it's OK." She cleared her throat and sat up straight. "My father is in protective custody in Hong Kong." She looked at me like she might burst out laughing. "Or he was anyway."

"Why is he in custody?"

"For his own protection," she said. I rolled my eyes. "You know all about that, don't you? He's a witness in a large corruption case involving high-ranking people. He's also a defendant, but he made a deal. Until the case is finished, he's basically been hiding."

"Which is why you're also hiding."

"Exactly. The people who don't want Dad to testify could come after me to get to him. At least, that's what he was afraid of a year ago. Especially after the fire."

"So what did you find out?" I said.

"Well, the case is resolved, at least my dad's bit. Two different people said it was settled."

"Which means you can go home?"

"Presumably. Somebody might could come after him out of revenge. But it's too late to, like, prevent him from testifying."

"That's big."

"Massive. And it's a big deal knowing when the case is over, and you can never tell from the media because it's China, and the official story has, like, zero to do with the real story."

"That's good news, right?" I asked.

She took her last bite and, as she chewed, picked up her half-smoked cigarette. "Yes, but. Thing is." She lit the cigarette. "I probably could have gone home six months ago. Once my dad testifies, it all changes and protective custody ends and so on. I could have gone back in, like, November. Skipped Unionville altogether."

"That would have been sad."

"Not for me. No offense."

Offense definitely taken.

She picked a piece of tobacco off her tongue. "But Manny never told me. Why?" She took a deep breath. "And what else is he not telling me?"

"Where is Manny?"

"Whenever he has to *deal with things*," she said, putting those words in quotes, "he goes quite far away. Paranoia and all that, doesn't want to be found. But now, I'm thinking, is there another reason he goes away?"

172

"It's understandable why he—"

"Actually, it's not. It's not fucking understandable. He's lied to me for six months? Longer, maybe? He keeps me in the dark, scaring the shit out of me so I don't communicate with anyone. That is *so* fucked up. And now he'll drag me away to some other crap town, when I don't even need to be hiding."

"Maybe you don't, but—"

She cut me off. "Look, if it was a few days, and he's gotta figure things out? OK, fine. This is six months, *at least.* Are you fucking kidding me?" She rubbed her temples.

"Can you trust these people you're talking to?"

"Exactly what Manny would say. Don't trust anyone. I'm sick of it. I'm making the decisions now. I've always been told, like, I make bad decisions. Tough shit. I'll make bad decisions and live with it."

She stacked our plates and forks and scraped the table crumbs into her hand.

"You don't have to go anywhere," I said.

"What d'you mean?"

"You don't have to go with Manny or back to Hong Kong. You could wait it out."

"Here, you mean?" I nodded. "In our little love nest?" I nodded. "Aren't you sweet? That's a delightful offer, and it could never work, but thank you, Bug. Much appreciated."

I probably should have let that go. "What do you mean?"

"What do I mean about what?"

"What do you mean it couldn't work?" I said.

"Come on, Bug. This is sweet, but it's not real."

"Feels real to me."

"Well, you believe in fairy tales. I don't."

"What do you believe in?"

She looked at me, deciding if it was a question worth answering. "Barely tolerable situations that occasionally get much worse for reasons beyond your control."

"So cynical."

"Piss off. I'm just saying, things aren't fixable, are they? They weren't going along great till someone screwed them up. It's not like that." She looked out the window, then back. "It's a lot of damaged, self-interested, occasionally well-meaning people doing the best they can in the moment. That's what we've got. There's not some, like, better world we could live in if we just tried harder. Sorry, too American for me."

"So no point in doing anything."

"No, you have to survive. Not insignificant, that. And, yeah, there's nice things. Music. Fags. Cute boys." She narrowed her eyes at me. "Come on, if I stayed on here, we'd hate each other. This is great—I mean it, it's fucking great—but only because it's about to end. If the end weren't in sight, we'd resent the hell out of it. And each other." She started clearing the table.

"You would."

"You would, too, though. I'm a lot of fun at arm's length. I'm not cute up close. Swear to god I'm not."

"I don't like cute," I said. "That's why I like you so much."

"Sarcasm. See, I am influencing you. But you should know, it's best to tease someone about things that matter quite a lot but not *all* that much, right? So, like, I can take the piss out of you for being a delinquent, but probably not for having a drunk mum. And probably not for, like, burning that little boy, right?"

"Probably not. Though you definitely have."

"Being cute is not a good one for me. Being obnoxious? Pain in the arse? Smelly, even? All great. But if you don't think I'm fucking gorgeous, keep it to your stupid self. And your drunk-ass mum, too."

I laughed and cringed. "Do you really want to know?"

"Probably not, no. And don't fucking feed my self-esteem. That's even more horrid."

I knelt down in front of her. "I'm gonna tell you."

"Oh, Christ, don't."

"If you took everyone—"

"Please, no!"

"If you took everyone in the world and lined them up by how attracted I am to them." Meili looked straight up at the ceiling. "It would be Meili. Then a huge gap." I ran my finger across her lips, her beautiful lips, puffy from our aggressive kissing and other things. "And then everyone else." She clenched her mouth. "I am desperately, helplessly, maniacally attracted to you."

She closed her eyes, and her mouth stretched into a half grin, half grimace.

"And I mean that in the shallowest possible way," I said. "You've got a lovely personality, but I'm talking about your face and your body."

She pulled me in and gave me a warm, wet kiss, her soft tongue and lips pushing gently against mine. I tasted something sweet and dark in her saliva, a denser layer of excitement rising from her depths.

"That's a fucking turn-on. You wanting me is a turn-on. Even though you're just lying to get in my knickers." She pulled me onto her lap and pushed my hand under her skirt. "Now get in my fucking knickers."

I fought to stay awake, reading on the couch as she made endless phone calls. Maybe we'd have sex one more time.

I was sound asleep when she tapped my forehead. "Guess what?"

"Whoa. Hi."

The slight panic of waking was offset by seeing Meili. Waking up to Meili—is there anything better?

"Guess what I'm the proud owner of," she said.

"Uh, don't know." I sat up.

"Come on, guess." She sat down sideways, put her legs in my lap.

"New calling card?"

"Bigger."

"Manny's car?" I wedged my fingers between her calves. So nice.

"You'll never guess cause it's completely ludicrous. I own a building."

"A building."

"Large one."

"What exactly is your building?"

"Ooh, that feels nice, doesn't it? *My* building. Thank you for that. Not sure—I'm picturing offices, apartments, little shops on the first floor."

"You own a building but you don't know what it is."

"It quite slipped my mind. Don't recall buying it, but apparently I did a couple years ago. This lawyer found it, a friend of Jia's mum." She smelled the contents of a glass, approved, and took a sip.

"How did you not know about it?"

"Someone's not allowed on the internet, is she? Interesting, right?" She squeezed my hand with her legs.

"Who bought it? Your dad?"

"I assume. Anyway, I'll find out soon. I'm about to assert my ownership."

Something was boiling in the kitchen.

"It's water for tea," she said, not looking up, somehow reading my thoughts.

"But you don't know what's going on," I said.

"What do you mean?"

"You can't just jump in, you have to be careful."

"Quite the opposite. I have to stop being careful. I don't know what's going on, you're right, and that's why I'm stirring things up."

"But there are reasons for all this."

"Reasons?"

"Reasons your dad bought it and didn't tell you," I said.

"I'd love to sit down with my dad and hear his explanation. But since he hasn't spoken to me in a year, I'll find out another way."

"You're stepping into a crazy situation you don't understand."

"I live in a crazy situation I don't understand. That's my life. This will get me out."

"I'm just saying there are reasons, and we don't know them yet."

"I can't believe you of all people would say that." She pulled her legs out, sat up straight. "You really think the adults have it all sorted, and we just need to fit into their elegant little plan? There's no plan, Jason. They're making it up, and not very well, either."

"What if you make things worse?"

"Worse than hiding out forever in some crap town? Can't imagine. Look, I've had nothing for a year, and now I have something. I'm going to use it." She squished a moth on the coffee table and scraped the corpse into the ashtray. "What?"

"Nothing."

"You're thinking something," she said.

"I'm comparing our crappy parents. My mom's a mess, obviously. But I have this image of your dad; he knows what he's doing."

She rubbed her moth finger on the couch. She was getting used to the Wilder house.

"My dad's amazing. Seriously. He's completely brilliant. He's also ten thousand miles away and not talking to me. His trial fucking ended, and he doesn't tell me? I can't . . ." She leaned her head back, closed her eyes. "Your mum may have an especially brutal way of it, but they're all lost, Jason. They're all lost."

THIRTEEN

MEILI WAS CRUSHING ME AT RUMMY. TURNS out, there's strategy beyond "Hey, I got three jacks." Rummy was the perfect time-wasting activity for her: competitive, not depressing like TV, and, most important, she could smoke, drink tea, and talk. We started after lunch and were still playing two hours later.

"What about this?" I said. I couldn't stop thinking about Meili's building. "What if the building is your inheritance, and your dad didn't tell you yet?"

"When do I get to ask questions?" Meili said, waiting for me to play.

"About what?"

"You ask me all these questions about my situation. I want a turn."

She laid down four tens. Ouch.

"There's not a big mystery in my life," I said.

"You're quite mysterious, actually. And casual about it, which only adds to it. Your mum, for example."

"My mom."

"She raises a son, and the son turns out to be a completely unusual man. How did she do it?"

"How did she raise me?"

"Yeah, and your father, too, if he was part of it."

"My real father?" Jesus. "He's not around. I mean, he's around, but not for me."

"So your mum, then, how did she raise such a special man?"

"Wow. Thank you. I guess. Gotta think about that."

I picked up and discarded. My turns were much faster than hers.

Meili poked my shoulder. "Answer the question." She laid a five-card straight. Five.

"Right, my mom. God." I had to put down my cards. Playing rummy badly was taxing. Now I had to think about my mom, too? "If I put aside all the craziness she's been through and put us through . . . I mean, is that even possible?"

"Is it?"

"I guess. If I put all that aside, she's really, uh, full. She always has a million projects and ideas and trips." I looked around for an example, but she had taken or I had put away all traces of her. "We used to collect posters for fairs and stuff. We'd take them off telephone poles. Anytime we were driving, I'd look out for cool posters, and no matter what, even if we were late or it was raining, she'd pull over and grab them." What happened to those posters? "She's got a lot in her, maybe too much."

"Too much for what?"

"Too much for her, too much for the world. Like with the drinking."

"She drinks too much?"

"No. I mean, yeah, she does. But some people drink to make themselves more interesting, right, cause they're boring sober. My mom drinks to make herself less interesting. And just . . . less."

"All that drinking must have been weird."

"Everything's normal to a kid. You adjust."

"How d'you do that?"

"You know, you adapt. Maybe your mom sleeps in the bathroom sometimes. OK. So, in the morning, you pee in the backyard, put a blanket over her, brush your teeth in the kitchen."

"Ohmygod, that's the saddest thing I've ever heard."

"Boys like peeing outside."

"No, little Jason putting a blanket on his mum cause she's passed out in the bathroom."

"Don't get all teary."

"It's heartbreaking."

"Pity is aggression. You know that."

"Ooh, so good. I'm going to use that." She drew a card she didn't like. "You're quite smart, Bug. Is it true you skipped a grade? Someone said that."

"Ha. Not exactly. My mom dropped me off first day of school, and they were like: 'See you at noon.' Cause it was half-day kindergarten. She freaked out. An hour later, they moved me to first grade cause she convinced them I was brilliant. But really she needed childcare. Sucked cause all my friends were in kindergarten."

"You did have friends, though, right? You weren't always on your own."

"Yeah, but it changed. Lots of kids stopped playing with me in middle school when my mom got caught driving drunk. And it's different when you're older. A seven-year-old from a messed-up family is sad. A fourteen-year-old from a messed-up family is dangerous."

"Dangerous."

"Bad influence. Lie down with dogs, you get fleas."

"God, is that a saying?"

"I've heard it to my face."

"People are shit."

"Yup. That's why I ignore them. The list of people I listen to gets shorter every year."

I watched the Maroneys' elderly mutt pee on our scraggly grass. He had a thing about marking our lawn, and Al, preposterously, used to rage about it.

"Who's on your list now?" Meili said.

"You."

"And?"

"Melissa."

"Haven't seen that one around."

"She disappeared when I started dating this gorgeous girl," I said.

"Are we dating? Have we been on a single date?"

"Does this count?"

"Seems to me we got drunk at a party—I did anyway—then moved in together."

"That's dating in Unionville."

She was cross-legged on the couch. Did I mention she was wearing underpants and a T-shirt? She looked at her cards, I looked at her thighs.

I giggled. "Actually it is."

"What?"

"That's how my mom dated," I said. "Come home from the bar with a guy, he lives with us till she kicks him out."

"You just wake up and he's there."

"No, in the morning, they sleep. You meet him when you come home from school and he's watching your TV, eating your food. Asking you: 'Why doesn't the remote work?'"

"Why *doesn't* the remote work? I press the buttons so hard."

"You have to stand right next to the TV."

"Then you may as well use the buttons on the TV. What's the point?"

"Exactly what the boyfriends said."

"God, I really am like them."

"You smoke more."

"And, in my defense, while I do eat your food and watch your TV, I'm not like: 'This is all fine.'"

"What does that mean?"

"I mean, it's a mess, isn't it? Your mum's drinking, you living alone. I see all that, I think: we should get you help, get your mum some help."

"We?"

"People. Me."

"That's not how it works."

"I'm just saying I can't believe no one stepped in." She took a sip of yesterday's cold tea. "What's so funny?"

"You have no idea."

"I'm being pretentious."

"You're being rich."

"Same thing."

"Not at all," I said. "Pretentious people think the way they see the world is the only way. Anybody who sees it differently is crazy."

"I do think people are crazy."

"You also think you're crazy."

"Certainly true."

"So you're not pretentious."

She stretched a leg. I watched the cut of her calf.

"But everyone here considers me this posh, pretentious—what d'you call it?—preppy."

"Well, growing up here, you meet a lot of obnoxious preppies who think they know everything." I didn't say: like Mr. and Mrs. Jenkins. "But poor people can be just as pretentious. Locals, rednecks, we love talking about how people from outside don't know shit. It's our favorite topic: 'What did the rich preppy do this time? Doesn't that prove we're better?' That's pretentious, cause it's narrow-minded and arrogant. But you're not like that, Meili. You"—I played three queens—"are just rich."

She drew a card but didn't play. "Which means what?"

"You see a person in a messed-up situation, and you think: they just need someone to fix it, someone like me. That's a rich-person thought."

She was quiet.

"What are you doing, Jason?"

"Come on, I'm just giving you a hard time."

"No, what are you doing in the Rubber Room and all that?"

"Um, staring at the new girl. Are you gonna play?" I only needed one card to go out. I'd still lose, but less badly.

"I'm serious. You've got this crazy intelligence. You say things I've never heard."

"Yeah, we're from different worlds, we know about different things. Come on, play."

"I don't mean you know *about* things. I mean insights, fucking truths."

"OK, thanks. Now play a card."

"Don't say thanks. My point is: What are you doing? What's wrong with you? Why are you throwing it all away?"

God, that question. *What's wrong with you, Jason?* Everybody asked that.

Ignore it. Wait for her to play.

"Come on," she said. "Why?"

You won't like my answer, Meili. Swear to god.

"Hello?" she said.

"Jesus, Meili. What's *wrong* with me? Really? I have no fucking idea. And maybe it's not just me that's messed up, maybe there's other problems." Somehow I was standing, my cards on the floor.

"No, I didn't—"

"And could you please just . . . just not say that? Could you please be the one person who doesn't go: 'What the fuck is wrong with you, Jason?' Can you imagine what it's like to hear that from you?"

"I'm sorry."

I wasn't done. "Things weren't going along great till I screwed them up. It's not like that. Shit was never gonna be good for me."

"I didn't mean that."

Still wasn't done. In fact, I was getting hotter. "I ask you questions cause I want to know you. You ask me questions so you can figure out what's wrong with me? Seriously? That is *so* fucked up."

"That's not why."

A car pulled into the driveway, jolted me out of my tirade. Stop yelling at Meili; protect Meili.

"Whatever. It's OK," I said. And then I had a Meili moment: make a joke when things are heaviest. "It's obviously not a touchy subject."

I wasn't as good at it, but that's an unbelievable move. Massive. To swerve, laugh about how dramatic I am, and still feel dramatic? Maybe the biggest thing Meili ever gave me. Anyone ever gave me.

"No," she said. "I'm not sitting here going: 'What's wrong with you?' I meant the opposite. You're brilliant. You're a genius. You know that, right?"

"No. I don't." I went to the window.

"You are."

"You say that cause you like me." I recognized the car.

"I do like you, Bug, which means I don't fucking lie to you."

"Great. And OK, wow, Stephen's here."

"Ooh, little Stevie, what a sweetheart. And look at me with no pants on." She headed to my room, presumably to hide.

188

I watched her knickers—I was angry, but it was Meili in underpants—till she was out of sight. Before Stephen knocked, I opened the door. "Hey, Stephen."

"Hi, Jason, what's up?"

I blocked the doorway, definitely not inviting him in. "Nothing. What are you up to?"

"Is Melissa here?" he said, holding a stuffed white trash bag, its red straps stretched thin.

"Melissa?" I said, trying to sound genuinely confused. "No. Haven't seen her in a couple days."

"Hm." Stephen tried to read my expression. "She asked me to bring her some stuff."

"Hey, Stevie! Come on in, darlin'," Meili called out, back in the living room wearing my sweatpants and flannel shirt.

Huh?

Stephen looked at me scoldingly. I shrugged and let him in. They did kisses on each cheek. Was that a Meili thing? I never got cheek kisses. Maybe it was a Stephen thing.

He handed her the trash bag.

"You're a doll, Stevie. Seriously. Bug, I forgot to tell you, Stevie got me some clothes. Girl clothes." She gestured at her current, ungirly outfit. "D'you want some tea or a snack or something? Sit, sit." She went in the kitchen to put water on.

"No, I'm good," Stephen said, not sitting. "I probably shouldn't stay long." He was trying to figure out the two very different welcomes he'd received. I was, too.

"Don't worry about Jason," Meili said from the kitchen

doorway. "He's a bit overprotective." She looked at me. "A girl can have a friend over, yes?"

"Sure, whatever," I said, closing the front door. "It's your life."

"Ooh, that's dramatic," Meili said, sitting on the couch and pulling Stephen down next to her. "The unspoken thing there is: or your *death*. I do worry about this one sometimes. If anything happens to me, Stephen, get an autopsy, know what I mean?"

BRAAAAAAAAANNNNNG.

Meili startled. "Shit, I will never get used to that. You gonna get that, Bug? I doubt it's for me." She looked at the clock, which she had set to Hong Kong time. 3:22 a.m.

"Hello?"

"Jason, it's Manny. How are you?"

"Hi, Manny," I said loudly, stretching the cord so I could see Meili. "I'm OK, how are you?"

Meili shook her head and mouthed "not here," which wasn't helpful since nothing would freak Manny out more than hearing that Meili was gone.

"I'm alright," he said. "Is Melissa there?" Still with the name.

"Yeah, she's sleeping. Didn't get much sleep last night. She conked out."

"I tried calling last night, but no one answered," Manny said.

"Oh yeah. Sorry."

"No one answered for four hours," he said.

Shit. "Yeah, my mom called, and she was acting pretty crazy, so after that, we just didn't pick up. I have to do that sometimes. Sorry." Like Meili said: lies, lies, and more lies.

He didn't love my explanation. "Don't do that again. I need to be able to reach Melissa."

"Alright," I said.

Meili was in the kitchen doorway now, watching me.

"Tell Melissa I'm talking to a lawyer about her arrest. It doesn't look great, but I might be able to work things out. I'll know more tomorrow," he said. "But we're fine so far. Nothing's come out publicly, so we're still clean."

"Great," I said. Talking to Manny was awful. I wanted to get off.

"I'll call later, OK? And thank you, Jason. I can't tell you how grateful I am for what you're doing."

Yuck. If he only knew.

"Sure, no problem. See you."

He hung up without saying goodbye. Of course.

"What'd he say?" Meili asked immediately.

"I'll tell you later," I said, nodding toward the living room.

"Oh god. Is it bad?" she said.

I shook my head.

"Really?"

"He was pissed that no one answered the phone last night. That's all."

191

"Shit, I saw these calls from a hidden number, should have known it was him," she said. "God, I just want to punch him in the mouth."

I loved hearing a girl say that.

She sat on the couch and switched her tone to bring Stephen back in. " 'Pissed' means drunk, by the way, Bug. He wasn't pissed, he was angry. Proper usage, please."

"Sorry, your highness," I said.

Meili pulled clothes out of the bag. "Lovely little sweater. That's great. Oh, and a skirt to go with it, that'll look nice."

"I thought you'd look great in those," Stephen said.

"This is all your sister's?"

"Yeah, she's at college. She won't miss them. She has so many clothes."

"Look at this!" She held a sheer dark-blue dress up in front of her. "Might look alright in this, d'you think, Bug?"

I nodded. It was pretty sexy.

"I thought one special outfit would be good, a going-away dress."

Going away? What else did Stephen know?

"I might not be going away," Meili said quickly. "Jason thinks we should shack up here like redneck husband and wife. Pretty kinky, right?"

"It's cool that you guys can live with no parents," Stephen said. "Must be awesome."

"It's pretty great. I was telling Jason it's a miracle to wake up in the morning and have a fag," Meili said. "I don't mean a fag like you, Stephen. You're not a fag, that's a terrible slur. You're a hot little queer."

Wow. I kind of knew Stephen was gay, but Meili *knew* it, joked with him about it.

"Speaking as a hot little queer, I'm jealous," Stephen said. "The things I could do if there were no parents in my house."

I had to say something. "Yeah, well, my mom still lives here. She's just . . . she's away at the moment."

Long silence.

"Cool. Where is she?" Stephen asked.

He was probably being nice, an innocent question to keep the conversation going.

"She, uh, she's visiting. People." So many lies. Screw it. I stood up. "I'm gonna take a shower."

After the hot water ran out, after I sat on the edge of the tub in a towel for a long time, after I heard Stephen leave, and after I shaved badly with lukewarm water, I unlocked the bathroom door and walked out.

Meili stood up from the couch. "Hey." She was wearing the gorgeous blue dress.

"Hey," I said.

She put her arms out and raised her eyebrows.

"You look great," I said.

"You're mad."

I nodded.

"Bout Stephen?"

"Let me get dressed," I said, and stepped into the bedroom.

"No, I love you in a towel. All drippy and fresh. It's like a cologne ad." She followed me into my room.

I looked for clean underwear. I couldn't do the smell test with Meili there, so I took my best guess.

"That's tasty, too," she said, lying on the mattress. "Tight boxers on those little buns." I ignored her. "Oh, come on. It's Stephen, he's harmless."

"Look, you can tell him whatever you want about your situation. Seems crazy to blab about it, but that's your call. But you can't tell people about my situation."

"I didn't blab about it, I just needed some clothes. And I didn't tell him your whole situation, I—"

"He knows I live alone. If that gets back to my probation officer, I go to jail. Nobody can know that, OK? Nobody. You are literally the first person I ever told." I pulled on jeans, and coins fell out of the pockets. Change was usually precious in my world. I hoarded it in my dresser, kept it for emergencies. But ever since Manny's fifties, I was dripping with cash.

"I figured it out, actually," she said. "I'm just saying."

"You're leaving, you're getting out. I have to live here, OK? I have to make it work."

"You don't have to stay here," she said quietly.

"What does that mean?"

"Maybe you could leave, too."

"Go live with my mom in Florida?"

"Yeah. Or somewhere else. With me."

What.

"You said that could never work."

"No, I didn't," she said.

"You called it a fairy tale."

"No, I said living here was a fairy tale. That's different."

"What's different?"

"Well, what do you think?"

I sat on the trunk that used to hold my toys. "I think I don't know what you're asking," I said.

"Do you want to go with me?"

Wow. I looked up at the ceiling. Be honest? "OK, yes. I want to go with you. Of course I do."

"Well, you can't. It's impossible. Too bad," she said quickly. "What? I'm kidding, I'm kidding. Easy, OK?" She rolled onto her side, and the dress rode up on her thighs. Intentional? "It means a lot that you want to, it does. I sort of can't believe it. Who wants to run away with an obnoxious, chain-smoking fugitive? I can't imagine."

Silence.

"But," I said, finishing her thought.

"But what?"

"There's a but. You're about to say: but it can't happen."

"I dunno, Bug. Seriously, I don't. Last night I found out someone I really trust is lying to me. Then I found out I own

195

a fucking building. I don't know what's next. I don't even know what's happening right now. Except one thing." She paused. "This dress. Is happening. Right now. I am wearing the shit out of this dress, not that you've noticed, and even though I'm basically, like, a chunky old Chinese man . . ." She gestured at her legs. "When I wear this, I'm a chunky old Chinese man in a super cute dress. Wouldn't you agree? And don't you dare fucking agree with that, because do you remember earlier when you were down on one knee and you explained how everybody else is ugly compared to me? Has that bloke left? Is he gone?"

Silence.

"Why are you so quick?" I said, not getting up from the trunk. Not yet.

"Dunno." She was quiet for a while. "Bit boring otherwise, isn't it?"

The phone rang. I shook my head, and Meili did, too.

"Not getting that," I said.

"No way," she said.

"I can't even hear it ringing."

"Yeah, it's so quiet."

I fell onto the mattress with her, and we kissed. Slowly and patiently.

And the phone kept ringing. Four different times.

We ignored it four different times.

FOURTEEN

THE NEXT MORNING, MEILI WAS UP FIRST, although she'd definitely been awake at two when I passed out. It had been another night of phone calls and long conversations in Cantonese.

"Sleepyhead, want some not-as-good-as-your-eggs?"

"I just realized I should go to school," I said. I also needed to send that FunZone form to my probation officer. Those two thoughts had jolted me out of a deep sleep.

"Are you joking? Not today. Too many exciting things going on. I'm fabulously rich, and I'm setting up a meeting."

"A meeting." I sat in front of Meili's dry and brown attempt at scrambled eggs.

"I tried to tell you last night, but you were completely out of it." I did have a faint memory of Meili talking as I pretended to be awake. "That lawyer in HK, she said I own significant assets. That was her word. *Significant.*"

"You have assets."

"More than one building. There's legal disputes with some of them, apparently, but the lawyer says she can take care of everything. Sort out the real estate, connect with my dad, fly me home, all of it. So I'm making a meeting."

"In Hong Kong?"

"Here, silly. Not with her, with her people. Those eggs are crap, aren't they?" I chewed and thought about how to answer. "Don't lie to me. Unless you want more sex. Ever. In which case, you should say they're light, fluffy, and amazing."

"Light, fluffy, amazing," I said. "You're gonna meet them here?"

"Not in the house. Somewhere, I dunno, nearby. Next week, I'm guessing. She was like: 'No problem, I'll send a car, we can make it all happen, blah blah blah.'"

"So what's really going on?" I stepped into my mom's room to retrieve the pile of mail. Don't let Meili see that room.

"Sorry?" Meili called from the kitchen.

"Why would she do that?" I brought the mail to the kitchen table, looked for the most recent letter from my PO.

"Do what?"

"Send a car."

"Why would she send a car?" Meili repeated. "To solve the problem."

"People do things for reasons. Like, is she your dad's lawyer?"

"No, that's a whole different thing," she said. "What are you doing?"

"I have to send that job form to my probation officer."

"From FunZone?" she said.

I nodded. I found a probation letter from three weeks ago. Good enough. "People don't spend money on cars and stuff to be nice," I said. "It makes me suspicious." I went into my room to find the signed FunZone form.

Meili followed me, cradling her mug of tea. "The money?"

"Yes." I checked my black jeans. Nope.

"The money for the car?"

I nodded. She tilted her head, squinted. She wasn't trying to figure out the lawyer's motives. She was trying to figure out what was wrong with me.

"I think this might be, like, a perspective thing," she said. "For some people, paying for a car is basically nothing. It's like: phone call, done. The money's no big deal."

"Money's always a big deal." I checked my backpack. Nothing.

"No, Jason, listen. There's people in the world who have a lot of money. Like, a gigantic amount. You can't imagine. It's a different universe. And, like, here, it sounds like a lot of money to send a car or something. But I guarantee you it's nothing. It's like a postage stamp. Less than that. It's like water from the tap."

I tried to imagine a life where ordering up a chauffeur was no big deal. Couldn't.

"Someone in Hong Kong has cars in America just standing by?" I said.

"Pretty much, yeah."

No FunZone paper. Shit. The probation envelope will have another form. Back to the kitchen.

"Seriously, Jason, you have no idea. There are places where there is so much money. It's nothing like this." Her hand flung out, indicating: What? America? Unionville? My cheap-ass furniture?

"Sorry, I try my best," I said.

"No, I'm not saying that. I don't mean you, I mean—"

"What?"

"This . . . this world. You know, Unionville, this whole environment," she said. She took her last gulp of tea. "You think I'm pretentious. I mean rich."

"No, I think you're"—I half giggled—"wrong. And I can't find the FunZone thing. Can you sign this?"

"What, sign Don's name?"

"Yeah, any squiggle is fine."

"Oh my *god*. Are you *serious*? Are you doing this just to torture me? I told you you should have done this from the start."

"I'm trying to stay out of jail, Meili. I don't care about the job now; I care about not being locked up. Maybe that's a matter of perspective, too."

She scribbled a decent imitation of Don's signature. "It is both ways, you know," she said. "There are things here people in that other world would think are utterly insane."

"Like?"

"Going to a hot dog stand on purpose to get in a fight. Or the Rubber Room, for god's sake. Are you really going in?"

"Have to."

"Seriously? Can't you say you're ill?"

"If I miss another day, the school could require a meeting with my mom. Then I'm screwed. And they could tell my PO, and I'm really screwed."

She scraped some food off the table with her fingernail. Ice cream? "So funny. We've both got secrets, haven't we? Hadn't thought about that till yesterday. We're both lying all the time, and we haven't got a parent within a thousand miles. We're like twins. Orphan twins." She looked up to see if I liked that. "Sorry for blabbing to Stephen, by the way. I didn't realize. I get so caught up in my own ridiculousness, it doesn't occur to me other people might have problems. And everybody's problems are the same size."

"What does that mean?"

"If you're, like, dying of cancer, you've got this massive problem." She held her arms up in a wide circle. "But if your problem is, like, your car won't start, you blow that up so it's just as huge, feels like a catastrophe."

"So you're saying I'm blowing up my problems."

"No, the opposite. I'm saying I'm such a fucking cow that I can't look outside myself and see that other people have problems to deal with, too. Doesn't occur to me." She took my fork and started eating my eggs, especially the brown bits. Maybe that was how she liked them. Egg fork in one hand, cigarette in the other. How could that not be disgusting? "Look, in my situation, there's two kinds of people. People are either useful or dangerous. That's it. One or the other."

"Which one am I?"

"You're both. That's why you're so interesting."

"What makes me useful?"

"You're tough, for one. That's always useful. And you've got this lovely house where I can hide out. But I like you, and that's dangerous."

"Why?"

She stopped and stared at her cigarette. She took a drag and looked at it some more. "I'm sitting here going: Should I tell him how ruthless I actually am? If you knew how ready I am to take advantage of"—she paused—"any person around me, you'd piss off. Or kick me out, rather, since it's your house."

"That makes me dangerous?"

"No, what makes you dangerous is that I care about what you think. Push comes to shove, I might not be ruthless enough." She grinned at me and stubbed out her cigarette.

"But why are we talking about this? It's a beautiful day, I'm rich, and you are . . . going to school?"

"Unfortunately." I looked at the clock. Crap. Five minutes to get ready. "Rubber Room's gonna be fun without you."

I went to get dressed.

"I wish I could give you some books, Bug, but I've got nothing here." She opened the door to my mom's room. "Oh, good lord." She immediately shut it and came into my room. "Here we go. What have you got?" She looked through my bookcase. "Lots of fantasy stuff, that's always nice." She pulled out three books, including *The Hobbit*. "Tolkien's great. I'll put these in your bag. And what d'you want for lunch?"

"You don't have to make my lunch."

"No, it's adorable. I make you lunch in a little brown bag, and when you take it out, everyone looks over—I mean, I know it's the Rubber Room, so it's basically Damn Harris and a pothead—but everyone looks over and goes: 'That Jason, he's gat a heyck of a waaaahf.'"

The accent was bad as ever, but I liked her joking about being my wife.

How crazy. I had known Meili for thirty-one days, one month exactly (yes, I counted). And I loved the idea of marrying her. Loved it. That's another thing we shared: a hope that we were about to be saved.

Maybe that's why things ended up this way. Two people with the same problem pulling in opposite directions.

My lunch did not inspire envy. At 12:25, the aide instructed us—me and Mike Kosnicki—to eat, and she left to get a tray from the cafeteria.

I pulled out:

> A bag (!) of cold macaroni and cheese
> An English muffin, untoasted, with jelly
> A can of orange soda
> A napkin full of raisin bran, no milk
> Two bananas
> Six Oreos
> And a note:

Dearest husband,

I know you are working hard at the coal mine. Please come home safe. Me and our seven children need you.

> *Your faithful wife,*
> *Esmerelda*

PS—While you're reading this, I'm walking around your house in my knickers. So there.

The strange thing about this lunch was not the food (or the lack of utensils, dear wife), it was how out of place it seemed in the Rubber Room. As soon as I arrived at school, I slipped back into my pre-Meili life. Sign in at the office. Walk with an aide to the Rubber Room. Take my seat in the third row. Pass the time reading. Be a menacing, surly presence in the school.

I was susceptible, a word I learned in tenth-grade Peer Group. Whatever was around me was true. I rearranged myself instantly and completely for the Rubber Room. Meili and our domestic fantasy seemed distant, imaginary. Was she living with me? Was I considering going with her to . . . where? Hong Kong? The Florida Keys? From the familiar silence of the Rubber Room, that was beyond ridiculous.

My life was here, obviously.

After lunch, Ms. Davies came to see me. Kosnicki was back in his non-Spanish classes, so we met right there at my table while the aide took a break.

"Hello, Jason, how are you?"

"I'm good." I made a point of spreading out the school-books I hadn't looked at all day.

"You've been absent."

"I was sick."

She waited for more information. I didn't give it.

"You need a note from your mother. You're already up

205

against the limit on absences, so make sure she sends a note."
I nodded. "How's your mom?"

"She's OK," I said.

Ms. Davies liked to say simple things, then sit quietly and wait for you to open up. Again, my secret: don't talk.

She nodded and kept looking at me. She raised her eyebrows and nodded some more. Didn't work. I said nothing.

"I sent her a letter asking if we could all sit down, and I never heard back," she said finally.

Shit. Somewhere in the stack of mail. I usually caught those.

"I'll ask her about it," I said.

Silence.

"The thing is, I'm told there was an incident over the weekend between you and Mr. Bellman." Ronald Bellman. "Can you tell me what happened?"

"We ran into each other at the VFW," I said. Full stop.

"And?"

"Ronny and some other guys came after me, and I defended myself." Not exactly true. In fact, a lie.

"Uh-huh," she said, nodding. "I'm concerned, Jason, because you are not going to graduate if we can't get you back into classes." She gestured at my books. "The work is not getting done, and we're running out of time."

"I understand," I said. None of this was news to me. She

made this speech every few weeks, mostly for herself. Nothing ever changed.

"I don't want you to say you understand, I want you to work with me to fix it, OK? And part of fixing it means no more incidents with Mr. Bellman."

That was too much. "Look, they're the ones that mess with me. I'm locked up in here because they won't leave me alone. You want this to stop? Talk to them."

She liked that. She went into her slow nod, wanted me to keep going, keep expressing. I didn't.

"Jason, I understand how this must seem from your point of view. But you have to remember the feelings in this community about what happened." *What happened* was guidance counselor–speak for me burning that kid.

"I get it. That's why I'm gonna sit in here till June, then piss off and get my GED." "Piss off," a Meili phrase, bothered Ms. Davies. "I mean, go away and get my GED."

"My job," she said, leaning in, "is to have you walk with your class on June twenty-fourth. Not just for your diploma, Jason. I want you reintegrated in this community. I want you back where you belong, which is in class with your fellow seniors."

"I want that, too," I said. "I'll go back to class right now if you let me."

"You can't go back as long as you keep choosing violence."

"I am not choosing it. Ronny's choosing it. Ask anybody."

She raised her eyebrows. "Jason, more than one witness—with no reason to lie—said you threw the first punch."

Well, shit. When you put it that way, it did look bad.

"You wouldn't understand." Every kid in Unionville knew the code about fighting. How come no adults knew it? "And who told you that?"

"Two students independently told me. In confidence." She lowered her voice. "Here's how bad it is. Both students said: 'Please don't tell Jason I said this.' They're scared you might come after them."

Fucking should be. Snitches get stitches. Lying snitches get worse.

And what about the racist thing Ronny said about Meili? Why wasn't that part of *how bad it is*?

She continued, "I also think that's why the victim didn't report you to the police. If he had, you would not be walking around today, as I'm sure you're aware."

Victim. Ronny didn't tell the cops for the same reason I didn't: he knows the fucking code.

So ironic. Know how this all started? Last summer, two guys got arrested for dealing weed and pharmaceuticals, and a rumor went around that my mom had snitched on them. People started hassling her, saying stuff to her when she was out, driving by our house and yelling in the middle of the night. One day, my mom and I were at the Sunoco, and this guy started talking shit. I told him to step off, not talk to my mom like that, and he got up in my face, calling me snitch-this and faggot-that. Whatever, I've been called worse. But then he grabbed my mom's arm. She's at the pump, and he yanks her arm, gas spilling on her shoes.

You listening, bitch?

Uh-uh. You don't put a hand on my mom. Sorry.

I pounded him. Middle-aged dude, big gut, I just dropped him.

Turned out, that was Ronny's stepdad. And the fun began.

OK, deep breath, Jason.

I tried to sound sincere. I tried to *be* sincere. "A lot of people hate me. So I have to protect myself. And when I do, they use that as a reason to hate me more. So you tell me."

"It *has* to *stop*." She tapped the table twice in front of me, on "has" and "stop," her fingers gathered together for maximum impact. Every meeting with Ms. Davies had a peak, a moral, a here's-why-we're-having-this-chat moment. "*Has* to *stop*" was that moment. "Whatever story you are telling yourself, whatever fantasy is justifying this violence, it is wrong. *Period.*" One last table tap.

Good news was: if I signaled my acknowledgment, we could start the wind-down.

I nodded gravely. *Yeah, I guess you're right.*

That must have satisfied her, because she leaned back

and said, "I need to sit down with you and your mom. Have her call me." A smile for a boy who's learned his lesson.

"I will," I said, reaching, preposterously, for my Bio textbook.

Ms. Davies stood up and headed for the door. "Is Melissa here today?"

So many truthful ways I could have answered that. *No.* Or *I don't believe so.* Why would I choose the one response that was a direct lie?

"I haven't seen her," I said.

"OK." Another smile from Ms. Davies, and a well-practiced wink. "Back to work, buddy."

I hadn't realized how much I was lying until Meili pointed it out. I thought I was protecting people, saving them from worrying about things that were, in the end, fine. I can't tell Ms. Davies about punching Ronny because she doesn't know how respect works in Unionville. And I can't tell her I live alone because she doesn't understand that I'm OK, that I'm better off without my mom and Al.

No one understands, that's what I told myself. Maybe that was the biggest lie.

I tried to read the Tolkien book to impress Meili, but it was too slow, too pleased with itself. I read enough to be able to discuss it with her later, then switched to *The Last Fortress*, the second book in my series. I was completely engrossed. I'd expected the Rubber Room to be torture today, *exquisite* as Meili would say. I looked up from *The Last*

Fortress and it was 2:29. An hour and three minutes had passed without me noticing, something that never happened with Meili in the room.

"Wilder!"

Todd the Bod, a hunky senior swimmer and lifeguard, nice guy, walked over in the parking lot. We played basketball together, back before everything. Todd was sharp: hair product, tight T-shirt, unlaced high-tops. He was trailed by a big dude, maybe a wrestler.

"Yo, Jason, man, what happened? You get busted?"

We did the clench handshake and shoulder hug. Todd smelled nice.

"No, I'm good, man. Keeping clean."

His friend stared at his phone, maybe trying not to talk to me.

"Saw you at that party, though, right?" Todd said. Was he there? "How crazy was that? Like thirty kids from here got arrested."

"Yeah, I hid in the woods," I said.

"Oh, shit, on the stealth tip." Todd socked his friend. "My man Randy here hid under a bed."

Randy finally looked up, noticed me, didn't have a problem with me. Which was nice. He nodded and grinned.

Todd leaned in. "Dude hides under a bed and passes out."

"I was pretty hammered," Randy admitted/bragged.

"Wakes up, fucking eight in the morning, everybody's gone." Todd poked me in the chest. "Makes. Fucking. Breakfast. No joke."

Randy shrugged. "Little cereal, OJ. Couple mavericks. You know, start the day off right."

A maverick is a partially full beer someone abandoned. Especially delicious the morning after.

"But, yeah," Todd said. "I was like: 'I wonder what happened to Jason,' cause I didn't see your bike here yesterday." He leaned in, got quieter. "And people were like: 'What happened to that girl, the DJ girl, your friend?'"

I felt him trying not to say "the Chinese girl," which I appreciated.

"Melissa," I said.

"Yeah, some people were like: 'She got deported.' Other people were like: 'Her family's so powerful, they just called up, boom, cops had to release her.' I was like . . ." Todd shook his head. "Pfffff, that's deep."

Not surprising that people were talking about Meili. But weird that their guesses were so close to the truth. Not that I knew what the truth was.

"She wasn't in the Rubber Room today," I said. "That's all I know."

"Crazy, man. It's like . . ." Todd watched some girls stretching on the track. "Fuck Kendall. Know what I mean? Fuck that whole town."

"Seriously," I said.

Another shoulder hug.

"Glad you got away, though. That's awesome." Todd headed to his truck, Randy's phone and Randy close behind. "Tell that DJ I liked her set."

Didn't he hear me say I hadn't seen her?

Or was I a shitty liar?

FIFTEEN

I SHOPPED ON MY WAY HOME. I BOUGHT groceries every day, just cause I could.

The phone was ringing as I walked in the kitchen. It was the middle of the night in Hong Kong, so Meili wouldn't be answering it.

"Hello?"

I dropped my bag with the mac and cheese, tea, ginger ale, bagels, and—yup, cause I could—a pineapple.

"Hello, I am calling for Melissa."

Formal. Weird.

"Melissa who?"

"Melissa Young."

"Who's calling?" I said. Pineapple goes in the fridge? Seemed right.

"Is this Jason?"

OK, that's a fucked-up way to answer my question. I stopped with the pineapple. "Who is this?"

"This is Melissa's father."

Holy. Shit.

"Oh, hello. Sir. Yes, I'm Jason. Sorry."

"Don't apologize."

"Melissa is . . . um, hold on." Where was she?

"Jason," he said. Could it be a trick? Somebody pretending to be her dad? "I understand you've been keeping Melissa safe. We are all grateful." His voice was warm, steady. He meant it.

"Yeah, well, she's . . . um . . . she's amazing." Ugh. "I mean, don't worry. She's safe."

"Can I speak with her?"

God, I hoped she was here.

Meili was curled up on my bed, asleep. Crash position, mouth open.

"Meili, your father's on the phone."

"What?" She was instantly awake, no transition. "You serious?" She was on her feet, smoothing her T-shirt (my T-shirt technically), head down, half jogging to the kitchen.

It was her father. I knew from her voice. Excitement, warmth, childlike glee.

I leaned against the living room wall and, without understanding a word, followed the entire conversation.

Meili gushed, giggled.

She talked about life here, suspiciously upbeat. I heard "Unionville," "Jenkins," "Jason Wilder." I was being introduced to my girlfriend's father. If she was my girlfriend.

She laughed, raced through questions for him. She wasn't like me, giving the minimum to reassure an absent parent. She was enthralled.

Then something sad and serious. She can't go home? She's in trouble for the drinking? Meili absorbed it, protested, gave up, protested.

And then something deeper and quietly shocking. Someone died? I heard her posture change, the tiny collapse of things taken for granted and now gone.

Short, flat answers. A final rush of words.

Silence.

The phone smacked the floor, slid along the linoleum.

A wail. Deep and long.

When my mom cried, you could rate it by how high-pitched she got. Imagine a strongman scale with a bell at the top for one-hundred-point sorrow.

This was different. This wasn't taking off into the sky, it was a crack opening underneath Meili, a crevice cutting her in half. When you split wood, the splitter goes in an inch, maybe two, then the whole log gives way at once. Meili was split.

She caught her breath.

I did, too, forehead on the living room wall. Let her be. She needs space.

Then a deeper, harsher, rasping scream.

Damn.

OK, give her a minute. I put down the pineapple I

was somehow still holding. Think about other things, let it . . .

No.

I marched into the kitchen. Meili was bent off her chair, frozen in midfall. I reached down to . . . hug her? Sit by her? No. I scooped her up, deadlifted her, tipping the chair, kicking the phone.

I half fell onto the couch with her in my arms. She let me hold her, let me in.

She screamed so loud I turned my ear away.

I never want Meili—or anyone—to be so betrayed and broken. But if we're gonna live in a world where that happens, I want this. I want her thrashing sobs and gut screams. I want to clench my body to hers and tumble. I want that velocity. I want my share.

Black River flows through the Notch, these great cliffs for jumps and the occasional death. When the water's especially high, you can shoot the rapids on your butt, bouncing off rocks and tumbling over two big drops.

I held Meili as she plunged through the Notch.

She buried her face in my shoulder, vibrated my chest with her wails. Hair, snot, tears, saliva. Everything flowed and tangled, paused then restarted.

After the fire, I'd wake up every morning and have a moment of peace. Then: oh, shit, I burned that kid. Meili cycled through crying, settling, then seeing the horror with fresh eyes.

Her moments of calm gradually lengthened, her breath slowed.

She slid off my lap, sat next to me. I waited, my arm around her.

Minutes passed, my personal record for *don't fill the silence*.

"I can't go home," she said.

Terrible news. For her. But I sure didn't want her to leave.

"I'm sorry."

"And it's worse. It's not to do with the trial. That's finished. It's to do with . . ." A sob. "Money. Fucking money. You believe that?"

Well, yes. When money's involved, people do crazy things. Tyler Beck's dad still walked funny because of some fight over a trailer worth, what, a couple thousand dollars?

"It was so fucking good to hear his voice," she said. "I can't even tell you. I miss him *so much*. I've been terrified something happened. Jail, another fire. Or something worse. I've been petrified."

"You don't talk about that."

"It's the only thing I think about. Ever. It's *right here*, every second." She put her fingers on her forehead.

Did I have that, something I thought about every moment and didn't talk about? Euhhh. Shudder.

"Is he OK?" I said.

"Yeah, thank god." Big exhale. "But he's lying, Jason. He's been fucking lying for so long. I can't . . . aaaaah."

She clenched her fists, shook her head. The news seeped in, but her body fought it.

"About what?" I said.

"Why I'm here. It's those buildings, that's why I'm stuck in America. I'm guarding the family fortune. He put them all in my name so the corrupt arseholes can't take them. He says they're *at risk. Vulnerable.* Can you imagine using those words with me? *I'm* fucking vulnerable."

I didn't say it, but I definitely thought it, probably because of the family I grew up in: Could Meili's dad be the corrupt arsehole?

"And there's more," she said. Resigned, methodical. "There was no fire."

"What?"

She ripped a sheet from a notebook, blew her nose in it, folded it. "Believe that? There were threats, apparently, legal ones and not so legal. But no fire."

"Your dad made it up?"

"Yeah. And he just now told me, like: 'Hey, good news, darling, no fire! Your stuff didn't get burned.'"

"Damn."

"Mm-hm."

"I'm jealous."

"What's that?" She picked up a mug, saw it was empty.

"Wish my fire got erased," I said.

"Oh, for fuck's sake."

"I'm just saying." I dug my hole deeper. Why? "I'd

love it if someone called up and said my fire never happened."

She sat up, got out of my arm. "If you didn't want a fire, all you had to do was not fucking start one. Is that so difficult to understand? I had *nothing* to do with my fire. Nothing. It sent me here and ruined my life. And now it's erased, never happened? Ruins my life again."

We weren't touching. Dammit. I rubbed my own arm—didn't help.

"He made up the fire to scare you?" I said.

"That's not what he'd say. He'd say he did it to protect me."

"The money, you mean."

"The what?"

"He made up the fire to protect the money, the family fortune. Not you."

I was focused on figuring out the mystery, not on how devastating it was.

Turns out: pretty fucking devastating.

Turns out, this was my equivalent of Meili saying, *Florida. It's gorgeous.*

No, this was worse.

Her face wrinkled up. "Yeah. That's it, isn't it? None of this was for me. Ever." Like throwing up in slow motion, tears started in her belly, bent her over as they squeezed up through her chest. "Oh god."

Meili had two reactions to the conversation with her

father. First, she was wrecked. By the call, the lies, the months spent apart from him. Meili, always quick, always direct, overheated completely. She was on the side of the road, steam pouring out of the hood, staring helplessly. That comforted me. It's how I felt most of the time, broken down and not sure why.

Then she switched to anger. Reckless, who-gives-a-fuck anger. That's also something I know about. But you don't start down that path unless you're ready to go all the way. Unless you can really bring it.

"Does Manny know?" I said.

She shrugged.

"I bet he doesn't," I said. "I bet he's in the dark, like you. That's the only way the plan works."

"Fucking bastard."

"No, I'm saying Manny's not a bastard. He's been misled."

"I'm not talking about Manny."

Right.

She lay down, curled up.

I rubbed her foot. And I felt—I would never tell Meili this—excitement. Possibility. Her collapse, the betrayal, it all made me relevant, necessary. Cause whatever else my fucked-up life had done, it taught me how to survive when the adults won't protect you.

She was silent so long I thought she was asleep.

I slid away. *Leave her be. She stays up most of the night, must be exhausted.*

I got halfway to the kitchen.

"What's wrong with our parents?" she said, as if we'd been talking the whole time.

"*Our* parents? Different things."

"No, it's the same." Her eyes were open, bloodshot and staring at the floor. "They've thrown us away. Walked away from their fucking child cause they've got more important things to do."

"Look, I'm not defending your dad, but he does take care of you. He sent Manny, he found you a family to stay with, I assume he sends money."

"That's not taking care of me. It's the opposite. It's hiring people so he doesn't have to."

She sat up, grabbed her tobacco.

Say something, Jason. "You're right" didn't seem helpful.

"Can you imagine?" she said. "If you had a child, can you imagine sending her away, not speaking to her for a year? It's unthinkable."

A drop of water landed on her half-rolled cigarette. She tossed it all into the ashtray, put her head in her hands.

"A year, Jason. A fucking *year*."

I sat back down, and she spun around.

"All for some money? *Money?* Are you fucking kidding me?"

Her shoulders shook, the tears streamed.

"Are you *fucking* kidding me?"

Could I imagine a parent thousands of miles away

from a kid, not knowing or caring what's happening in his life?

Yes, Meili.

I could.

Meili's conversation with her dad did not bring us closer.

That night, we had a long, surreal argument. Much of the argument was about (a) whether we were having an argument, and (b) if we were, what the argument was about.

My position was that we were having a discussion—not an argument—about the pros and cons of meeting with Anthony Holt, a guy sent by that Hong Kong lawyer. I thought it was a terrible idea. If your dad ships you off to another continent to hide money, there must be real danger. I suggested alternatives. *How about I meet Holt first and check out whether he's legitimate?* I didn't know how I would do that exactly.

Meili said if your dad ships you off to another continent to hide money, you get to do whatever the fuck you want. *When you've been thrown away, you don't owe anyone anything.* She said we were arguing about who gets to make decisions in her life: her or "all you men," meaning, as far as I could tell, her father, Manny, me, and her uncle. At one point she included Ms. Davies, who, though technically not male, was "part of the whole power thing." First and only time I've been accused of conspiring with my guidance counselor.

Topics we covered: Whether using your child to hide money was cruel but possibly understandable, or just cruel. Whether Manny had put me "in charge" of Meili or "in service" of her. Whether the name "Anthony" indicated a sneaky or reliable person. Whether owning a bunch of disputed real estate made Meili powerful or vulnerable. Whether being in jail, something I knew about, was worse than hiding your identity, something Meili knew about. Whether it was harder to have a drunk mom a thousand miles away or a devious dad ten thousand miles away.

Here's how ridiculous it got. I said, "I don't even know what we're fighting about" so many times that Meili started lip-synching it.

We switched rooms, closed doors on each other, paced, came roaring back with: "But how can you say . . ."

When she could no longer bear the repetitions, the infuriating dead ends, she went to sleep on the couch. It was agony. I lay in bed, facing away from the door, replaying and continuing our argument. She moved to the bed at 3 a.m. With her near me, though not curled around me, I nodded off a couple times.

I crawled out of bed in the morning to shower. When I came back in, she sat up sharply, peered around the room. She never liked what she saw when she first opened her eyes. She lay back down and pulled the blanket over her head.

I'd learned not to reach out in the morning. Let her initiate, especially after last night.

I got dressed and searched my bookcase for *The Forgotten Sea*, sequel to *The Last Fortress*. Having a great series helped in the Rubber Room.

"You going?" she said from under the blanket.

"Every day."

"Seems a bit much."

I found *The Distant Island*, two books ahead in the series, but it would do.

Don't initiate. Let her talk first.

"You going to miss me?" she said, eyes open, covers down by her chin.

A brutal question. *The* brutal question. God, could she leave? I dodged it.

"Technically, between 8:07 and 2:41, I will miss Melissa Young, not you," I said.

"Can't stand that one. Such a snob," she said, smiling slightly. "Looking for more great literature?"

"I like my series. Piss off."

"No, it's great. Better than watching TV. I really don't want to watch TV again. So depressing."

"Maybe you should . . . not watch it then," I said.

"You scholars are so rational. That's not how it works."

"Scholar's gotta go."

"No! Get over here, Bug."

I lay down next to her. She put my hand on her chest and turned so I was spooning her, the thing I'd wanted all night. I felt her heartbeat, urgent and sturdy.

"What happened last night?" she said. "Did I call you a Nazi?"

"Among other things."

"God, what are we like?"

"I think I called you a nightmare," I said.

"A *fucking* nightmare, 's what you said." She craned her neck around and looked at me from the corner of her eye.

"Sorry." A smarter boy would make a joke: *But really you're a dream come true.* But a smarter boy wouldn't be exhausted, hungry, and late for the Rubber Room. "Nazi's gotta go," I said.

She gripped my hand tighter. "Don't." I slid out of her grasp, and she groaned. "I can't be*lieve* you're going to school again."

In the kitchen, I scanned for the fastest breakfast and lunch. She yelled from the bedroom, "Go to school again, hooligan!"

That was the last calm thing she said to me.

Before I left, I looked in. Meili was on her back, head tilted to the left, mouth open. On each exhale, she made a tiny "huh." If I was completely still, I could hear it from the doorway.

Here's how it started.

It was Frosh-Soph Field Day at UHS: goofy outfits, relay races, and hollered chants. I was really out of the loop. While

226

freshmen screamed through an obstacle course outside the Rubber Room windows, I thought about Meili.

And her buildings.

Significant assets gave me a tingle. Whatever was screwed up in Meili's world and my world, significant assets could fix. It was like that stack of fifties from Manny, like those manic moments when my mom got a windfall. The money tilted me, made me imagine.

With money, we could . . . what?

Leave. We could go. No Manny, no UHS, no probation officer, no Aunt Sophie, no Ronny, no cold mac and cheese. Our whole situation could be bought out, replaced.

My mistake, or maybe my question, was thinking of *our situation*. Did we have a situation? Or did we have two separate, shitty situations that intersected in the Rubber Room?

Eating my lunch (crackers, jar of peanut butter, two bananas), I thought about Manny coming back. Do we tell him? Manny would know what to do. He could *handle himself*. But maybe he was in on it. Meili definitely wasn't trusting anyone, except, insanely, this Anthony Holt guy. Once she calmed down, I'd convince her not to meet Holt. And then, who knows, maybe we take those *significant assets* and live some other place, some other way. Maybe we smash our problems together and solve them both. But I had to convince her there's—

"Jason, you have a phone call in the office," the aide said, sandwich in one hand, intercom in the other.

That's how my time in the Rubber Room ended.

Phone call. My probation officer sometimes called the school when my phone was shut off. But my phone was working. I rooted through my backpack for the probation form, the kind of compliance that kept him happy.

I walked through the echoing, scrubbed halls, face-painted Field Dayers hustling past.

I passed my old locker, which was so close to Ronny's my locker privileges had been revoked. Right then, I didn't care. And not in a fuck-Ronny way. I was above it. I was beyond this claustrophobic school, this small-minded town. *Too tight*, Meili said. Such a big world out there. I felt sweet toward UHS, almost nostalgic.

We had assets. Meili and I could—maybe—leave together. I would actually miss this place.

I should have savored it, should have strolled laps around the school, since Field Day meant the hall monitoring was relaxed. And since it would be the last time I was permitted inside the building.

"Hi, I'm Jason Wilder, I have a phone call."

The secretary brought out Ms. Davies, who had her serious face on.

"Jason, a doctor called concerning your mother." What? She guided me into her office. "They need to speak with you directly. It's line two. I'll be right out here."

They. That word got me. Permission to take her off life support, donating organs. Those are the things "they" ask you about, right?

I sat in the soft blue chair facing Ms. Davies' desk. No school district furniture for kids who came to talk with her: this was puffy and leaned back. Made you want to stay.

I pressed LINE 2.

"Hello?"

"Jason, it's me."

"Meili?"

"Oh god, Jason," Meili said, out of breath. "I'm so sorry. I just—it's all messed up."

"What's going on? Where's my mom?" I said.

"No, it's nothing to do with your mum. I'm sorry, I just had to get you on the phone. I've got a meeting with the guy, but it's all wrong. I needed to hear your voice. I'm scared, Bug."

"What guy?"

"The guy! Holt, the guy from the lawyer, he came to meet me."

I caught Ms. Davies watching me through the door, and she looked away.

"I thought that was next week."

"He just showed up, and he kept calling, like: 'I'm here now, you have to come talk to me.' He says I'm in trouble, the buildings aren't really mine, there's lawsuits, and, I dunno, I'm scared."

"You don't have to—"

"He shoved these papers under the door and said I'd been served. What does that mean?"

He came to the house? Was he still there?

"Hold on, Meili. You don't—"

"I'm scared of leaving, Bug. I'm scared they're gonna, like, take me with them. This guy's not playing around. And I'm scared of these papers, Jason, I don't even want to touch them."

Papers, right. I knew about papers. "You can touch them. Once he says those words, it's over, so you might as well read them."

In retrospect, maybe those papers were the whole story. The idea that there were—what, assassins? kidnappers?— looking for Meili seems pretty over the top when you think about it. I don't know much about real estate, but I know a silly amount about serving papers. If you avoid being served, you avoid a lot of legal problems. Maybe the scary stories and the fleeing from town to town were her father's way of making sure she never got served. How messed up is that?

"God, I don't want to read them." I heard her lighter flick. Must have been rolling a cigarette this whole time. "He wanted to come in, kept pounding the door, but I was too scared. I told him to go to Stewart's, and I got in the car, but I freaked out and came back in and called you. I'm sorry. It's all fucked. Manny called, and I'm scared he knows about it, too."

Sometimes my vision shakes. Fights won't do it, even getting arrested didn't. But when those guys put bottle rockets in my house, threatened my family, everything wobbled. It happened during this call, same feeling: don't come after my people, my home.

"I'll be there in five minutes," I said. "Don't go anywhere."

"I've gotta go, I've gotta talk to this guy. I've been putting him off, and he's really angry. I just didn't want to, you know, have them whisk me away, and I never said goodbye or anything."

"I'm coming, Meili." I was on my feet. "Don't go anywhere."

I opened the door so quickly I startled Ms. Davies.

"Jason, is every—"

"I have to go." I was already hustling toward the hall. "It's my mom, she's in the hospital."

Ms. Davies tried to slow things down. "OK, Jason, what hospital? We can get you there."

"No, I have to go."

I was down the hall in full sprint, my shoes slapping the shiny floor.

I had my keys with me, so I ran right past the Rubber Room and out the double doors to the parking lot. Please, god, let my bike turn over.

It didn't.

I pushed it hard till I was running alongside. I jumped on, and it started. I kicked into gear and roared out of the parking lot.

I pulled off onto my road, gunned it into my driveway, and left the bike running.

Manny's car was gone. Shit.

"Meili!" I shouted. Inside, the phone was ringing.

I banged on the back door, which, turned out, was unlocked. Not good. I never left the door unlocked, even when I was home. I entered the house braced to meet someone I didn't want to see.

Kitchen was empty. Meili's notebooks and pens were gone.

"Meili!" I raced through the house, looking for her but careful. Each door I opened, I had both flavors of adrenaline in my muscles: hope that Meili was there and fear that someone else was.

Phone still ringing.

Her stuff was gone. All of it, even the clothes Stephen brought. Like someone had swept in and erased her presence. Whatever papers that guy served, she'd taken them. My vision wobbled.

At least the kitchen still smelled like tobacco, the smell that nauseated me back on Brandt Hill.

Phone still ringing. Could be her.

I picked it up. "Hello?"

Static and a voice in the background.

"Hello?" I repeated louder.

The phone cards were gone. And the scribbled-on take-out menus.

"Jason? It's me." Not Meili. Manny.

Shit. Of course.

"Jason! Is that you?" Definitely Manny's voice.

I looked for evidence of Meili: a pen, a hair tie, a fucking cup of tea. Nothing.

"Yeah." Goddammit.

There: her shark-tooth necklace under the couch. I pocketed it.

"What's happening? What is she doing?" he said.

OK, which lies was I telling Manny again? And Manny was . . . bad? No, just misled? I was too jacked-up to remember how to talk to him.

"Are you there? Listen, Jason, she's—"

I hung up.

I just hung up on him.

I couldn't listen to Manny, couldn't add more layers to this fucked-up moment.

Out the back door to my bike, still idling. No helmet, just go. The phone started ringing again. I turfed the lawn and shot out into the road.

Breathe. Focus. What was happening? Stewart's, a meeting. What if she wasn't there? Gone, erased, "whisked away" was the phrase she used. That would be a disaster. The end of everything.

Oh, god.

She had to be there. Had to. And then, really, how bad could it be? Some scary guy was threatening her, bullying her? Worst case, I take him on and Meili runs. If you don't mind getting hurt, you can solve most problems.

It was a fast fall from the glory of walking past my old locker. Manny's voice, my fear that someone had broken in, Meili's stuff gone. I was doing sixty on Black Rock Road. My insides were speeding up, too.

Then I saw the parking lot.

A bunch of cars and pickups, a medium-size lunch crowd. Manny's Ford was on the side of the building. Thank god, she's here.

But then, parked right up against it, pinning it in so it couldn't leave, was a silver SUV with someone in the driver's seat.

That settled it.

When I think back—something I did a lot in the weeks after—that was the moment everything became inevitable and, in a way, easy.

Because if there's some argument in Stewart's, all messy and debatable and he said/she said, I can't really help.

But if this is how it is? You park your SUV behind Meili's car? You pin us in so there's no turning back? Then I can be very useful.

Useful and dangerous. That's what she called me.

SIXTEEN

I PARKED ON THE OTHER SIDE OF THE LOT. NO hurry, no drama. I played innocent, checking my bike for a moment, then letting my gaze casually drift over. The guy in the SUV was clocking me.

I didn't mind. I just thought: you *should* be worried about me, asshole.

Out-of-state plates. Somebody drove a long way for this meeting.

I walked to his driver's side, stood there, didn't say anything.

The tinted window glided halfway down. "What do you want?"

Definitely not Anthony Holt. It was his lackey. I had hoped for an overweight driver, a guy who eats Oreos and does word-search puzzles. This guy was fit and wired. No candy wrappers, no magazines, fucking protein shake in the cup holder.

"Gotta move my car." I played the hard stare, stay still and don't say much. You can scare city people with that. Problem was, this guy did it, too, maybe better.

"You rode a motorcycle." He nodded toward my bike.

"Yeah, and now I gotta move my car, so back up."

I turned away, got a few steps.

"That's not your car," he said.

There are a few ways to play this moment. I figured he couldn't afford a fight with some kid in the parking lot, so I escalated.

"What did you fuckin say? What did you fuckin say to me?"

Primitive, but effective. Makes the other person accept or decline the fight. It works in response to literally anything. Try it.

Can you pass the ketchup?

What did you fuckin say? What did you fuckin say to me?

No response from him. Just a stare. The tinted window slid shut.

I walked around to Manny's trunk. My whole scene would look a lot weaker if I couldn't unlock the car. I felt under the bumper.

Come on, Manny, you said there was a spare key.

There. Taped high in the corner. Found it.

I unlocked the door, started the engine. A sleeper has an advantage here: it makes noise. I gunned it.

Brog-og-og-og-og-og-graaaaaaaaaaaaang.

Not your grandma's Ford Tempo.

Lackey didn't move. I put it in reverse and jerked back a few inches.

Finally, the SUV glided backward, smooth and noiseless as the tinted window.

I spun the car around and parked next to my bike, away from the building so it couldn't be blocked in.

I hopped out, locked the door.

Yeah, that's right, Lackey, I'm not leaving. I'm just getting started.

And then, right as I entered Stewart's, his SUV door opened.

Shit.

Ding-dong. Come out fighting.

I've replayed this scene so many times in my head and for other people. It's become cinematic, with tiny moments highlighted, different camera angles. It's all so etched now, so written and rewritten, it's hard to remember that it was live, pulsing, and undecided.

Meili sat at a two-person booth near the counter, facing me. She glanced over, then turned back to the mostly bald white man across from her.

There were other tables eating, a mom with her kids, three working guys, a couple, an older man alone. (I don't think I saw the old man, but he appeared later, so I've

237

pasted him in there.) I didn't want any of these people to get hurt.

I rushed it, walking right to Meili's table. Lackey would be in any second.

"How you doin?" I asked, careful not to use either of her names.

"You're here," she said, locking eyes with me. The table had piles of official-looking papers and one messy Meili notebook.

"Uh-huh," I said, matching her obviousness.

She widened her eyes and tilted her head toward the guy. He wasn't looking. She shook her head, like: "Not good."

"It's nice to see you," she said.

I bet.

I turned to him.

He was big, with enormous hairy hands, wearing a button-down shirt over an undershirt. Something about the undershirt told me I did not want to get hit by this guy. He looked at me and decided I was a nuisance, not a threat. He took a sip from his soda.

Ding-dong. Lackey. Goddamn. I needed more time.

"I saw your car out there," I said to Meili.

"Yeah," she said. She was wound up, waiting for me to do something, take control.

"Somebody parked you in. Right up against your bumper."

"What?" Meili squinted at me. That scared her.

Lackey arrived, stood between me and Big Hands. Two on two.

I turned back to Big Hands. "It was your SUV blocking her in. That's what your driver said."

Big Hands looked at me, and I got upgraded from nuisance to possible problem. "Did he?" he said. He knew Lackey wouldn't say that, and he knew I knew it. His stare told me all that. But there was something comforting in his voice. It was soft. He was powerful, no doubt, but he wasn't cut out for what was coming. He had the voice of someone who spent a lot of time in front of a computer. I'd rather fight someone like that. "And you are?" he said.

"Friend." I matched his low word count. I still didn't want to get hit by those big hands. I said to Meili, "I'll make sure he stays out of your way so you can get out."

Lackey looked to his boss for orders. Big Hands, rolling his eyes a little, nodded toward the door. What did that mean? "Move the car"? "Get this kid out of here"? "We're leaving"?

I looked at Lackey, like: "Can we go now?" I wanted him to walk out first. He didn't like me, but he liked me better out in the parking lot, away from his boss.

"I can move my car," Meili said. She wanted to come with me, get the hell out right now. Can't blame her. She started to stand.

This was the one way things could have ended well,

right? Meili says, "I'll be right back," we walk out together, take her car, gone.

I could see it. Still can.

But Big Hands stopped her. He put his hairy fucking hand on her. Meili's arm wrinkled as she pulled against his fat fingers. He pushed her back into her seat.

Uh-uh.

That was it.

Can you believe this fucking guy? Big Hands, your day just ended.

But first, I followed Lackey out.

This was my advantage. Don't start the fight before you start the fight. And when you do, go fast, go hard.

I lagged a couple steps behind. I grabbed the sugar pourer from an empty table, one of those heavy glass ones.

I spun around and took two quick steps, rising like a volleyball player for a smash.

My arm arced high and slammed the canister on the back of Big Hands' fucking head. It shattered in my hand, and his face hit the table hard.

Meili screamed, covered her face from the flying glass and sugar.

I grabbed the back of his head and smashed his face on the table. His nose broke. I lost my grip on his head because there was so much blood, mine and his, mixed with sugar, bright red spreading into the white crystals.

"Jeezus!" Meili yelled. His blood was sprayed on her shirt and her papers. "Shit, Jason! What are you doing?"

People jumped up. Yelling. That heavy, brittle charge that passes through a room where someone is being harmed. Everyone off-balance.

Except Lackey.

This was the moment Lackey lived for. I pictured his long, useless days, driving around, waiting in the SUV, clearing the way for important people to walk into restaurants. He wasn't cut out for that. Too much downtime, too much brain time. This was the shit he loved.

And, sadly for us, this was the shit he was really good at.

Let's pause to admire his quick read of the situation: I am the Hostile, Meili is the Asset, Big Hands is down. His first move was so brilliant and thorough, I have to recount it precisely.

Yes, I like this stuff. I like how people fight, the way some people like cars or college basketball. I believe in it. The things you want, the ideals you hold, the people you love, that's all well and good. What you do when the shit goes down, that's what decides your future. How you move through Stewart's at 1:15 on a Thursday is what you have to offer, what separates you from the whiners and yammering grievance keepers. And, honestly? Most people are so disappointing. They're weak or obvious or opportunistic. So many tough guys fear a fight till it's obvious they can win.

Then they pile on, gang up on people who are already down. You'd be surprised how many men love beating someone who's on the ground. That's all you need to know about them.

Lackey was not like that. Sadly, he was glorious.

Lackey shot a hand into his boss's armpit, stopping him midfall. He wrapped my neck up with his other arm. The side of his face was wide open. I came up hard with my right fist and landed what I thought was a brutal punch on his chin. It didn't do a lot, other than pushing some glass deeper into the meat of my thumb.

He could have turned and fought me face-to-face and definitely beaten the snot out of me. But I was not the Asset; Meili was. Beating me down while Meili ran out would have been a disaster for him. Satisfying, but a failure.

After my fierce but apparently inconsequential uppercut, Lackey looked at me for the quickest instant. Not angry, not even annoyed. He scanned me to measure how much attention I would require. What percentage of his violence was necessary to subdue this kid?

Not a lot.

Big Hands was steady now. Lackey released him, and his left arm yanked me toward his body as his right landed a blow on my torso like a brick shot out of a cannon. Ribs—in the plural—cracked. My breathing stopped for the near future. And he was already turning toward Meili.

My seventh-grade rec basketball team thought we were

hot shit. Then we went to a tournament and got destroyed in four straight games. Annihilated. That's what fighting Lackey was like. I thought I was good at landing punches and taking punches. Turns out I was only rec-center good.

Meili was trying to stand, clutching some papers. "Stop it! Just stop it! What are you doing?" she yelled. "Get out of here!"

Lackey kicked my legs out from under me—I was already bent over from his punch—and I dropped to the floor, still not breathing. He braced a leg against Big Hands and pulled Meili out of her seat with his other arm.

Impressive. In the three seconds since I jumped Big Hands, Lackey had put me out of commission, stabilized his boss, and secured Meili. He sailed undisturbed through the room, the universe bending itself around his objective.

Not breathing feels like an emergency, but it isn't. Unless your airway is blocked, your body will find a way to breathe again soon. As long as you don't panic, you're at least a couple minutes from passing out, a couple more from brain damage. I got to my knees and pushed away the fear. I was just underwater. I had plenty of air to last me for a while. My ribs hurt, but adrenaline was already taking care of that.

Big Hands was awake but not in any rush to get up. Lackey deadlifted his boss to half standing.

Meili was pulling her arm away from Lackey, saying, "Let me go. I have to go." With her free arm, she frantically grabbed more scattered papers.

The smart move now would have been to get a broom or one of those metal napkin holders, something that could do real damage. Lackey had so many things on his to-do list I could have landed a good head shot. But I saw his hand on Meili, saw her struggling to get away. I knew where Lackey was going: get the Asset and his boss into the SUV and get the hell out. So I went straight at him. I came up from below, launching myself at his head. I landed one nice punch on his cheek—he turned at the last second or it would have been his nose—and wrapped my other arm around his neck. I sent the whole tower off balance, and he stumbled to his left, all three of us half falling into another booth.

My side (not the broken-rib side, happily) slammed into the Formica table. On a normal day, that injury would have been a big deal. Everyone around me would have stopped, ice would have been found, maybe a visit to the ER. There would be lots of, "Wow, that looked so painful" and "I can't believe the table didn't break." But in the moment, I barely noticed it. Much later, I saw the imprint of the table edge in a long diagonal bruise.

Big Hands, no longer propped up, slumped over. Lackey, bless him, tried to catch Big Hands, but then swiveled and drove an elbow into my gut. I let out a groan, a gurgling, involuntary yell. People in the room groaned with me, the way people watching a fight do when a blow seems particularly brutal or dirty.

"Stop it!" Meili was yelling. "Get out of here!" Not that Lackey was listening.

I got to my feet and tried to make space to land some hits. One-on-one with Lackey, I didn't like my chances. But with him distracted by Meili, I thought I could do some damage. I led with my glass-free left hand, but he dodged it. He couldn't dodge my right into his gut, though, and the force of my fist pushed him back into Meili. He grabbed at me with his free arm, but I ducked and came in hard, my right elbow cracking into his jaw, followed by a sloppy-but-on-target left to his temple.

Someone came flying into my line of sight, and my first thought was: Big Hands? Up and at 'em that fast? Then somebody was on my back, tackling me.

And this is where I say: god bless Unionville.

It's a messed-up town, and I didn't love living there, didn't love how I was treated. But people in Unionville are ready to fight. We don't wait for the cops, sometimes we don't even bother with the cops. We will happily interrupt our lunch break to put a hurting on somebody.

Two guys pinned Lackey down, trying to get Meili out of his grasp. Two others held me. I pushed them away, saying, "I'm cool, I'm cool." Probably helped that they knew me.

Everyone was yelling.

"Cut the shit, guys!"

"You're done, man, you're fucking done!"

And other obnoxious fight talk.

Meili scrambled out, slipped, stood up, and grabbed her bag.

Another thing about U-ville: people got guns. *Ding-dong.* I turned my head reflexively. Someone else I needed to fight? It was the old man holding a shotgun, a handgun tucked in his waistband. We hadn't been fighting long. Gramps must have jogged out to his truck.

"Alright, let's settle this down, people," Grandpa announced, not sure who was fighting who, walking carefully toward the mass of bodies.

Meili had the same instinct I did: Get on the other side of Grandpa. Get the armed man between us and the bad guys.

There was a lot of yelling now, ten different people in charge, telling everybody to "Hold on!" and "Settle down!"

Meili grabbed the last of the papers from the floor and ran toward the door. Grandpa stopped her. Given the arsenal he was carrying, it was a bit menacing.

I limped over to her.

"Where are you going?" I said. "I can take you." I had my breath back. When did that happen?

Sirens. People gathered in the parking lot, looking in. That was a favorite Unionville pastime: stand near some crazy shit so later you can say, "I saw the whole thing, and, man, let me tell you . . ."

"No, Jason, it's not—" Meili started. "Oh my god, look at you."

I reached out with my left hand. My right was a bloody, sugary mess. She pushed my hand away, looked out at the arriving police car, and closed her eyes.

"Shit . . ." She turned back to me. "This is not good. You're out of control, Jason."

"It's OK, we can . . ." I started, but I didn't have any ideas. It was the adrenaline talking. It was not OK. We couldn't.

"Listen to me! You're out of control." Meili leaned in close. "I'm sorry, Bug. It's for your own sake. Really. It's better for both of us."

"What's better?"

"I'm sorry." She pushed me away and said to Grandpa, "Sir, it's not safe for me here. I need to get away from this man."

Grandpa misunderstood. When I took a step to follow her, he turned to me and raised his gun. Like I was the problem.

And Meili slipped past.

Jesus.

"She's not talking about me. I have to go with her," I said. I had my hands up, reasonable and calm.

People cleared the way for Meili as she hustled out.

"Son, take it easy," Grandpa said. "You're staying right here. Police are gonna sort this out."

"No, I'm *with* her. She's talking about that guy." I gestured back toward Holt and Lackey. Either one. A glob of red sugar dribbled off my palm onto the floor.

Ding-dong. Meili was out the door.

"Wait!" I yelled, no longer calm.

"Sit down, son. Nobody's leaving till the police get here." That was obviously false. The central person of the whole incident just walked out.

Ding-dong. A cop opened the door and froze. Grandpa laid both guns on the floor, saying, "Officer, glad you're here." He put his hands up and stepped back, keeping his body between me and the guns. "I was securing the area till you arrived."

Strange situation for the police. They're called because of a fight. An old man, strapped, claims he's on their side. The cop was wary.

Bad news for me: I knew this cop. Or, rather, he knew me.

"Down," the cop said. "I need both of you down on the floor."

"Yes, officer," said Grandpa.

"I'm with her," I said, pointing outside. "I have to go with her."

"Lie down, hands behind your head." He put a hand on his gun.

"You don't understand, I'm—"

"Down, Jason!" he shouted, and the gun was out.

Fine. I lay down on the smelly linoleum, my face right on the worn-down path. I arched my neck to see the back of Meili's legs through the doors. She was wearing the red skirt she wore at the party a million years ago. Or was it a week ago? Less? Unbelievable.

The cop picked up Grandpa's guns, saying, "Relax, everybody, just relax."

Sunlight glinted off the police car windshield.

A second cop came in and blocked my view.

When he stepped away, the back of Meili's legs and the back of Meili's red skirt were gone.

SEVENTEEN

THINKING EVERYTHING IS ABOUT TO GET straightened out is exhausting.

It's the worst thought to have as you lay facedown in handcuffs for close to an hour, as you see the assholes you fought walk out of Stewart's one at a time, as you get asked ridiculous questions, questions that can only be answered with: "You've got it all wrong."

That sounds like the guilty guy in the movie. So, instead, I said, "I want to talk to a lawyer." Which also sounds like the guilty guy.

Eventually, I said, "Unnnhhhh," because the pain kicked in. With the adrenaline wearing off, I had a catalog of intense injuries all over my body, and they took turns screaming the loudest.

But the worst part of that hour, and the trip to the hospital, and the endless questions, and the trip to juvenile jail, and the more endless questions, and the drugged not-sleep on my cell bunk, was the feeling that everything was about to get straightened out.

I want to go back and get rid of that feeling. I'd keep the fractured ribs, the stitches, the twelve pieces of glass removed from my hand and the three pieces still in there. The thing that caused the most pain was wondering, every time someone entered the room or a phone rang: Is this the moment when people finally realize what's going on?

I wasted phone calls calling my house, thinking Meili might be there.

Where the hell was Meili? Or Manny? Or her aunt and uncle? Somebody would show up soon.

That thought never died. It shrank and hardened.

I could understand, sort of, why Meili did what she did. Maybe it was *for my own sake*. Maybe those guys would have come to my house with more than fists if I wasn't securely locked away. But at some moment, that danger passed. At some moment, Meili and Manny had to come forward and tell everyone what happened. That would be *better for both of us*, Meili.

I tried to explain it all to my skeptical, overworked, court-appointed lawyer. Here's how well that went.

"Melissa called me at school because she was in danger. I went to Stewart's, and these guys were threatening her, trying to take her away." I was earnest and serious at the beginning.

We met in a cheerful room that's not what you're

picturing. New carpet, comfortable-enough chairs, bright lighting, a window. None of juvie is what you're imagining. It's a boring cement dormitory, pleasant and anonymous except for the doors that lock from the outside, the screaming, the fistfights. You had a *room* in the *facility*, not a *cell* in a *jail*. But we all called them cells cause it sounded tougher. And cause that's what they were.

"According to their statements, they were meeting with Melissa to discuss financial matters," Jeffrey Malcolm—*please, call me Jeff*—said, pulling some pages out of his huge stack.

Why do prosecutors all have sharp suits and fancy haircuts and defense attorneys have rumpled clothes and overgrown hair? Is there a dress code?

"That's right," I said. "Melissa's father is in trouble, and he put a bunch of real estate in her name. Those two guys found out where she was, and they were threatening her."

"Explain," he said, reading but paying attention.

At this point, I realized I didn't really know the story. I was inventing, or at least filling in, a lot of details.

"It's simple. They want Melissa so they can take her family's assets," I said.

"Who are 'they'?" he asked.

"People connected to her father's case."

"His case," Jeff said. The more dubious he got, the slower he talked. "And who is her father?"

"I don't know his name. He does business stuff." A

terrible sentence. An I-don't-know-what-I'm-talking-about sentence. I was exhausted, injured, pissed off. "I mean, real-estate stuff."

"Do you know where he is?"

So exasperating. "No one does, that's the whole point!" I yelled.

He paused, a slow-down-the-crazy-person pause. "We would need to confirm all of this with Melissa."

"Yes, definitely," I said. I leaned back in the chair and tried to be a Good Client. My chair was chained to the table leg, presumably so I couldn't pick it up and throw it at Jeff. So many maniac-proof rooms in the world. In my world.

"But we can't locate her," he said.

"Of course not. She's terrified." I tried not to yell.

He switched tacks, pushing some pages across the table. "What's bad here is the victim states you attacked him un-provoked. And we have uninvolved witnesses who back him up."

That sounded like Ms. Davies. *Witnesses with no reason to lie.* Why was I in so many situations where I technically threw the first punch but, really, I was attacked?

Maybe I was a hooligan.

Go to school again, hooligan.

"You're not giving me a lot to go on here, Jason. I under-stand that, in your mind, you were protecting Melissa. I believe you . . . acted on that belief." Jeff did have one twisted skill: convincing bad people he empathized with their crazy,

253

evil decisions. "But the court is not interested in what you thought. The court is interested in what you did. Now, the two victims are not especially sympathetic, and we have eyewitness testimony that the second one grabbed you in a threatening way before you hit him. If that holds up, we can probably get charges related to him dropped. That leaves charges related to Mr. Anthony Holt, and the best we can hope for there is the ten-month suspended sentence from your earlier arson charge. I think there's zero chance we'll get below that, and I'm guessing the prosecutor, particularly if it's Bill Burke, is going to push for more." He paused for emphasis, as if "Bill Burke" might change my mind. "That's why a plea deal is absolutely in your best interest. Taking this to trial could go badly for you. Very badly."

"What does 'very badly' mean?"

He slid a page over to me, the charge sheet I'd already seen. "There are serious charges here, felony charges. That's bad enough, and on top of it, you're on probation. You've had your second chance, Jason. From a prosecutor's point of view, you're an arsonist who sent a young boy to the hospital, and now you viciously and publicly assault two people. And beyond those arrests, it's my understanding you've been in several altercations in the interim, *including other fights at Stewart's.*" He tapped the table on that last one.

For the record: fuck table tappers. Every one of them.

"Those were different. That wasn't about Melissa, that was the other stuff, the fire," I said.

"Exactly. It's a continuous string of violent acts, many taking place at a family restaurant, instigated by you."

"It wasn't all at Stewart's. We also fought at the VFW." I channeled Meili, smiling sarcastically.

That confused him, and he turned back to his papers. "If we are going to trial, I need more than stories, I need evidence."

"Like?"

"Testimony from Melissa Young." I shrugged. "Testimony from members of her family. Evidence she has been harmed or threatened in the past. Medical records, 911 calls, a friend saying she felt she was in danger." I shook my head. "Court records of her father's case. A statement from her father. Evidence that someone is trying to take her assets illegally. Anyone who overheard their conversation in Stewart's and can confirm Melissa was being threatened."

I had none of that. Nothing.

He continued: "You must have talked to someone, a friend or family member."

"About this? No, it was secret."

"About Melissa. You must have confided in someone, bragged to your buddies, right?"

Here's a sad fact. The only person I could think of was Manny, a guy I saw exactly four times.

"I don't have buddies."

"None?"

"None."

He leaned in with that sympathetic guidance counselor nod, eyebrows raised. We're Learning a Lesson Here. I wanted to lean in, smile, and head-butt his greasy, smug face. Everyone who makes that face deserves a broken nose.

Don't head-butt your lawyer, Jason. Really, don't.

"What convinced you, Jason?"

"About what?"

"That Melissa was in danger. That you had to protect her from these men."

"What convinced me? I believed her," I said. "She explained it, and I trusted her."

He didn't say anything. He just let my words sit there.

No further questions, Your Honor.

That night, I did what I always do when I'm in trouble. I didn't call my mom. I had phone privileges between 6:15 and 7, so every night at 6:15, I told myself: time to call Mom. Then, all I had to do was waste thirty-five minutes, and I could say: It's too late now, we need more time to talk and connect, I'll call her tomorrow for sure.

The best way to spend those thirty-five minutes was on either bunk—no cellmate yet, I mean *room*mate—reading a fantasy novel. I could get wrapped up in the story, keep one eye on the clock, and reasonably tell myself I had lost track of time.

The worst way to spend those thirty-five minutes was

thinking about Mom. Thinking about her seeing me here. About how she bawled when she visited me in jail after the fire. Thinking about the endless apologies: "I'm so sorry, baby. I've been a terrible mom. I'm never gonna forgive myself."

She always got ahead of me. When I was mad, she'd beat herself up till I'd start saying nice things to her. When I needed her help, she'd break down crying, and I'd end up comforting her. That's what drunks do, according to the Alateen group I'd attended one and a half times. (She pulled me out in the middle of the second meeting when she found out it wasn't a required part of her DUI sentence.)

So maybe it was her. She made conversations hard, all tangled up.

But really? Truly down deep?

Maybe it was me.

That night, for thirty-five minutes, I thought about Jeff's question: What convinced me Meili was in danger?

He nailed it with that question. How, specifically, did I know Meili was in trouble, that she was at risk? If I told that story, Jeff would be convinced. And Jeff could convince the judge, the prosecutor.

That's when I got serious about the writing.

Everybody had given testimony except me and Meili. I wrote our story from the first day in the Rubber Room. From: *That's not your name.*

I wrote on everything. I filled a notebook the social

worker gave me, then tore blank pages out of books no one was reading, then traded for a second notebook. On my third night inside, way too late, I wrote on napkins.

It's incredible how much you remember when you get focused. The different angles of Meili's two front teeth. The taste of her mouth after she drank tea. The rainbow reflections off the sunglasses of the power-washer guy at FunZone. It was a movie in my head, I could direct it, edit it, rewind, zoom in.

I'd show Jeff my movie. I'd show him what convinced me.

Writing made the hours fly by. Guys started calling me Professor. Hilarious.

Then I worried. Could I get it all on paper? And could Jeff make sense of it? I gathered everything I'd written, every scrap and notebook and ripped sheet. It was bad. I was the crazy client who drops a stack of random, hoarded bullshit on his lawyer. Paranoid diagrams of how the president was tracking me, secret messages in McDonald's ads, all scrawled on the back of trash-picked envelopes.

I had to clean it up, simplify it. My tenth-grade literature teacher used to challenge us to "say it in a sentence." Tell the essentials (that was her word) of *Twelfth Night* or *The Bluest Eye* in one sentence.

Young man sacrifices himself to help girl with a British accent and a troubled past.

Bad boy and on-the-run girl fall in love in small-town America and are torn apart by circumstances.

I could copy it over into one notebook, maybe two. The story had to be clear, so Jeff could get me out of here.

So I could find Meili.

So it would not be:

Violent boy ruins his life right when he feels hopeful for the first time.

I borrowed a pen light and wrote all night before my second meeting with Jeff. My hand hurt, my writing got sloppy. I raced to get the last bits into my notebook. I skipped breakfast, not a good idea unless you had money at the commissary.

At 10:15 a.m., I dropped three notebooks on the table. I had tucked several pieces of nicely folded paper into the last notebook. It wasn't perfect, but it wasn't crazy-person, either.

"Good morning, Jason."

"Good morning. I wrote it all down."

"I'm sorry?"

"I wrote down everything that happened, everything that convinced me Melissa was in trouble, it's all there."

"OK. Why don't you have a seat, Jason." He was trying to slow me down. I was sped up. No sleep, no food, fourteen straight hours of writing. If only my teachers could have seen me.

I sat down quickly. "You have to read it. It explains everything." Why wasn't he reading it?

"We have things to talk about," he said.

Of course we do. "I know, I know, I know. That's what I'm saying: It's all in the notebooks. All the important stuff."

A stack of case files teetered on the table, all of Jeff's locked-up clients. He was killing maximum birds with one visit.

"Great." He shifted tactics. "We'll definitely talk about the notebooks. Are you alright, Jason?"

"Yes."

"You look exhausted." He didn't care, exactly; he was concerned he couldn't bang out an efficient meeting with me.

"Because of this! I've been up all night. But it's totally worth it cause I got it. I got the story."

"Good, I'm glad."

No, you fucking aren't.

"Now, I wanted to start by asking about our plea deal," he said. *Our* plea. I nodded. "Have you thought more about what I said?"

"What part?"

"Pleading to lesser charges, taking the ten months minus time served. A little over nine months. Earn some credits inside, maybe eight and change."

Eight and change. Me locked up for two weeks was a bunch of pennies you wouldn't bother to pick up.

I didn't want to get mad. I looked at the notebooks. Maybe I could get him to notice them by staring at them. My stack of papers versus his.

"I talked with the prosecutor, Jason. He's charging you as an adult, OK, this is not like your earlier case. But he put this deal on the table. It's an excellent deal. Now, we can't wait forever." He took two crisp papers out of his WILDER, JASON file. "He gave me a one-week window on the offer. This was yesterday. So read it carefully, ask me any questions, and then we'll have a few days to think it over."

We. As if he was going to give it serious thought, weigh the pros and cons for a day or two.

This was not the lawyer I wanted. I wanted the lawyer who couldn't wait to chase down leads, poke holes in the official story, hand the witness some shocking document and ask, "Is this not your handwriting, Officer?"

I had the lawyer who made deals with the prosecutor as quickly as possible so he could move on to some better case.

Stay calm, Jason. You worked hard on this. Don't blow it now.

"How about this?" I looked at Jeff for the first time. "I'll read that, and you read this." I pointed at my notebooks.

"OK, well, I can't read it all right now."

"Remember last time, you asked me: What convinced me Melissa was in danger? I thought about that so much. It was a great question, the best question. So I wrote it all out, it's all in there. I swear, read it and you'll understand."

Jeff nodded, for real, and picked up my notebooks, which, compared with his pile, looked totally reasonable. "Alright. I will. I want to understand, Jason. I want to understand how you got here. And I promise: any information in here that helps our side, I will use it to the fullest extent of my ability to get us the best possible result."

I liked that lawyer. That was the lawyer I'd hoped for.

"Thank you." I could feel a sob rising, but I pressed it down. "And I'll read this and think about it. Definitely." I stood and took the two clean, white papers. Maybe they only seemed clean compared to my scribbled notebooks.

Jeff looked at his watch. "Today's Tuesday, I'll be back Friday. That'll leave us plenty of time to make our decisions."

"Thank you. I appreciate you reading all of that. Sorry about the handwriting. I think it's gonna help you, you know, get it."

"Getting it is good. I want to get it. And thank you for reading the plea offer. I think we can find our way to the best outcome. Not perfect, but the best we can."

I never bothered to read the plea deal. As soon as Jeff started looking into things, as soon as he started asking the right questions, everything was going to change. I pictured us someday laughing that we had ever considered a plea. Jeff would shake his head and say, "I can't believe I almost let them lock you up for eight months."

And change.

EIGHTEEN

THAT NIGHT, I CALLED MY MOM. I FELT BETTER about how things were going, and I wanted to see if she had any news. From Meili.

I assumed Meili would never call me directly, too dangerous. Maybe she would get in touch with my mom.

I requested phone time at 6:30, hoping to hit her sweet spot between annoyed-but-sober and sweet-but-wasted.

The phone rang once and she picked up. All the calls were recorded, so it started with a beep and a long announcement about the recording.

"Jason, baby, I'm so glad to hear from you. I've been so worried."

"Yeah, sorry. It's hard to make calls here." Not really.

"What happened? Aunt Becky tells me you got arrested."

"Some crazy stuff went down. But I'm OK. You'd be proud of me, Mom. I did the right thing, I protected someone. And the lawyer says I might get out soon." That was a lie. What I meant was: once the lawyer checks out my story, he'll work on getting me out.

"I'm glad. You know I want the best for you, baby."

"Has anybody, uh, contacted you?" The real question.

"The juvenile court folks never called here, they probably think I'm still in Unionville. But, like I said, Aunt Becky called, and she tried to explain the whole thing to me and, you know, I got real worried, I tried to read about it on the internet. Anyway, our neighbor's internet is down, and you never know when it's gonna work. But Al talked to them, and I think it's gonna get fixed real soon."

So like my mom. Ask her a crucial question—a simple question—and she detours into some bullshit about her problems.

"Nobody else called you or wrote to you? Maybe a friend of mine? Have you checked your messages?" A chronic problem for her. She dodged calls from debt collectors, so she let messages pile up, especially if she didn't recognize a number.

"Not that I know of, no," she said. "But I'm so glad to hear your voice, and so glad you're getting out of there."

"Maybe. I don't know yet."

"You tell that fabulous lawyer to get my baby home, OK?" The wind-down. That was quick. Meant she was drunk.

"I will."

"You're my baby, you know that, right? I'm always gonna be here for you."

"I know, Mom. I love you."

"Love you, too, sweetie. Call me, OK?"

"I will."

Click. Beep. Recording ending.

The next day, I had visitors. Plural.

Sweet, pale Stephen, wearing a well-fitted hoodie that I imagined was his stylish attempt at jail-friendly clothes, and Butchie. Butchie? One of my sort-of enemies.

This was another way I could hear from Meili: she sends a mutual friend. Took her long enough.

They sat at a table in the way-too-bright visiting room, Stephen utterly out of place, and Butchie trying to look comfortable, which seemed more desperate.

There was a raucous family at the main table, four kids, maybe siblings, a mom, and a grandpa, all visiting this goofball guy who had tried to tell me jokes when I first arrived in jail. I thought he was coming on to me. Turns out, that's just who he was. The young kids were loving it, laughing and all talking at once, competing for his attention.

Butchie chucked his chin at me. Cool, gangstery gestures and language all felt ridiculous in jail.

"Hey, Jason." Stephen smiled a little.

I sat across from them. No barrier separated us, but we weren't supposed to touch. "Hey, guys. What, uh, what are you two . . ." I stopped myself. "Thanks for coming."

It really was nice of them. There aren't enough delinquents in Unionville to justify a facility, surprisingly. So I was in Essex, a good forty-five minutes away.

"I should have come earlier, but it was . . ." Stephen said.

"No worries. It's good. I'm . . . I'm good," I said, answering a question no one had asked with a lie no one believed.

Butchie stared down at a spot on the table between me and Stephen, tracking us without seeing us.

"How are you guys doing?" I asked. Let them bring up Meili.

"I'm good," Stephen said.

Butchie looked up suddenly. "I got your bike."

Huh. "My motorcycle?"

Butchie nodded.

Stephen said, "That's why we came. Butchie told me about your bike, and I said, 'We should go tell Jason.'" Something in my expression made him explain more. "I mean, I wanted to come anyway and see how you're doing."

Gross. Don't.

Butchie perked up, happy to tell his story. "It was at Stewart's, where you left it. But I guess no one knew what to do with it, so it sat there."

A little girl was chased around our table by the goofy guy, who fake-whispered, "Beep-beep. 'Scuse us!"

I waited till they got back to their side of the room, then said, "Was there anything on it? A note or a message?"

"No. I mean, not by the time I got to it."

"What Butchie's not saying," Stephen explained, "is that some people messed with your bike, so he got it and rode it to your house."

Butchie nodded. "I couldn't ride it. I put it on a trailer. It's in your shed. I locked the padlock, so it should be safe. I mean, I think it's fixable. There's just some . . . physical damage."

But no emotional damage. Phew.

"Thanks, man," I said. "What was damaged?"

Butchie shrugged, looked over at Stephen, who said, "Some people, like, smashed it. The mirrors, the speedometer . . ."

"Slashed the seat," Butchie added, helpfully.

Damn. "Who do you think did it? Ronny and those guys?" I didn't want to accuse all of those guys since Butchie was obviously not involved.

The family started singing "Happy Birthday."

Stephen shook his head. He had to half yell to be heard. "A lot of people are upset about . . . what happened."

"Yeah, me too," I yelled back. "You don't think I've been going crazy in here?"

The song ended with applause. Butchie clapped.

Stephen said quietly, "I know we're not supposed to discuss the case, but . . ." He looked at the sign with all its rules, maybe to avoid looking at me. "It's just that people were freaked out. Theresa's mom, she was there, she was in Stewart's and saw the whole thing, and Theresa said she couldn't stop crying about it. The fight was so brutal, she was just like: 'That boy, that violent boy.'" He looked to see my reaction. I tried not to have one.

Screw Theresa's mom.

One way to know you have a problem: you hear people think you're violent, and you want to pop an elbow into their pretty little cheekbones.

Breathe, Jason.

Change the subject.

"Did she contact you?" I didn't need to say who.

Stephen shook his head. Maybe lying?

"I need to get in touch with her," I said.

He nodded. *Yeah, you do. And good luck.*

No one spoke. Even the big table was quiet.

"Do you know how I can reach her?" I said.

Stephen shook his head. "She left."

Left.

"I want to make sure she's OK, that's all."

"For sure," Stephen said in a voice that meant: bullshit.

"It's not . . ." I said. I wanted to justify something, but I couldn't find it. It just hung there.

We all waited for someone to speak, to think of something. The family was filing out while goofball watched and waved, big smile on his face.

Stephen instinctively reached for his phone, which wasn't there cause you're not allowed to bring one in. He looked around for a clock. "We should probably get going," he said.

Butchie, who had been waiting for someone to say that, stood up immediately.

"Yeah, thanks for coming, guys," I said. "And thanks for taking care of my bike."

"Let me know if you need anything," Stephen said, but didn't mean.

The sob started to come. I clenched my gut hard, pushed it down. I didn't risk speaking cause I wasn't sure what would come out.

"See you, man," Butchie said. And right before he turned to go, I saw his worried face look back at me, eyes narrowed, lips pursed.

And that boy, that violent boy, walked back to his cell.

I was only there ten minutes, then this announcement:

"*J. Wilder to see Jason Wilder.*"

A typo, right? Someone put my name twice.

That's why I didn't prepare, didn't think about how I looked.

The visiting-room door buzzed. I pushed it open.

Jay Wilder.

Jay Fucking Wilder.

Jay Ain't Nobody Wilder.

"Jay-SON! What's going on?"

He always put the accent on the second syllable cause that was the joke: I was *Jay's son*, so he named me Jason.

Ha ha.

People who do shit like that should not have kids.

"What's up, man? I came to see you." He stared at whatever helpless facial expression I was making.

"Hi, Jay." I never called him Dad, just Jay.

"How you doing, man?" He leaned forward, hairy elbows draped on his jeans. Tucked-in plaid shirt, clean sneakers, close-trimmed beard and stache. Jay had been, probably still was, a hit with the ladies.

"Good." One syllable. I was dumbstruck. And what do you say when people ask you that? I'm in jail. My shit is horrible.

"I was thinking about you in here, man. I wanted to come out, you know, see how you're holding up." He looked around, shook his head. "It's a hell of a thing, huh? Doing time's a hell of a thing."

I shrugged and, weirdly, shook my head at the same time. Whatever-slash-no.

"Look at you. Grown-ass man, you filled out real good. What's going on, man? How are you? How's your mom?" Jay's conversations had a racing impatience I used to get caught up in, the seductive feeling that I was so interesting he couldn't stop asking me things.

I avoided the first two questions. "She's not good."

"I heard she's down in Florida, right?"

I nodded.

"It's nice down there, man. I bet she likes it."

Just like Meili. You tell someone your mom fucking abandoned you and went to Florida, and all people say is: "Florida, so pretty."

"It's not going well." I don't know if I really thought that. But I didn't want to let Jay off the hook. *Everything is terrible*, that was my position.

"She's a real crazy lady, isn't she? Beautiful person, though. I hope it all works out for her."

I made a neutral "Hm." Like: "Huh, you said those words."

The room was echoey, lifeless because that happy family was gone. Or maybe because my fucked-up family was here.

"What about you? Finishing school?"

"I'm in here."

"Before, though," he said. "You're what, senior? Junior?"

"Senior."

"The finish line."

"I wasn't gonna graduate. Even before this."

"You can get your GED in jail. Lot of guys don't know that."

"I'm not in jail. I'm in custody."

"Yeah, I know, how's it looking?" Jay put his hairy arms

on the table, laced his fingers together, ready to get serious. "What's your lawyer say?"

"I should take a plea."

"They always say that. Plead out, do your time. But"— his knee was bouncing—"I don't want you in here. Look at you, man." His voice dropped, cracked a little. "God, I don't want you in here."

A sob swelled in my gut. No fucking way. Not in front of Jay.

His face wrinkled up. Whoa. Jay Wilder crying? Thank god. He took the sob. I could relax.

"When your mom told me, I was just . . . I know what it's like." He took a big breath. "I don't want this for you."

"I'll get it straightened out."

He squinted and nodded too quickly, too many times. "Yeah, yeah, you will," he said. His thick wrist smeared the budding tears sideways. "Whew, sorry. Anyway, what else? What else is there, man? You wanna hear what I've been up to?"

"No." I said it so quick, I might have said it while he was still talking. Every possible Jay Wilder sentence that starts "You wanna hear . . ." is a no.

"Fair enough." He put his hands up like I was being un-reasonable. *Real crazy*, as he would say. "I don't need to talk about myself. That's not why I'm here."

"Why are you here, Jay?" I liked using his first name. Man to man. Loser to loser.

"I heard what happened. I'm your father, I wanted to come down and see if—"

"You're not my father."

"I'm your father, Jason. Believe me. I got the paternity test and everything."

Jesus. In my family, shit just gets dropped in conversations. My mom would casually mention "the hepatitis" or "those harassment charges."

I ignored "paternity test."

"You're a guy my mom used to date. You don't know me."

In my mind, that was: BOOM. Time for deadbeat dad to break down and ask for forgiveness.

"I did more than date her." Oh, you had sex with her? Sweet. "But, look, I'm not here to talk about the past."

I snorted.

"What?" he said.

"Guys like you never want to talk about the past."

Again, POW. Was no one hearing these takedowns?

Jay glided past it. "I want to talk about how you're gonna get through this. Cause it can get deep when you're inside. Real deep. There's things you might not even realize you're doing and then, bam!" He pounded the table, and I almost jumped. "Now, you look like you can handle yourself. I heard—whew—I heard what you did to that guy, I was like: 'Damn.'" He nodded with an approving frown. "Guess that's what happens when you piss off a Wilder, a grown-ass Wilder."

"We're not supposed to talk about that," I said, tilting my head toward the rules.

"I'm just saying, I get it. I don't need to tell you how to handle your business. I wanna talk about the code on the inside. I wanna give you some advice, cause if you come at people the wrong way, you make a lot of problems for yourself."

Fucking advice.

Hey, everybody, and especially people who are basically fucked-up failures, here's an idea: don't give advice unless someone specifically asks for it. And if no one ever asks you for advice, that's because you don't have your shit together.

I honestly think I've never asked for advice. Not once. But, damn, did I get a constant stream of it from people who were nothing like me (my teachers, my lawyer) or from walking disasters like Jay.

"Here's two phrases you're gonna use a lot," he said. "One: 'I keep to myself.' Anytime someone asks you what you do, what you're into, you say: 'I keep to myself.'"

A woman came in, my mom's age, done up a little, plump arms pooching out of her blue dress sleeves. She sat at a table far away from ours, pointedly looking at her nails. Too dignified for this place, or so she wanted to think. Wanted us to think.

Nobody's too good for this place. Nobody's too good for anyplace.

"The other one is: 'I don't take sides.' If there's a beef, or some racial nonsense, you say: 'I don't take sides.' And then you shut up, you don't say anything else. 'I don't take sides.' Period." Jay casually turned his head to look the woman up and down, decided she wasn't worth it, turned back. Definitely a guy who still hit on women daily.

I was trembling. When did that start? I sat on my hands.

"Hopefully, that keeps you out of the bullshit. But there still might be somebody who wants to test you, especially if you age out of juvie. This is real important." He leaned in so no one could hear his precious secret. "Somebody pushes you, tries to provoke you, you ignore it, understand? Then, a day or two later, you find another guy. Not a top dog, not some big boy, cause that looks like a power play. But not a little man, either, get somebody in the middle. You pick him out, and you jump him, out of nowhere. No reason, no warning. It's a statement piece. You're saying, one, I can handle myself, and, two, you never know when I might go off. Cause if they mess with you and you hit back, they're in control. They're making you fight. But you come out of nowhere and drop somebody? Nobody wants to touch that. Make sense?"

Where to begin?

"I'm not gonna do that," I said.

"Hopefully, you won't have to. I'm just saying you might need to make a statement if people test you."

The jail-side door buzzed, and a skinny guy sulked in, drooping shoulders, eyes on the ground. A loud asshole back in the cells, always talking shit; here, he was tiny, hollow. He slumped into a chair across from the made-up lady, faced sideways, didn't say anything.

"That's not me, Jay. I don't do stuff like that."

"I mean . . ." He shrugged, let out a little laugh. "Yes, you do. Let's be honest."

"What?"

"What happened in Stewart's, that was a statement piece."

"You don't know what you're talking about."

The dressed-up woman was sobbing. Neither of them had spoken a word.

"I'm just saying, you went off on a guy—or two guys, right?" Jay said. "They had no idea what was coming. That's your statement."

"That's not what happened," I said. "You weren't there, you don't know."

"No, no, no, you misunderstood. I'm not judging you. I respect you. I'm saying you might need to do that on the inside. One time." He leaned back. "Good news is: do it where the guards can't see, I guarantee nobody talks. I guarantee the guy will say: 'Oh, I fell down and hit my head.'"

Like Ronny. *We were just playing.* Like me.

"I'm not—"

"Key is: don't go after a big man. You don't want the general, you want the corporal."

"I'm not like that," I said.

"And no weapons, right, cause then—"

"I'm not like that!"

He leaned back. "I'm trying to help. That's all."

"Don't help me."

Makeup Woman was shaking and blubbering now, wet sobs spasming out of her lipsticked mouth.

"I'm worried about you, man," Jay said.

"Don't worry about me. Don't think about me. Leave me alone."

"OK. OK." Hands up again. "Are you angry? Fair enough. If you're angry, just say so."

I remembered Manny's line. I said, "When I get angry, Jay, you won't need to ask if I'm angry."

He slapped his knee and pointed at me, big grin. "See? That's what I'm talkin' about. That's the stance right there. 'You don't *want* a piece of this.'"

Fuuuuuuuuuck.

Ms. Davies, the guidance counselor, wouldn't let male students use the word "frustrated" when talking about our feelings, because if she did, that was the only feeling we ever mentioned.

Dear Ms. Davies: I feel frustrated.

Stop trying to burn him. Change the subject.

"What happened to your ear?" I said. There was a bunch of nubby scar tissue on the crest of his left ear, translucent like a Tootsie Pop.

"Had an earring in there, ended up getting torn out." He squeezed it, and I thought it might burst. "Don't mind, though. It's like a tattoo."

The earring *ended up getting torn out.*

My mom put me on the phone one time, I was eleven or twelve, made me ask Jay why I wasn't going on a youth-group trip. "The money thing's gotten a bit weird, kiddo," he said. "Trips and stuff are gonna take the year off."

I should talk like that.

Hey, Jason, why are you in jail?

The law-abiding thing's gotten a bit weird. Freedom's gonna take the year off.

"Tattoos, though," Jay said. "Stay away. Straight up. No matter how bored you get. You want a tattoo, go to some-body on the outside, a pro with a real kit. Man, if I . . ." He grinned, hoisted his leg up on the table. "You wanna see how dumb your fa—how dumb this guy is?" He pulled up his jeans to show a pale, pimpled calf. Torquing it around, he pointed to a blob. "Guess what that is?"

I shrugged.

"Seriously, guess. What's it supposed to be?"

"Whale?"

"I get that a lot. Whale, fried chicken leg. One girl said it was the bubble in comics where the characters talk. Said I should write something in it. Anyway, this dude had no business inking anybody. I assumed it would fade out, but the thing's clear as ever." He slid his leg off the table. Then, quietly: "So stupid."

Makeup Woman started wailing. "Heaaaaaaaaaaahhhh . . ." Long, wet, high-pitched. Skinny Guy looked at the floor. Neither one spoke or moved. She wailed till she ran out of breath, gulped some air, and started again. "Heaaaaaaaaaaaaaahhhh . . ."

Jay pursed his mouth, sniffing his top lip. I remembered that from when I was little. Huge man tensing up, smelling himself.

"So what's the answer?" I said.

"What's that?"

"What was it supposed to be?"

"Fighter jet, a guy in the cockpit unloading on some target. I made a drawing. Dude just couldn't copy it."

I felt for him. A little. He went to jail when he was nineteen, but he was really just a kid, scribbling cartoons of fighter jets, asking some clown to ink it on his leg.

I imagined describing that to Meili.

They're all lost, Jason.

Some more than others, Meili.

"Heaaaaaaaaaaaaaahhhh . . ." the woman wailed again.

"Jeezus," Jay said, leaning back and looking at the ceiling. "You see what I'm saying?"

Uh, no. Jail is hard? Prison tattoos are stupid? I should do a "statement piece" on this bawling woman?

"I put some cash on your commissary," he said. "I know

how important that is. Five or ten bucks at the commissary can save the whole day, right?" I shrugged. "I'm gonna do that every month. I don't want you having to trade for stuff or fall behind with any—"

"Heaaaaaaaaaaaaaahhhh . . ."

"Are you kidding me?" Jay looked around for someone to make the woman be quiet or at least agree that it was ridiculous. "Come all the way here for visitation, and this is what you do? Come on."

She looked over at Jay, tears striping her face, sob aftershocks puffing out her cheeks. But she got quieter.

Jay threw a couple indignant shrugs for a nonexistent audience. "I mean, come on."

"I won't be in here next month," I said. "It's a big misunderstanding."

He nodded the slow nod that means: nah. "A lot of guys think that. Hell, I thought that. Realistically, though? You might need to put in your time."

It's a bad sign when a lifelong bullshitter like Jay tells you: "Don't bullshit yourself." Or maybe not. Maybe he was the one person who could spot it.

"Anyway, you get out eventually," he said. "What then? You been living here without your mom, huh?"

"Not supposed to talk about that," I said.

Jay leaned in. "That's a lot, man. How do you do it?"

"How do I do what?"

"Doing this all alone. It's a lot for one guy to carry. Your—"

"Heaaaaaaaaaaaaaahhhh . . ."

"Seriously?!" Jay stood up like the woman was specifically wailing at him. "What the hell?" She started another wail, this one seemingly inspired by Jay, and he shouted over her, "Enough!"

Skinny Guy looked up for the first time, but not at Jay, at me. Dammit.

The door buzzed, a guard came in, a burly woman with a grandma face. Your third-grade teacher in body armor.

"We should go, Jay," I said.

"Is there a problem?" the guard asked Jay.

"Yes, ma'am, there is. Trying to have a dignified conversation with my son here, and these people are making that impossible."

"Sir, this is not a private space. You share it with other visitors."

"Exactly. That's why *we* are talking in normal voices and keeping our problems between us. But these two—"

"Jay, you should just go. It's late," I said.

"This is not a private space, sir. If you're not comfortable, I can escort you out."

"I'm perfectly comfortable. It's *these* people who are making me uncomfortable." Nice Jay logic.

"Sir, you need to keep your voice down."

"Keep *my* voice down? What about her? She's been screaming since we got here." Not true.

"Sir, keep your voice down, or I will escort you out."

"Fine, I'm leaving. I'm out of here. I'm not gonna sit here with people screaming and crying. 'Oh, poor me! I have to come visit someone in jail! Boo-hoo!'"

Mocking a woman who's crying in jail. Damn. That is dark.

The guard put herself between Jay and the crying woman and, without touching him, herded him toward the door.

"We don't need this. We don't need this shit, Jason." He yelled over his shoulder. "Push-ups! Push-ups and sit-ups!"

Push-ups and sit-ups. Wow, Jay Wilder. Nice to see you, too.

The door closed. And there we were: me, Skinny Guy, and Makeup Woman.

Oh, god.

I stood, waited to be buzzed out. For a long time.

It was silent. Jay's ejection had the surprising effect of quieting Makeup Woman.

I had to say something.

"Sorry about all that. It's . . ." It's what, Jason? What exactly is it? "He's been under a lot of stress."

What? Did I fucking say that? Apologize for a guy I haven't seen in how many years? The absurdity bubbled up, and I started giggling.

Uncontrollably.

Just me in the shiny visitation room, laughing my ass off while a skinny sociopath and his devastated mom try— and fail—not to stare.

The door finally buzzed. I slipped through, back to my cell, my breathing calm, my hands no longer trembling.

Ah, jail. What a relief.

NINETEEN

WHAT DO YOU CALL SIDEBURNS ON A GIRL?

Sideburns?

One more memory of Meili, not sure when or where. She's looking down, reading, maybe writing. The tiny hairs by her left temple swoop down and up, converging as they tuck behind her ear.

The hairs spread mathematically, proportionally, like a scientific graph; like contours on a map, they split and merge. I stare, searching for the flaw, the stray hair.

Finally, Meili—absorbed, annoyed, resigned to being stared at by me and a thousand others—says, "What?"

She tucks the hair back, and the map is gone.

"We need to talk, Jason. And, for the purposes of this conversation, I'm going to ask you to be objective."

Jeff was back Thursday, a day early, which was promising.

He had papers in front of him, but not the notebooks. He was direct, stern, his frumpy clothes tucked in tighter.

"I want to consider the evidence," he said. "And I want you to tell me what you make of it objectively."

"OK."

"What brought you to Stewart's last Thursday, June first?"

"What brought me? Melissa. She called me."

A thin rectangle of sunlight cut across Jeff's papers, a little blinding. I had one of those from the tiny window in my cell, used it to track the day. Sunlight in the metal sink meant dinnertime.

"We'll refer to her as 'Meili Wen' from now on," he said.

Wow. He knew her secret name, though he mispronounced it: "Mealy."

"Where were you when you talked to her?" he said, glancing at his pad. I could only make out a few words of his loopy handwriting: *parking lot, sergeant, transcript.*

"At school, in the office."

"What did she say?"

I sat up straight, mirrored Jeff's posture. "She said this man came to find her, and she was scared and it was all wrong."

"Wrong?"

"He came to meet with her, but she wasn't expecting him that day."

"They were having a meeting," he said.

285

"Sort of. But really, he came to her home, and he was threatening her."

"Her home." His replies came quickly. This wasn't a conversation, more like an interrogation.

"My home. Where she was staying."

"He threatened her? What did he say?"

"She didn't tell me. He was acting threatening."

"Did she say those words: 'This man is acting threatening'?"

"I don't know if she used those words, but that's what she was saying." Ugh. You sound like you're bullshitting, Jason. "She wouldn't let him in the house, that's how freaked-out she was. She would only talk to him at Stewart's, in a public place."

Somebody was singing in the cells. Badly.

"Why did she call you?"

"She needed me. She was going to Stewart's, and she needed me."

"Needed you to do what exactly?"

This was like we were in court, a practice run.

"Protect her?" I said.

"Are you asking me or telling me?"

"No, that's what she needed."

"Did she say those words?"

The phone call was frantic. All I knew was what I felt afterward. Rage, panic.

"That's what she meant," I said.

He underlined something, moved down his list. "What did you do then?"

"I ran out of the school to my bike."

"Uh-huh. And you rode to Stewart's?"

It felt good to practice, imagining people listening intently, the prosecutor worried about his case, wondering if he should object. I was the serious, decent guy, answering every question.

"Yes. I mean, no, first I stopped at home."

"Home?"

Was this news to him? Didn't he read my stuff?

"Meili called me from my house. I was hoping she would still be there."

"Why were you hoping that?"

"Because I could help her, I could protect her. Convince her not to meet the guy."

"Why didn't you want her to go to this meeting?"

Meeting. It sounds so official and appropriate. What about ambush, setup, trap?

"It was a terrible idea."

"You addressed this in your . . . account." Nice word for my stack of scribbles. "Meili wanted to return home to her family. Are you saying that's a terrible idea?"

"No, that's not what I mean."

"What do you mean?"

"She didn't know this guy. She was going too fast."

"Too fast for . . . you?"

"Too fast to be safe."

"Who did you think this man was?" He came in close, got still. This was apparently a crucial question in his cross-examination.

"The whole problem was: we didn't know. And in Meili's situation, you don't meet with someone you don't know. But are you asking me to guess? Who do *I* think he was?" Jeff nodded. "I think he was after these buildings Meili owns. Her dad put buildings in her name, and this guy wanted them."

Jeff leaned back, took his foot off the gas. "You're not far off. Meili Wen does own considerable real-estate holdings, and many of those properties are in dispute. Mr. Holt indicated there is ongoing litigation concerning alleged fraud and the rightful ownership of seven properties. They've been trying to find Meili and work this out for over a year, according to him. So you can imagine the sense of urgency from his point of view."

"See? I was right."

"In part. But you're assuming the meeting was somehow—"

"No, I was right. These corrupt assholes are after her. I told her if she came out of hiding, they'd be on her."

"Jason, look at me. Nothing about this meeting was illegal or inappropriate. Mr. Holt was communicating legitimate business concerns to Meili Wen. I'm sharing this information about their business relationship, but, frankly, the court is not at all concerned with that. The court is concerned with the moment a criminal act began, the moment when you attacked Mr. Holt. That is what we are here to discuss. Is that clear?"

I hate when they do that. I hate when you explain the big picture, and they say: "That's not what we're talking about." All the power of teachers and cops and lawyers and counselors comes from that one move: "We're only here to discuss X." Nothing I want to talk about ever fits into X.

"I was right," I said.

For the third time.

Put it on my tombstone.

"Being right is easy, Jason."

Good sentence, Jeff. A messed-up sentence, but a good one.

"Everybody's right up here," he said, pointing to his temple. "You have to be right out here." He swept his hands to indicate the room, the world. He waited for me to protest, then sat up straight. "Let's keep going. You arrived at your house. Meili was not there."

Back in court. Answer the questions, Jason.

"She was gone. Her stuff was gone."

"Because she was leaving?"

"She was thinking about leaving," I said. "But not like that, not all the sudden."

"From there you rode to Stewart's?" I nodded. He slowed down, overenunciated. "And following a brief conversation with Meili Wen and Anthony Holt, you attacked him. From behind. Unprovoked."

Not a question, a statement.

"No."

"No what?"

"It wasn't unprovoked."

"Did he hit you or threaten to hit you?"

"No, it's not that. He . . ." *He started it* wasn't quite right. How do you say this to a judge? "They made their intentions clear."

"How, Jason?"

"They blocked Meili's car in. His driver was in this SUV, and it was right up against her bumper so she couldn't leave."

"You said this in your account." He paged through the file till he found something. "Neither Mr. Holt nor his driver mentioned this, but assuming—"

"Of course they didn't."

"Assuming the driver did park there, did you ask him to move?"

"Yeah, I told him to."

"And did he move?"

"Eventually."

He spread his hands, little shrug. "That's grounds for assault? And remember, we're talking about assaulting Mr. Holt, who wasn't even in the parking lot."

Holt. Fucking Holt.

"Holt grabbed her."

"Grabbed who?"

"He grabbed Meili's arm when she tried to stand up."

"Did he injure her?" I shook my head. "Did he threaten to injure her?" No. "Did he restrain her for more than a few seconds?" No. "Did Meili say, 'Let me go'?" Nope. "So a car in the parking lot moves when asked, and a man touches Meili's arm. That provoked your attack?"

"When you put it like that, it doesn't—"

"How should I put it, Jason? Tell me." He was relentless, like a real prosecutor.

"These guys were dangerous."

"You made them dangerous, Jason. In your mind." He pointed at my mind. "Look, I don't care what you say outside this room, what you tell other people. I need to know what happened."

Outside this actual room? Or outside the court? Jeff was confusing. Maybe that was on purpose. "OK, wait, are we still pretending we're in court?" I said.

A sigh. "We are not in court. This is a private conversation between you and your attorney, Jason, a completely protected conversation. I need the truth."

"I've told you the truth."

He grimaced, slow-blinked. "Jason, I read your notebooks, I looked into your story, and some of it simply does not add up. I believe Meili Wen was staying at your house. And as I'm sure you're aware, her guardians, the Jenkinses, didn't know that. I believe she called you at school on the day in question. I believe she was upset. I'm willing to believe Mr. Holt was pushy with her, even confrontational, based on the circumstances surrounding the meeting. But from the moment you arrive at Stewart's, it does not add up. The violence, the anger do not add up."

He waited for me to respond. I didn't. Anyone who thinks anger can be added up, balanced out like an equation, has never been angry.

"When it comes to the fighting, Jason, nothing makes sense."

I chuckled.

"What?" he said.

"That's actually pretty true."

"Your entire story checks out, *except the fighting*." He opened my notebook, then thought better of it. "You say Ronald Bellman started fights, but school records indicate you threw the first punch. Repeatedly."

"Landing the first punch isn't the same as starting it."

"In the eyes of the court, it is." He liked that one, let it sit. "Here's another question: Why did your mother go to Florida?"

"Ask her," I said.

"I did. But why do you think she went?"

"I don't know, to get clean, I guess. Her and her boyfriend, Al. And Al had some business idea, an old buddy of his who lives down there."

He leaned in and spoke slowly. He had a whole

repertoire for dealing with difficult clients, and he was using all of it. "On March fifth, Al Pettit, your mother's boyfriend, filed a restraining order. You remember that, right?"

Fuckin Al. I shook my head.

"You'll remember it because it is against you." Two sheets of paper. "He alleges repeated acts of violence against his person and property, and verbal threats against him and your mother. The only reason it didn't land you back in jail is that he filed it in Florida." He turned it around to show me.

"I don't need to see that." Fuckin liar, that Al. From day one. I would never threaten my mom.

"Because you saw it March twentieth when it arrived via Certified Mail."

Al would get drunk—obliterated, eyes pointing in two different directions—and start throwing shit, bullying my mom. Put a hand on her a couple times, so, yeah, I put him in his place. And then *I* get the restraining order? Nah, fuck that.

I shrugged. "Maybe. Don't remember."

He sighed and sat back, giving me the what-are-we-gonna-do stare. "I need you to be truthful with me, Jason. I can help you."

"I've told you the truth. I swear."

"What you've told me does not align with the facts." He opened his palms to indicate the papers.

"These are *papers*!" I swept a bunch of them onto the floor. "You want papers? I gave you fucking papers that prove I was right."

He leaned down, out of range, and picked up his folders.

"These are not just papers. These are statements and eyewitness accounts from people with no reason to lie."

That phrase. Everyone has a reason.

"How do you know they have no reason to lie?"

He sighed. "Why would they lie, Jason?"

"I don't know. I'm just asking: How do you know? Are you inside their heads? Do you know everything? Do you know Meili's dad? Do you know the people in Hong Kong who are trying to take him down? Do you know how powerful they are?"

"If you are telling me there is a conspiracy reaching from Hong Kong all the way to multiple eyewitnesses in Stewart's, it is my opinion you are having trouble discerning fact from fantasy. And it's therefore my recommendation, as your attorney, that we get you evaluated."

The fuck? I shook my head slowly.

"An evaluation cannot hurt your case in any way," he said. "And it can significantly help. There is no downside, no assumptions are made simply because an evaluation—"

"You need to find out the truth!" I slammed the table.

He realigned himself in his chair, feet on the floor. That wouldn't matter. I could be on him so fast he'd never make it to the door.

"And how do I do that?" Someone looked through the narrow window. Jeff consciously ignored it, a gesture for my fucking benefit.

"Find. Meili." What could be more obvious?

He flipped through his papers. Maybe this was progress.

"I know you felt a strong connection to Meili Wen. As I understand, you came to see her as a kind of lifeline, someone who could save you. Would you agree?"

"Ask her. It was more than that." People don't know. They don't know how it feels to have that weight taken off you, that loneliness, that separateness.

"Uh-huh. Sometimes when we attach special significance to a person, when we see them as saviors, we begin to act in ways that are incongruent, even contradictory. They become, in a sense, too important. We can't let them get hurt. Or let them out of our sight. Or, maybe, we can't let them leave."

Don't let her out of your sight, that's what Manny said. I think he did, anyway.

"Look, before you psychoanalyze me," I said, "talk to her. She'll tell you."

I didn't say this, but you know what? If Jeff had someone like Meili, someone amazing and ballsy, and they really connected, he wouldn't want her to leave. He would do whatever he could to keep her. Would he smack around some city dude in an SUV who's taking her away? I think so.

But Jeff never had anyone. Obviously.

"I can't talk to her now, but I do have reports of what she said. First, this." More papers. "I pulled out every eyewitness recollection of what Meili said during the incident. Repetitions are multiple witnesses reporting the same thing."

He switched to courtroom voice, flat and overarticulated like a computer saying "Press one for the operator":

"Jesus, what are you doing?

"Shit, Jason, what are you doing?

"Shit, Jason! What are you doing?

"Stop it!

"Stop it! What are you doing?

"Stop it! Just stop it!

"Stop it! Get out of here!

"Get out of here!

"Get out of here!"

Jeff cleared his throat, showy, like this was an important speech. My vision wobbled.

"Oh my god, look at you.

"This is not good.

"It's no good.

"You're out of control.

"Listen to me! You're out of control.

"I'm not safe here.

"I need to get away from this man.

"I need to get away from him.

"I need to get away from him."

He put the papers down. "When I read this—when

anyone reads it—I hear a young woman who is frightened, but not of Anthony Holt. She is scared of you, Jason. She is trying to get away from you."

These words, these hateful words, he gathered them all together and put them in my face?

No.

Sorry, Jeff.

You can't do that, Jeff.

"I also spoke with Sophie Jenkins, Meili's so-called aunt. She had a phone conversation with Meili after the incident." He pulled a page out of his stack.

What? Why didn't you start with this? My vision shook harder.

He leaned back with the precious paper. "Ms. Jenkins paraphrased the call, and she was quite clear on certain points. Quote: 'Melissa was very upset, she was worried that she might go to jail.' Et cetera, et cetera. Quote: 'She said she hadn't done anything wrong, it was all that Jason boy's fault. I asked her . . .' Here it is: 'I asked her why he would do something like that.'" Jeff looked up. "Meaning you. Quote, 'Melissa said he completely lost it. He was totally off it.'"

Even through my growing head rush, I could hear Meili say those words. They sounded ridiculous in Jeff's boring American voice. Ridiculous and weak.

"Quote, 'He was out of control. I've never seen him like that. I've never seen anyone like that. He was vicious. Terrifying and vicious.' End quote."

I couldn't let this pass. I couldn't let Jeff or Meili or Mrs. Fucking Jenkins get away with this.

We're done here. *You're* fucking done, Jeff.

"Give me that paper," I said. My voice must have sounded different, because Jeff froze.

You want to say I'm a brute, I'm that violent boy? Fine. Take a fucking number.

But don't come between me and Meili. Don't say shit about us. Don't you dare step between us unless you want to get hurt.

"Excuse me?" He couldn't hear me, couldn't accept he was no longer in charge.

My mind was made up. There's a moment when you just know what comes next. We had passed that moment.

"Give me. That fucking paper."

In the end, Jeff gave himself up. He chose this moment to lean in and do a stern, I'm-in-charge move. Incredible.

"You need to listen!" He pointed his hairy finger in my face.

Come here, Jeff. You're making it easy.

He poked the air in front of my eyes, barking, "If Sophie Jenkins testifies in court, you are going down, and there's nothing I or you or . . ."

Blah blah blah. So weak. Who listens to someone like this?

I watched his finger.

Poke, poke, poke. In and out of the rectangle of light. I had to time it right.

". . . and if you continue making . . ."

I shot my hand up and grabbed his wrist. I flipped it over, pinned it to the table, twisting him sideways. He screamed, fell off his chair.

And I saw the pen.

Jeff's Bic on the table. They didn't allow pens in the Rubber Room because they could be weapons, right? It's weird, but I never would have thought of the pen if the Rubber Room didn't have that rule.

A squeal from Jeff, the kind of sound that guys who never get hit make. I thought lawyers loved a good fight. Dude was useless.

I gripped the pen, thumb on the pointy blue cap.

Footsteps. Yelling in the hall.

Jeff fought to stand up, his free hand flailing, papers scattering.

They're right about pens. The blue tip of a ballpoint is sharp enough to pierce a shirt and blunt enough to do real damage when it hits.

An alarm went off.

Maybe five or six clean hole punches before Jeff's shoulder muscle holds on to the ink part.

Someone was on the door.

But no one talks about that. Judges, lawyers, all they talk about is what I did.

Jeff screaming.

No one talks about what I didn't do. They don't give

trophies for Not Stabbing Your Lawyer with a Pen, but they should.

I didn't stab Jeff. I didn't. Even though it took a while for the guards to get in there. They might could practice a bit.

I was still looking at Jeff, pen in hand, still not hurting him, when the door flew open.

Three guards tackled me.

I watched from the bottom of the pile as they picked Jeff up and hustled him out.

Eventually, they tased me, more pain than I've ever felt. A lot more, like exploding in slow motion.

They added "attempted assault with improvised weapon" to my charges. And took away all my pens.

Attempted. Like I tried and failed.

I fucking chose not to hurt Jeff. He was a shitty lawyer. He had little balls of spit in the corners of his mouth. And he mispronounced Meili's secret name.

But thank you, Jeff. You changed everything.

You're why I can *put down the Bic.*

That's my phrase.

Put down the Bic, Jason.

TWENTY

I CAN'T BELIEVE YOU SAID THAT.

[*Said what?*]

You said I lost it.

[*You did lose it, Bug. You've got to admit. That poor man.*]

I was protecting you. Protecting us.

[*In your mind, you were.*]

That's weird.

[*What?*]

Same phrase my lawyer used.

[*'S true, isn't it? You just fit everything into your little story.*]

It's your little story. I'm not the one who started this.

[*I forgot, it's never your fault, is it? Like those boys you keep attacking and then claiming they started it.*]

You wouldn't understand. That's not your world.

[*Actually, I do. I understand when someone's lying.*]

I didn't lie.

[*Really? What about your mum and what's-his-name, Al?*]

I left that out. That's not lying.

[*Leaving out that they were so scared of you they moved a thousand miles away is a fucking lie. Sorry.*]

I couldn't talk about it. I'd end up back in jail.

[*Well, now I see why.*]

Why what?

[*Why your parents were terrified. You really are scary.*]

Sometimes you have to be scary.

[*Is that what you tell yourself? Is that how you explain bashing that poor man's head in?*]

That guy was your problem, Meili. I was solving your problem.

[*Solving my problem? Are you serious? You made it a fucking problem. And, to be perfe'tly honest, you might want to focus a bit on your own problems. Cause they're major.*]

Yeah, I have plenty of problems now. Thanks to you.

[*Oh, please. I didn't do this to you. You were like this.*]

Like what?

[*Angry. Violent.*]

You're not the sweetest person, either.

[*So sorry. Should I smile more?*]

You don't even see it.

[*Oh, I'm a bit twisted, I admit it. I'm up-front. You're much more dangerous. No checks and balances, trying to play the hero.*]

Don't say that. After all I've done.

[*All you've done is put a man in hospital and put me in danger.*]

Don't say that.

[*I'll say what I think, thank you very much. And right now, I think you should take a step back. You're a bit scary up close.*]

Alright, deep breath.

Put down the Bic.

Be honest.

I never thought you'd do that.

[*Do what?*]

Leave.

[*Leave Stewart's?*]

Unionville. Everything. Me.

[*Were we supposed to live happily ever after? Because, just to be clear, I don't recall saying that. I don't recall promising to spend my whole life in Unionville packing your lunches and raising horrid little babies. And I don't recall saying: 'Please come and savage this poor man I'm talking to.' When did I say that, exactly?*]

You just left.

[*silence*]

[*What was I supposed to do, Jason?*]

[*silence*]

Stay.

[*silence*]

You were supposed to stay.

[*silence*]

[*silence*]

Sob.

Jesus.

I should swerve, make a joke about how dramatic I am. Can't think of one.

Sob.

Say something, Meili.

Sob.

Unbelievable, right?

Imagine you give up everything to protect someone. Imagine you are completely fucked, and she is free and clear. Imagine waiting a whole day for her to visit or call or write, an endless, excruciating day. Imagine the outrage, the are-you-fucking-kidding-me wound it opens up.

Multiply that by 107 days I've been in juvenile.

And I still can't get an answer.

So I practice.

I'm getting better. At first, she barely said a word before I went off or started sobbing. Now, we have a good argument. A discussion.

I'm getting her voice well, really sounds like her. She makes good points, too. *No checks and balances.* Ouch. That's nice, Meili.

My celly Glen said I had to stop "talking to myself" in our cell, so I walk the hall or sit in the square of sunlight by the commissary. I wear Meili's leather necklace on my wrist—they confiscated the shark tooth—and carry her Big Don signature in my pocket. And I talk to her. (And I do push-ups and sit-ups. Seriously. Thanks, Jay.)

She makes me laugh. There was a hilarious bit about her aunt cursing like a sailor. Guys stared, I was laughing so hard.

And I get multiple sobs now. Every time it gets deep, or Meili makes a joke about us having sex, a gut sob rises up not once but a few times. That means something.

Know what my mom used to say? "It's never too late." She always told me that. Her favorite example was this guy Bear who lived down the street, big biker dude with the beard and the boots, sketchy people coming by at all hours. He had a girlfriend who did witchcraft, actual witchcraft, and a scary son named George. And Bear was dealing drugs, hard stuff, nobody messed with him. We used to dare each other to go to his house on Halloween. One day, Bear gets busted. Federal dudes, the jackets with the big letters on the back, they raid the house, and he gets eighteen years. It's a lot, cause he's gotta be fifty, right? He might die in jail. Then, a couple years later, little George murders a guy. Shoots him in the face with a shotgun.

Here's what Bear does: he testifies against his son, tells the jury all the psychopath shit George did growing up. He's like an anti-character witness, puts his son away for life, and, in exchange, Bear gets out. Comes back, kicks out the clean-cut family living in his house and settles down with this woman Carla. And you know what? He's happy as hell, sweetest guy you ever met. They go to the Gulf every winter, bring back shells for the neighborhood kids.

My mom would see Bear planting a bush in his yard—he's gardening, for god's sake—and she'd say, "It's never too late, Jason. It's never too late for any of us."

[Can I say: that's horrible.]

What?

[I don't . . . I can't even begin. I hate everyone in that story.]

Snob.

[Especially your mum. She'd actually tell you that story, like, at bedtime or something?]

She'd invite Bear over to tell it while he tucked me in.

[Piss off. Is it true? Is it even true?]

No, it's true.

[Then what's so funny?]

I'm picturing Bear rocking me to sleep, big old beard smelling like Kentucky Fried Chicken gravy and biker pussy, and I'm nestled in, sucking my thumb.

[silence]

[See, that's it right there.]

What?

[*Gravy and pussy. 'S fucking brilliant. You get me with the details, Bug. I'm all hot and bothered.*]

[*silence*]

[*Seriously, that nasty beard, it's, like, erotic to me. Whot? You OK?*]

Sob.

Another sob.

Another.

The commissary line is getting long, guys are right up against me, annoyed by my talking and now my crying. Time to walk. I'll get stamps and tea later. Thanks to Jay for that, too. Dude's actually putting money on my commissary. Never too late for any of us.

Back to my cell, see if Glen's there. He's decent enough, couple DUIs and a vehicular manslaughter, all by the age of seventeen. That's what he says, anyway. Who knows? Nobody tells the truth in jail. Maybe anywhere.

I hear him down the row, practicing his "drumming." He wears headphones and plays along with punky music, stuff I've never heard before.

I keep walking. If I'm moving, guys leave me alone.

I've stayed clean. And I didn't have to do my *statement piece*, Jay. I'm peaceful, so far. Peaceful guy doing time for arson and assault.

I see dudes starting shit, sometimes with me, and I

think: man, put down the Bic. Young guys in here stalk around, waiting for an excuse to go off. *What're you saying? You got a fucking problem?* Uh, no. I don't. You have a fucking problem.

Doesn't feel like putting out a fire, either, feels like not lighting the match. Yeah, not the best analogy from someone with an arson arrest. Or maybe it is.

Hilarious, right? So many people must have watched me get into shit and thought: The fuck is wrong with Jason? I sure don't know the answer to that. Yet.

And I can't celebrate too much, cause it's jail, and I don't care about these people and their beefs. If it was outside? With people I care about? I honestly don't know. Guess I'll find out.

But I can say this. If my younger self walked in here—and I mean myself like four months ago—I'd think: that kid's obnoxious, he's trying to get hit.

Meili said that once. I think she did.

Meili. Where were we? The Bear story. Hot and bothered.

Right. Her body.

Jail is a lot of things, and here's one. It's the exact symmetrical opposite of having sex with Meili. Everything jail drains, sex with Meili drenches.

I pace, and I practice.

I still have seven months (and change) in here, plenty of time.

You need something to live for in jail. A lot of guys, it's their family, wanting them to see their son free and clear.

For me, it's this conversation. Somewhere—Fat Deer Key? Hong Kong?—Meili opens the door, and I start the conversation. I know every possible swerve. I know my own swerves. I know I'm not vicious. I'm not vicious, and I'm not terrifying.

The door opens, and I see your face, Meili.

I see your face, and I can put down the Bic.

Cause I'm not gonna hurt anyone.

I'm not gonna hurt anyone.

I'm not.

ACKNOWLEDGMENTS

Gratitude to my agent, Rebecca Stead, true artist and advocate, and to The Book Group.

To my editor, Joy Peskin, superb collaborator who asks the right questions, and to the team at FSG: Nicholas Henderson, Aimee Fleck, Kylie Byrd, and Jennifer Sale.

To Kate Klimo for twelve years of patience and support. Look, Kate, I made a book!

To Amy Smith and David Brick, my artistic family. You made me the artist I am.

To Jesse Tiger and Nico Wolf, brilliant readers and storytellers. Someday, I'll let you read this.

To the choreographers, dancers, directors, makers, and thinkers of my artist community: Nichole, Christy, Heather, Kate, Niki, Christina, Devynn, Mark, Dan, Whit, Jaamil, Matt, Dito, Jeb, Anna, Mark, Rick, Lorin, Pierce, Melissa, David, Scott, Byron, Maiko, Ishmael, Tere, Cynthia, Richard,

Susan, Olase, Meg, Kelly, George, Makoto, Debbie, Nick, Ashley, Michaela, Raph, David, Bill. I can't imagine myself without you.

To Kathleen and Tom for forty-eight years of love, and for accepting my swerves.

And to my first reader, Elizabeth. [perfection]